The
White
Cockatoo

Also by Mignon G. Eberhart
in Thorndike Large Print ®

Three Days for Emeralds
Casa Madrone
Next of Kin
Alpine Condo Crossfire
Fighting Chance
Another Woman's House
Two Little Rich Girls

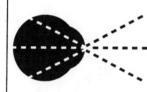

This Large Print Book carries the
Seal of Approval of N.A.V.H.

The White Cockatoo

Mignon G. Eberhart

Thorndike Press • Thorndike, Maine

Published in 1993 by arrangement with Brandt & Brandt
Literary Agency, Inc.

Thorndike Large Print ® All Time Favorites Series.

The tree indicium is a trademark of Thorndike Press.

The text of this Large Print edition is unabridged.
Other aspects of the book may vary from the original.

Set in 16 pt. News Plantin by Melissa Harvey.

Printed in the United States on acid-free, high opacity paper. ∞

Library of Congress Cataloging in Publication Data

Eberhart, Mignon Good, 1899–
   The white cockatoo / Mignon G. Eberhart.
    p.   cm.
   ISBN 0-7862-0083-9 (alk. paper : lg. print)
   1. Americans — Travel — France — Fiction.
   2. Mining engineers — France — Fiction.
   3. Large type books. I. Title.
   [PS3509.B453W45 1993]
   813′.52—dc20
                                        93-29320

To

NELLE RICHMOND EBERHART

and

CHARLES WAKEFIELD CADMAN

with thanks for many songs and for,
especially, that one song which is my own.

CHAPTER I

The thing began, as it ended, with the white cockatoo. His name was Pucci, and he gave me a doubtful glance from his shining black eyes and sidled nearer, peering over my arm while I wrote, as if what he saw might confirm his suspicion. He cocked his head on one side, ruffled up the pale yellow feathers of his crest, and watched my pen in a knowing fashion while I filled out the card of arrival which the hotel clerk — who, he had already assured me, was also the manager — had handed me. The card had thoughtfully been printed in two languages, French and English, and I filled in the blanks rapidly. Date: November 29, 1931. Surname: Sundean. Christian name: James.

At place of residence I hesitated; I wouldn't say Moscow, for I loathed the place, and as a matter of fact I had not been in Moscow but north of it. My thoughts hovered indecisively over various possibilities: New York,

Chicago, Denver. The card plainly said "Permanent residence," and permanent residence was a thing I had not. The cockatoo's waiting black eyes, no less than the consciousness that the swarthy, fat manager across the desk was noting my brief hesitation, nudged me to decision, and I wrote New York. Occupation: engineer. Arriving from: Berlin.

The cockatoo scratched himself vigorously, his curved beak under one wing; he withdrew it hurriedly to watch me push the paper across the desk and to write my name also in the open register which the manager was holding toward me. The page on which I wrote was entirely bare except for an ink blot, and it gave me what, I later found, was a quite correct impression that in November there were not many guests at the hotel. This time I did not hesitate at place of residence. The cockatoo was reassured only when I put down the pen; he uttered a hoarse murmur which was unintelligible as to sound but distinctly congratulatory as to tone, reached up his gray-blue claw in a nonchalant way to remove a soft white feather which had clung to his beak, and took another sidelong step toward me.

The manager said: "Pucci, Pucci!" in a caressing way and looked at my signature on the register.

He was a short, fat fellow, darkish and inclined to glisten. He wore four heavy rings, all set with stones, one of which was a very dubiously cut diamond, and his creased and rounded waistcoat would have been considerably improved by a trip to the cleaner's. I was at a loss to guess his nationality; there was a touch of the German about him and, faintly, of the Italian; his gestures were French, and there was something vaguely Hebraic about his full red mouth and his dark eyes, which were set just a hair's breadth too close together above the coarsely aquiline bridge of his nose. It was therefore something of a shock when he met my eyes again, beamed broadly, rubbed his fat hands together, and said:

"I, too, am an American." His hand was across the desk toward me, and I put mine in it and withdrew it as soon as possible: his was rather unpleasant; damp, perhaps.

"Glad to see you. Glad to see you," he went on heartily. "Many Americans come here during the tourist season. They come to see the palace and the old Roman ruins. But not many during the winter. So your home is in New York?"

I was obliged to say that it was. After all, New York as well as any other — or better, as far as choice goes.

"Mine is in Chicago. My name is Lov-

9

schiem. Marcus Lovschiem. Well, well. I've got a brother in New York. He took out his papers of citizenship the same year I got mine. He is in the bootlegging business and," he added simply, "he's doing very well."

I thought it possible; indeed, probable. But I wondered what this self-styled American citizen was doing here in a small, forgotten French town, managing a tourist hotel, wearing enough rings to do credit to any gypsy horse trader and caressing a white cockatoo. Surely he hadn't found pickings in France — especially during the cold winter months — anything like what, with his affiliations, he might have found in Chicago. He knew my thoughts. I was to discover that he frequently knew one's thoughts.

"You are asking yourself why I am here? Ah —" he lifted his fat, dark hand from the cockatoo's crest to point roguishly at me — "isn't that right? You are saying to yourself, What is this American doing here, managing a hotel — and a hotel which must be dull enough during the winter — when he might be in Chicago, making some money?" He shrugged and dropped his hand again to the cockatoo. The jewels on it flashed under the none-too-bright light that hung above the desk. "Circumstances, my friend. Circumstances. This post offered itself, and I took it, gladly." He sighed so hugely that the buttons on his waistcoat rose and fell, and the cockatoo eyed them sharply. He repeated, "Circumstances."

I had no reason whatever to suspect as I did that the circumstances were unsavory. But I was not his friend and had no intention of becoming that, and I dislike roguishness. Moreover, I was tired and cold and hungry.

I said no doubt and that I should like a room with a bath.

On this he became thoughtful. Rooms with baths and, he gathered I meant, hot water — he paused tentatively here and looked pensive when I indicated that I had meant, decidedly, hot water — rooms with baths were a little difficult. The hotel was old, I surely understood, and while it had plumbing, still, the plumbing had been added many years after the hotel had been built and was not, even now, quite adequate. I could have a bath, yes; I could even have a daily bath if I insisted, which would be only five francs a day added to my bill, but a room with a bath was difficult.

It was here that, wearying, I reached toward my bag. And there occurred a rather strange thing.

He didn't try to keep me.

It is a long and lean season, winter in A—, with few tourists braving, for more than a night or two, its bitter, incessant wind, yet this manager was apparently quite willing to see a paying guest walk out of his hotel and go to another. It did not, however, occur to me at the moment as being strange. I was preoccupied with another affair.

Such small things decide one's destiny. Things that are wildly and absurdly out of proportion with the train of events they involve. Everybody knows the drama of those moments of decision; the word that, eventually, revolutionizes a whole life; the turning left when it might have been right, or right when it might have been left that has at its end a heartbreak or a triumph, the chance speech, the chance glimpse, the chance encounter — life is full of them, and everybody knows the heights and the depths to which they lead. What I'm trying to say is that at that moment it was for me a faint, delicious smell of roasting meat. It was as prosaic as that; weirdly prosaic in view of what followed.

I did not like the manager. I did not, somehow, like the air of the place, but the smell of roasting meat assailed my hunger, and I dropped my bag. Later I was to think that instinct was warning me to leave and even giving me a slight shove in the direction of the door by offering reason for its warning. At the time I was only conscious of my hunger and weariness and the smell of dinner cooking.

Lovschiem had not spoken. When I dropped my bag and faced him again I surprised a look in his dark eyes which fled back at once into the murky depths from which it came, but which nevertheless I was to remember.

I said:

"But you do have an empty room with a bath?"

"Yes," he said, barely reluctant. "But it is over there, across the court." He motioned toward the door which led into a large square courtyard, which I had barely noted, getting out of the taxi which brought me from the train and crossing toward the lighted door of the lobby, as being a cold place of bare, gray-white paving and walls, with dark-blue shadows moving here and there as the rising wind swayed the shrubs and vines that grew densely in the corners. It was enclosed on three sides by the hotel and on one side by a wall with an arched entrance. The north wing, directly opposite, loomed a black bulk and looked desolate and secretive, rising there in the shadow.

"It is, as you see, the north wing, and a little chilly perhaps when the mistral blows. It is a nice room, however, and it has a bath. But people do not like the north wing in winter, and it is quite deserted."

"Let me have it," I said. "When will dinner be served?"

He told me and summoned a porter. I saw no one save the porter as I followed him and my bags through a cold and rather barren-looking lounge, with wicker chairs and a bare floor and a few anemic-looking potted palms, toward the lift. It was a very small lift, so small that the porter was obliged to take me up to the second floor and then return for my bags while I stood in the upper hall and waited.

The hotel was, I saw at once, much larger than my hurried glimpse of it through wind and dusk had led me to believe. But I did not, at that time, particularly note the curious architecture of the place.

The lounge was a kind of inside court, extending upward past two stories and their railed passages, which made encircling galleries, to the skylighted roof. We left the lounge well and apparently the main portion of the hotel and wound our way through half-lit, carpeted corridors, down a little flight of steps, and around several unexpected turns until we reached the north wing. There we turned abruptly through a door and walked along a very cold and narrow passage with closed, dark doors on one side and a wall of windows on the other till we reached at the very end of this unprepossessing passage the room that was to be mine. And there was not a sound to be heard save the wiry little porter's footsteps and my own heavier ones and the little sighing flap of his long white apron and the occasional rattle of one of the many windows or murmur of the wind.

Neither did I note then the room, beyond receiving a vague impression of outdated elegance and vastness and chill.

The water from the bathroom taps, however, did prove to be faintly warm, and perhaps half an hour later I started to retrace my steps through those confusing corridors to find the dining room. As I stepped outside my room and closed the door behind me I paused a moment.

Directly opposite me and across the shadowy court I could see the lights of the lobby; from its glass-paned door and its window bold rectangles of light spread themselves whitely upon the paving of the court. The wind was steadily rising, murmuring and sighing and creaking windows and shutters, and it waved the dense vines and shrubs in the corners of the court so that they made black-blue shadows which fled anxiously across the white blocks of light. The courtyard itself was faintly lighter than the shadows, owing to the light from the lobby and dining-room windows, as well as to a rather dim and wavering light which was hung above the arched entrance and which, as the wind swayed it, waked more fleeting blue shadows into life.

Immediately at my left as I stood facing the lobby was another glassed door, and, idly curious, I moved toward it, glanced through the glass, laid my hand on the latch, and stepped through the door onto a sort of landing which led upon a narrow, winding flight of iron steps.

It led to the courtyard below. It was thickly concealed at night by the engulfing shadows of the dense vines that grew in the corner, and the potted glycines, as well as the shadow of the courtyard wall. I don't know why the steps aroused my interest; perhaps I only wanted a breath of fresh air after the chill mustiness of my room. At any rate, I descended a few steps and paused again to view the shadow-ridden court.

Just below me someone was talking. In the lull of the wind I could hear the voices quite distinctly, although I could see neither of the speakers. Lovschiem, probably, rating a servant, for the lobby was empty, and it sounded like Lovschiem's voice telling someone in crisp English that he'd be damned if he let it happen again. The other voice replied that it wouldn't happen again.

"Are you sure?" said the voice I took to be Lovschiem's.

"I'm sure. It's certain. I know exactly where it is."

"No blunders. I'll have no blunders."

"No. I promise you."

"Good, then, I leave it to you." Lovschiem paused, and, this man of hybrid nationality, uttered the one Spanish word I knew which was *"Mañana,"* and which I remembered vividly from various dealings with Mexican laborers.

"Mañana," said the other, and Lovschiem, a dark shadowy bulk, stepped out from the shadows and shrubbery directly below the stairway and walked across the flickering black and blue and white of the court and into the lobby, where he stood at the desk, stroking his white cockatoo. The other speaker had vanished, or rather remained invisible, a furious gust of wind swept through the court, waving the light and shadows madly, and I shivered and decided it was not the kind of night on which to stand on light iron steps to admire chiaroscuro, be it ever so effective. Moreover, it was surely time for dinner.

Since then I have recalled with some interest that it was a faint distaste of Lovschiem which sent me up the steps again, and through the long winding corridors along which the porter

17

had led me, down the main stairs beside the lift, and finally to the lounge, rather than take the much shorter and easier route across the court and through the lobby — distaste of Lovschiem and the certainty that if he saw me he would try to engage me in conversation. If I had descended the remaining steps and followed Lovschiem directly across the court and into the lobby, things might have had a very different ending.

I lost my way almost immediately upon leaving the straight, window-lined passage of the north wing, and had to be set straight by a maid. She spoke no English, and my French was worse than none at all, for it dated from school days and had not been used since. She finally led me back to the corner where I'd taken the wrong turning, and then, giggling, to the corridor leading to the lift and main stairway.

The lounge was still empty, and the bar had not even a light, but in the dining room adjoining the lounge I caught a glimpse of the bright-eyed little porter apparently doubling as a waiter, for he was hurrying across the room with a steaming tureen of soup in one hand and a napkin properly across his arm.

He looked harassed, but after disposing of the soup, trotted to meet and seat me with an air of alacrity. He brought me the wine list, showed me a written menu which offered no choice, and hurried away.

There were only three other people dining.

Directly across from me sat a woman with a kind of war-horse look about her nose, and terrifying wide, black eyebrows; she was dressed in black, silky-looking stuff with quantities of beads and bracelets and brooches, and she looked, in spite of being rather angular in line, a little stuffed as to clothing, as if she had a great many layers of other clothing underneath the black silk. She was reading the *Daily Mail* with a lorgnette and considerable disapproval. I surmised she was English, but I was wrong, for she turned out to be Mrs. Felicia Byng from Omaha, Nebraska, and I might say here that I never did know exactly why she was touring the country or why she had taken it into her head to stop in A—. In many respects she remained to the last a woman of mystery.

Across the room sat a priest, youngish, with a dark brown sweater pulled over his black, tightly buttoned soutane. His claim to distinction appeared to lie in a rather ghastly red beard. His hair was cut *en brosse* and was of no particular color; thus the sight of his fiery beard was in the nature of a shock. The beard was thin and long and delicate-looking, not thick and virile, and was faintly repellent, though I didn't know exactly why. He was partaking of soup through the beard with unpleasant determination, and I shifted my gaze hurriedly back to the wine list in my hand.

But after a moment, simply because there were so few people in the room, and the little porter — or, rather, waiter — was trying to serve Mrs. Felicia Byng's soup and getting rather involved with the *Daily Mail*, which she obstinately refused to stop reading, and there was nothing else to do — after a moment, I say, my eyes drifted idly to the only other occupied table, where a woman was seated whose back was turned toward me.

Drifted idly but paused with interest, for it was, I saw at once, a very beautiful back. Not that I saw it fully: anyone wearing an ordinary dinner gown would have been courting pneumonia in that draughty dining room, which was more like a refrigerator than a civilized room in which to eat. But she was wearing a black velvet coat affair which fitted so tightly and smoothly that it exposed the slender, graceful lines of her shoulders and back. I could see, of course, her slim white neck and her hair, which was brown with gold lights in it and was soft and pleasant-looking, and one hand, which fulfilled the promise of the shoulders, for the wrist was delicately turned and fine, and the hand was young and slenderly made, with lovely pink-tipped fingers.

Below the folds of velvet and the black lace of the gown she was wearing I could see one ankle and foot. Indeed, I could hardly help seeing it, for she wore bright scarlet slippers with silver straps and silver heels. Her ankle was slender, too, with delicate fine lines, and the moment my eyes reached her foot with its nice instep I knew she was an American. It was a beautiful foot, and the slipper was well made.

I was not, I must add, as enthusiastic as this sounds. The thing was, I had spent the last two years in Russia and recently had visited Poland and Germany and then France; I had reached the place where thickish shoulders and stocky ankles and wooden wrists seem a not unusual thing in women. I had not forgotten that my countrywomen have clean-limbed figures and beautiful slender feet, but it had been some time since I had seen one of a type which is not uncommon in America, and my delight at seeing it now was purely impersonal. An engineer is rather impersonal about women, anyway; he's got to be. At least, so far as marriage is concerned. There's no getting around it, marriage and engineering don't go well together. Not, anyhow, until the engineer has gone much further in his profession than I had.

Well, I have described the three people in the dining room besides myself somewhat at length, because we were all of us dragged into the affair.

The erstwhile porter served my soup, and the dinner progressed quietly, with the exception of Mrs. Felicia Byng's insisting on speaking to the porter in what must have been bad French when he understood English perfectly well, and becoming visibly irritated when he failed to understand her requests — although it developed she wanted ice water, so he may have understood her all along.

And with cheese there was an incident which I alone, I think, in the room saw.

I was sitting facing the windows, which, in turn, faced the court. They were curtained with lace up to about the height of a man's shoulders, and across the lace someone had pinned some kind of shabby brown velvet or velours in an effort to keep out any vagrant currents of cold air — an effort which, I might add, was entirely without success. The outside shutters had not been closed, and I was looking idly at the black, shining window, which reflected, above, the crystal-bedecked chandelier, and thinking that the wind was increasing in violence, for I could hear it rattle the shutters, when I suddenly perceived that I was looking straight into the face of a man, and that man was Lovschiem. That is, owing to the lace and velours I could see only the upper half of his face, but it was unmistakable.

The rather disturbing thing was he was staring with curious intensity at the woman with the silver heels. He stared and stared, and his fat face became more distinct and looked whiter against the black of the night behind him, and his eyes became darker and smaller and glittered. I put down the glass I held, and the motion caught his eyes, which flickered to me and vanished in the same half second. He vanished so swiftly, and the windowpane was left so black and shiny and blank, that the face was like a mirage — there at one instant and then completely gone.

It had been Lovschiem, in flesh, however: I was sure of that. But if a man wishes to look in the windows of his own hotel I suppose he may do so, unpleasant though his gaze may be.

I loitered a little over some pears, rather hoping the girl with the silver heels would leave first, so I might get a glimpse of her face. Not that it mattered particularly, except that I had told myself that her face was apt to be quite plain and ordinary and disappointing. She had such a liberal supply of beauty of figure that it was against reason to expect

23

much in the way of beauty of face. But she did not move, even after the porter had cleared the table and disappeared.

I rose at length, reflecting that, after all, it was better to let the vision of beauty remain without running the risk of disillusionment, and that the room was growing colder and colder.

The lounge was deserted, and the parlor was dark. I told the porter to light a fire in my room and serve me coffee and a brandy there.

The night had increased in violence while I sat at dinner, and it seemed to me that the rambling old house had become, strangely, a part of the tumultuous night and was sharing its violence. It shook and rattled and swept bitter drafts through the corridors, and when at length I opened the door that led into the window-lined corridor of the north wing, the cold rush of air swooped upon me like some frightened creature let loose. I was glad enough to see the porter when he followed me a few moments later.

"Do you think it will burn?" I asked, watching him lay kindling. He glanced dubiously toward the chimney, said something about the mistral, and shrugged and pulled down his mouth in that splendid French gesture which utterly disclaims responsibility for what may occur. It said quite definitely, "You asked for

24

this fire, and here it is, but the mistral is blowing, and there's no telling what may happen. However, happen what may, it's on your own head." He arranged a small piece of wood and lighted a match.

"There aren't many guests at the hotel?" I said.

"No, monsieur. Not at this season. We have now Miss Tally, Madame Byng, Père Robart, and yourself. That is all." He blew vigorously at the small beginning flame. He had combed what hair he had in wet black strands over his white bald spot, and it glimmered in the firelight. His alert dark face grew scarlet before a flame shot up, and he took a breath and sat back on his heels with his dark eyes now catching lights from the fire and his white apron draped over his knees. "Miss Tally" (it was only perceptibly Mees) — "Miss Tally, she is the beautiful lady in the dining room tonight. The one with the red slippers. Madame Byng, she is the —" he hesitated doubtfully and finally said neatly — "she is the other one."

So she was beautiful. It gave me a little glow of satisfaction to hear that. Of course, the porter's notion of beauty and mine might differ; still, he had done politely all it was possible to do for Mrs. Byng. It didn't matter, of course: it was only that it seemed, somehow,

25

pleasant that she was beautiful.

A shutter banged, and the porter skipped to his feet and across the room, pulling open the long window and letting in a blast of wind that set the flames to dancing madly and smoke billowing into the room while he endeavored to fasten the shutter more securely. I judged he did not succeed, for he gave another shrug and left it, fastened the window again, and drew the thick red curtains across it.

When he had heaped wood on the fire and gone I sat lazily before the hearth. The fire was burning well enough, though a little fitfully on account of the wind. I stretched out my legs and relaxed comfortably. After all, it wasn't a bad place. A little too empty of people, perhaps, and too silent except for the wind, but not bad.

My gaze wandered idly about the room, over the thick, worn red carpet, the old chairs with their satin upholstery and what looked to be hand-carved frames, the fancy crystal-bedecked chandelier, the great somber wardrobe, the gilt-framed mirror above the fireplace, the gay French clock on the mantel — not much clock, but elaborately surmounted by the figure of a man on horseback in bronze.

It must have been just about then that I fell into a doze, for the last thing I remember was looking at the figure in bronze, so perfect and complete, with the horse's mane and tail waving, and the rider's hat and cloak swept back, and even his gauntleted hand and the long sword it held quite perfect in detail. I remember thinking how ugly it was as a clock decoration and how large — the sword alone must have been five or six inches long, and the rest of the figure in proportion — and that was all, until I waked suddenly to the fact that the wind was driving smoke down the chimney and into the room, that the shutter was banging furiously, and that I was cramped and chilled.

I rose, yawned, realized I'd been asleep, saw by my watch that it was past twelve, and decided to go to bed. The wood had apparently smoldered for most of the time, and so was not quite burned out, and the swoop of the wind was driving now quantities of acrid blue smoke into the room. Hoping the wind would swirl round again, and that very soon, for you cannot sleep in a smoke-filled room, I went to the door, opened it to let the smoke out, and stepped into the corridor, glancing down into the court.

It was a night to bring out the witches. Indeed, you'd have been willing to swear that they were already out and were whirling and surging madly up and down and through and around the court in a furied witches' Sabbath.

The light under the arch was tossing, black shadows were flying grotesquely; the thick shrubs and vines in the corners had come alive and were flinging themselves violently about, the corridor windows were rattling; the lobby across the court was dark, and not a thread of light was shining through any of the shuttered windows — there were only that small tossing light under the entrance arch and those wild flying shadows. I wished suddenly that I had chosen a less desolate and wind-swept place. Instinct is always stronger when you are about half asleep: I disliked the old hotel, disliked particularly the witch-ridden courtyard. It was quite suddenly sinister. That seems a fanciful and imaginative word and, God knows, I'm not a fanciful or imaginative man, but it was the only word that was apt. The place *was* sinister. It threatened.

And then all at once the wind was wailing louder. It was wailing in my ear — no, not wailing, it was sobbing. It was sobbing and saying, inconceivably:

"Let me in. Oh, please. *Let me in.*"

CHAPTER II

Her fingers were scratching and fumbling at the door beside me. Then her face turned from looking over her shoulder and showed me whiteness and wide dark eyes and blowing hair, and she beat on the door with her fists and sobbed again: "Oh, do let me in."

I got the door open, and she whirled in, and I closed it against the wind. She followed the light into my room like a child running from the dark, and when I followed her she was kneeling before the fire, stretching out her beautiful hands toward it, and her silver-heeled slippers made spots of light against the carpet. Her eyes flared with terror and met mine, and she said with a gasp: "Shut the door."

I shut the door into the corridor. There's one nice thing about not having much money: you aren't suspicious.

When I turned she was still holding her hands toward the fire, which had fortunately

29

righted itself and was burning cheerfully, and the light shone gold on her tossed hair and on her face and caught dull gleams from her velvet cloak. Her forehead was fine and wide, and her nose small, straight, and a bit arrogant; her lips red and trembling, but her chin firm.

There was still a little brandy untouched, and I gave it to her and pulled up a chair for her to lean against and waited. Presently her breath stopped coming in gasps and her lips steadied themselves. She turned and looked at me and smiled a little tremulously.

"I'm so sorry," she said. "You see, I've just been abducted."

Her dark eyes held mine for a moment, and then she turned back to the fire as if she had said all there was to say. I pulled myself together.

"You can't mean that."

She turned to look at me again, and I saw immediately that she did mean it.

"Shall I call the police?"

"The police. Oh, no. No. I don't think they could do anything about it. Anyway, I've escaped. Quite —" her voice wavered upward and she caught herself and said without trembling — "quite uninjured."

"But I must do something. The police —"
She made a decided gesture with one hand.
"Oh, very well, of course, I won't call them

30

if you don't wish it. But something ought to be done. It might —" I was about to say it might happen again, but I checked myself in the face of her fright.

I don't remember that I had need to convince myself that she was telling me the truth: there simply wasn't any doubt in my mind. I said: "Isn't there something I can do? Shall I call a maid? The hotel manager? Anyone? Can't I do something?" I moved toward the bell and she must have thought I was moving toward the door, for she turned around in fear again and said with a quick catching of her breath:

"Please don't leave. Just for a moment or two. I shall be all right again in just a moment. I — you see, I'm out of breath. I've been running. He was following me."

Something carried me to the door and into the corridor; it was not my reason or volition, for I had no wish to become entangled in abductions. She reached the door to the stairway as soon as I did and had both her hands on mine on the latch. She was frightened, for her face was white, and she looked through the glass in a terrified way, but she begged me to go back.

"Do believe me. Do believe me. He's gone. He must have gone as soon as you opened the door and let me in. He wouldn't stay

31

about, waiting to be caught. Besides, I can't thrust this upon you."

Her breath was warm and sweet and very near my face; her shoulder was thrusting softly against me as if to push me back in spite of myself; her hands were little and cold and strong, and she used some kind of scent that was faintly like gardenias.

I said, "Nonsense," and lifted her hands and moved her not too gently to one side; she was fairly strong under her slimness, and determined. But as I wrenched the door open and the wind howled upon us she seized my arm again and cried, her lips near my ear so I could hear her through the tumult of wind and creaking windows and clattering shutters:

"*Won't* you understand? It will be very difficult for me if you do this."

I looked down the steps. I could see only as far as the first curve, and that but dimly. Of course no one was there, and the courtyard was only alive with shadows. If she felt like that about it — after all, the decision must remain with her. She was standing so close to me that I could feel her body tremble with cold.

"Go back into my room and try to get warm." As she hesitated, I added: "Oh, I'll do as you say, of course." It satisfied her, after one searching look through the half darkness to find my eyes, and she went back to the light and the fire while I closed the door to the stairway.

She was sitting again on the floor before the fire when I followed her. She looked very sweet, sitting there with her small scarlet slippers showing and their frivolous silver heels shining, and her hands outstretched again to the fire, and her bright hair tumbled.

"Please don't look like that," she said. "As if I had cheated justice. I don't know how to explain all this to you. It must sound very lurid, thus far. But you must see that I can't involve you. And after all," she added unexpectedly, "one's abduction is one's own affair."

"It's very fortunate that it turned out in a way which permits you to say that."

She looked at me quickly.

"Don't think I'm flippant. I'm — I'm badly scared. Perhaps in a moment I can thank you properly. Just now I should like to get good and warm at your nice fire. I can face these chilly, long, dark corridors to my own room with a better grace when I'm warm. Isn't it curious that just being cold can do things to your courage?"

She stopped abruptly, as if that were at the moment too dangerous a topic, and said quickly: "I am Sue Tally. I'm staying here,

33

of course. You just arrived tonight, didn't you? Do sit down. And smoke if you like. I'm intruding unforgivably; the least I can do is want you to be comfortable."

I wanted to tell her she was not intruding. I wanted to tell her I was feasting my starved eyes just watching her. I wanted to tell her she was a damned little fool not to let me go after the man myself or call the police.

I said my name was Jim Sundean and would she have a cigarette.

She refused and watched me light one. Her small nose sniffed a little, and she said in a pleased way:

"Why, that's an American cigarette!"

I nodded.

"You wouldn't believe how difficult it's been for me to get them. Of course, here in France it's easy enough, if rather expensive, but in Russia it was practically impossible. At least, where I was."

"You've just come from there?" Her face looked softer; less rigid and white with terror, as if talking of everyday matters were restoring her poise. A sharper onslaught of wind banged the loose shutter at the window with a sudden loud clap, and her eyes leaped to mine, and she went white again, and I said hurriedly:

"Just a loose shutter in the wind; there isn't anything. Yes, I've just come from there. I

34

was there two full years, without leaving. It was on a job. I'm an engineer. It was rather awful. An old friend of mine, Jack Dunning, and I arranged by letter to meet here for a winter trip through southern Spain. I'm a week ahead of time. I don't know where Jack is at the moment." She was looking, I was glad to see, more natural again, and I went on: "I hope southern Spain is warmer than it is here. Less wind."

She smiled a little.

"It's the wind here that makes it so cold. The mistral, you know. But it is terribly hot here in the summer. That's when the tourists come. They arrive in flocks; all America must have been here at one time or another. In the summer it is white and hot and dry. I liked it at first. Now I —" I felt she was going to say she hated it but she said merely — "now I don't like it. What do you think of the hotel?"

"It's rather large in the winter, isn't it? The handful of guests must rattle around like so many peanuts."

"We do rather rattle around. Especially when the summer staff is dismissed. Just now there are only the cook, one porter and one maid, the manager, and Madame Lovschiem, his wife. And you and Mrs. Byng and a priest. And myself, of course. It is very quiet and lonely in the winter."

I must have looked a question, for she added: "I have been here about a year. You see — my mother was ill and died here. Madame Lovschiem and her husband have been very kind to me and to my mother."

She didn't mention any other family she might have had or where her home in America had been. As if she wished to change the subject, she slipped to her feet and looked at herself in the mirror, patted her hair, which was cut rather long and parted in the middle, so that the ends curled gently just below her ears and gave her the look of a beautiful medieval page, and she told me about the hotel. It had been, she said, an old and very elegant family residence; the people who had originally made a hotel of it had bought the place, lock, stock, and barrel, from the owners, which accounted for the handsome furnishings.

"Of course," she said, "it has been changed from time to time, decorations renewed." She tipped her head and looked at the wall paper. "The wall paper, for instance. That, now, looks like a fresco artist's nightmare. There is a private salon next door that has the original old satin brocade on the walls. The room is seldom opened, but you might like to see it. There's a piano in it, as big as a barn, on which a long ago Pope is said to have sung

36

a mass. I doubt that — however."

I made a sound of agreement, and she went on swiftly:

"There's a story about these old clocks, too; that they were bought in preparation for a visit from Napoleon. He liked clocks, you know; but I doubt that one, too. Even the most passionate clock lover wouldn't want half a hundred of them. Oh, you have the sword clock. It's the only one in the house."

Her pink fingers touched the little sword and slid it gently out of the bronze soldier's grasp. I must have looked surprised, for she laughed for the first time and flourished it. "Didn't you know it was loose? It's sharp, too." She ran her finger tips along the edge. "Like a dagger."

She stood there touching the toy sword. Her bright head was bent. Her velvet coat was buttoned as tight as a basque to her chin, its skirt fitted her slender waist and hips and then flared long and full. Our attempt at conversation had steadied her, but it hadn't altered the situation. I walked over to her and stood there leaning against the mantel. Something to my astonishment I heard myself saying:

"I want to help you. Won't you let me?"

She replaced the little sword slowly.

"You have helped. I don't know how to thank you. I'm not really, I think, in any danger." She hesitated and turned to look directly up at me. It is yet impossible for me to put a name to the quality in her gaze that was so compelling; I only know that I stood there without finding words, so strong was the feeling that there was something very momentous about her look.

After a time — probably only a few seconds — she went on gravely: "Perhaps I'd better tell you what happened tonight. It must have been around ten o'clock when I went out. I was restless and wanted to walk in the wind a little before trying to go to sleep. Oh, I often go out on the bridge and watch the river for a time at night; it's always been perfectly safe. But tonight — well, tonight . . ." She put her hand to her throat but went steadily on:

"Tonight a car passing me stopped. A man got out. I started to walk away, but he caught me. He tied something over my mouth and around my wrists and put me in the back seat of the car. He was hurried and I think frightened at what he was doing, and of course I struggled. Then he got into the front seat and drove and drove and drove. I thought we were miles from A—. I was in a panic, naturally, but I worked so frantically that I got my hands loose and the scarf from my face. It must have been more than an hour that he drove. Finally he stopped."

She stopped, too, and took a long breath. "I had planned what I would do. As he got out the front seat, I got out the back seat, on the opposite side, and ran. The wind was blowing, and it was dark, and he didn't hear me open the door, and it was a moment before he found I was not there. I was running, of course, and saving my breath to scream as soon as I should see a light anywhere. Then I saw a light, and it was the light at the entrance of the hotel. I didn't stop to think how strange it was, I just ran. The gate was locked, of course; but I knew the way in. He was after me."

Something must have come from my throat then, for she stopped, gave me a questioning look, and then went on.

"He could see me under the small light. He was so close, and there was no light in the hotel, and he, too, knew the way into the court. Then I saw your light. I ran into the shadows and up the stairway. I think he wasted time looking in the courtyard for me. I don't think he heard me call to you; the wind was too loud. But I'm afraid he saw me against the light. You can see your light from the court, you know, when the door is open. And that's — that's all. Except that I want you to tell no one — especially the Lovschiems."

"Who was the man?"

"I don't know."

"It wasn't anyone you had seen before?"

"I'm not sure. I couldn't see him."

"It wasn't Lovschiem?"

"Oh, no!" she cried. "It wasn't Lovschiem. He is so — fat, you know. This man wasn't fat."

That somehow made me see the struggle and the ugliness more clearly. She said quickly: "Don't look like that. I'm not hurt, except for the fright. And I escaped."

I said that the fellow ought to be killed. I believe I said I would enjoy the job of doing it. I said several other things, equally trite and melodramatic. As I finished I disconcertingly recalled that when she told me of it first I had asked her if she wanted me to send for the police.

"I've troubled you enough," she said. "I can't thank you. Now I'm going."

"But wait. Look here. Are you sure you'll be safe? I can't let you go like this."

"I shall be perfectly safe."

"It might happen again, you know. Let me call Madame Lovschiem."

"No. No. I shan't go for walks on the bridge again — at night, anyway. And there's no need to call Madame. She must not know. I'll lock my door." An expression of consternation crossed her face. "My key," she said. "I left my key on the board in the lobby before I left."

"I'll get it for you. Stay here. What number is it?"

"Nineteen. But —"

"Don't leave until I return."

The corridors were still dimly lit. I had reached the lift and stairway before I remembered that going across the court would have been quicker — but then the door from the courtyard to the lobby would probably have been locked. I glanced over the railing into the lounge as I went past, but it was a black well with a lightish strip along the floor from the faint light of the corridor back of me. I had no trouble getting down the stairs, for I could follow the railing, but when I had once crossed the twilight of the faintly lighted strip in the lounge I was in complete darkness.

Thus it took me some time to fumble about in the blackness for the electric light switches, and all the time the wind was rattling and shrieking in the court just outside. I couldn't find a match in my pockets, and although in hunting for the light switch my fingers encountered the key board, I couldn't, of course, tell which key was nineteen. I don't know just how long it was; several moments, at least, when I finally encountered the switch. Touching it threw the little lobby into a light that looked bright but probably wasn't. And even after that it took a moment or two to convince myself that not one of the keys hanging so trustingly on the board on the wall bore the number nineteen. There was a hook labeled nineteen but there was no key hanging on it.

I finally snapped out the light. The switch was near the door into the courtyard, and I glanced through the glass. The court was still black with flying shadows, but there was a light — it was from the door of my own room. The door was open. The light streamed out.

And at that very instant a dark figure flashed across the light, was silhouetted for a fleeting moment against it and was gone. I caught only a glimpse of a dark figure, but I was sure it was Sue Tally's, for there was the sharp black outline of her velvet cloak, tightly buttoned like a basque at the top, with long flaring skirts. It was sudden and clear and then gone completely.

The door of the lobby was locked, but the key was in it, and I had unlocked and opened the door and was running across the court-yard. The wind took the breath out of my lungs, and my heart was pounding by the time I had reached the little winding stairway. The shrubs growing about it reached out and clutched at me, and the railing was icy cold. It circled around and around while I thought that at any rate I had seen no pursuing figure. I reached the landing.

One step more to the door. I could see no one against the light streaming from the still open door into my room.

I took the step. There was something on the landing. I was stumbling. I was plunging down upon it. I was confused with it and couldn't extricate myself.

My hands were pushing against it and I was kneeling. I brought my hands up and tried to see them through the dim half light. They were wet, and I could barely see that they were darkly stained.

CHAPTER III

The next few moments are not very clear in my memory. I managed somehow to get the door open and the limp thing dragged through it and into the corridor, and then I could see it in the light from my own room. It was a man. I did not know who he was. He was dead. I knew that at once. And it was a very ugly death, for he'd been stabbed. I remember saying to myself: "Don't touch anything, this is murder. Don't touch anything."

Then I was in my room. No one was there: Sue was gone. I was pressing the bell with my thumb. I finally released the button, noted that my thumb had stained the white button in a perfect and gruesome thumb-mark, and hurried to the bathroom, where I washed my hands. And then I came back to the bell and washed it, too, with a corner of the towel, and rang again.

All the time I was washing the bell I could see the face of the dead man leering out from the surrounding darkness of the corridor. His eyes were open and his mouth was open and I felt as if he were about to speak to me. I hadn't seen anyone look like that since 1918, and instead of feeling calloused and cool about it, the sight had awakened a whole train of subterranean awareness that I had succeeded in pushing into limbo.

I was still pushing the bell and wishing the dead man wouldn't stare so, and in the same moment cursing myself for being so shaken, when I heard the door away down at the beginning of the north corridor open. I stepped out into the hall, avoiding a hand which had fallen slowly outward. Lovschiem himself, fully dressed, wavered out of the gloom. He quickened his footsteps when he saw me and then suddenly began to run heavily as if he'd seen the figure at my feet.

He didn't ask me anything for a moment. He just fell on his fat knees and stared at the dead man. Then he felt for a pulse and touched his face and leaned further over to see if there was any breath at all in that sprawled body. I stood watching him. Finally he leaned back and faced me. And if ever a man's face showed stark livid terror it was Lovschiem's at that moment.

He had to moisten his thick mouth a time or two before he could get any words out, and I remember how sweat stood out on his frightened face and glistened in the light. But his first question was not what I expected. For he said:

"Did you kill him?"

"My God, no."

He stared at me, dark eyes glittering from the sagging livid mask that was his face.

"Then what happened? He didn't kill himself."

"I found him. There on the landing. I dragged him into the corridor and saw he was dead and rang."

He looked at me disbelievingly. For a long moment we stared at each other above that ugly thing on the floor, while the wind howled and the witches darted madly about the court as if in high carnival at the fell thing they had witnessed.

Finally he lowered his eyes. He reached out a hand to the small ornamented hilt of the knife, drew his hand back as if it shrunk from touching the wetness about it, and then stretched it out again. The jewels winked evilly at me. I said:

"You'd better leave it alone, hadn't you? It seems to be murder. And the police won't want things touched."

His hand fell back, and his face, turned up to me, looked faintly green. It was as if the word police shocked and terrified him as much as the murder. After another long moment he mumbled:

"The police. But the police — I am ruined. I am ruined! There's no need to call the police. I can't have gendarmes nosing about. I —" He recalled that he was speaking aloud and to me and checked himself with a quick sidelong look at me.

"It's murder," I said. "You'll have to call the police."

His narrowed gaze measured me, tried to plumb my own eyes. It was not pleasant, standing there, watching his fear-sweated fat face and his eyes calculating. Finally he said:

"I was thinking of the hotel. Anything like this is very bad for a place. Do you know the man?"

I shook my head.

"I never saw him before."

It must have been convincing, for after searching my face for a moment as if testing the truth of my denial he said:

"I don't know him either. I never saw him before. He certainly had no business in the hotel."

If my words sounded entirely true to Lovschiem, his sounded equally false to me. I don't know why I knew he was lying with all the oiliness and ingratiating manner at his command, but I knew it. My foot was very near his fat thigh, tight because he was squatting there by the dead man, and it was all I could do to keep from kicking him for his lies and his unction and his oily certainty that he was deceiving me. Then my gaze shifted again to that dead face, and I felt no desire to do anything.

"You'd better call the police, then," I said.

Lovschiem, satisfied that I had accepted his word, was leaning over the man again.

"Ho — look here. Someone's robbed him. Pockets emptied, nothing anywhere." His hands no longer shrank; they were instead ghoulishly eager in their search. It was as if Lovschiem expected to find something that had been overlooked. If so, he failed, for presently he looked at me again. This time his eyes were angry and little and vicious. He said: *"Who are you?"*

Later I was to ponder over that crazy inquiry. Then it enraged me; I was angry, shaken, tired, cold, and I was still in the grip of a nightmarish experience.

"You know very well who I am. If you are innocent of this affair, call the police at once. If you don't, I will. *Keep your hands off that man!*"

I had spoken too late.

He had dragged out the knife and was holding it up into the stream of light so we both could see it. It was dark, and a slow drop was forming on it. But it wasn't a knife at all.

It was a small dagger like a toy sword. It *was* a toy sword, and I had seen one like it only a little before.

Lovschiem recognized it, too. He got heavily to his feet. I preceded him, however, into my room, and we both were at the fireplace staring at the bronze clock. It was quite unbelievable, of course, but still it was true. The little bronze soldier's gauntleted hand was empty, and the sword was in Lovschiem's fat hand. Or at least, I thought, a sword just like it.

But Lovschiem dispelled my sprouting hope of that at once. He said with just a gleam of ugly triumph:

"There's only one like it in the house. No, Mr. Sundean, you killed him yourself. You were very stupid about it. More stupid than I should have believed of you, for you've the face of an intelligent man. But you killed him."

There are things that leave you so stunned that for just a moment you feel numb — as if suspended in a void. I knew I was standing there in that bedroom, I knew I was looking at Lovschiem's fat face, more normal now and less frightened, and I knew that he was holding the dagger between his thick fingers. The thing that was so unreal and made everything

49

else unreal was his accusation.

"And you want me to call the police," he added, with what approached a smile. "Ah, you are a very stupid man indeed to think that that would establish your innocence."

It was still difficult to speak. But all at once things were real enough. A sudden memory had come to me with all the reviving influence of a stream of icy water. Sue Tally had stood there, almost where Lovschiem was now standing, holding that sword and running her pink fingers along its sharp edge and saying that it was like a dagger.

Then I had left her alone in the room. I had gone through the long corridors to the lobby, and when I had glanced from it I had seen her figure cross the light from my door and vanish into the darkness of the corridors. And immediately afterward I had found a murdered man beside that very door, and he had been murdered with the dagger I had last seen in Sue Tally's fingers.

I was no longer stunned. Things were painfully clear and real.

But the trouble was I didn't know what to do. I wasn't resourceful; I wasn't quick-thinking, I wasn't anything I ought to have been. I simply didn't know what to do. So I stood there looking at Lovschiem and said nothing.

A small satisfaction was that my look irritated Lovschiem and apparently made him uneasy. He said — and I was faintly pleased to note that he said it with a note of anger:

"You Americans, you are all alike. Straight eyes, straight noses, straight chins. How can anyone tell what you are thinking? Poker faces, that's what you call them. I suppose you are proud of your silly poker faces. Now then, shall I call the police?"

There was only one thing to say.

"Call them at once. I don't know how that dagger got there. I don't know who the fellow out there is or who killed him. I know nothing about it. I suppose you'll accuse me; but you'd better get them here at once."

He was visibly disconcerted. He stared at me and then took another step toward me, peering into my face.

"Who are you?" he said again. His voice was almost a whisper, yet it held an undercurrent of intense anxiety. Again, somehow, the question touched off my smoldering fury. I stepped quickly nearer.

"See here, Lovschiem, I told you once who I am! And that I didn't kill this man!"

He backed away a step or two and someone from the corridor gasped shrilly:

"What is it? For the love of God —"

"Grethe — hush!" Lovschiem's voice

51

smothered the woman's cry. I whirled.

It was a woman, now, kneeling by the murdered man. A woman in a yellow shawl whose fringes dropped from her shoulders. She lifted her hand to hold them back so they should not become stained. Her red hair was drawn in a great knot at the back of her neck. She was staring at the dead man, and her mouth was moving.

Lovschiem, the dagger still held carefully between two fat fingers, left me and advanced quickly toward her. I followed him and saw her turn her horrified face up toward him and heard her gasp:

"So, you've killed him."

By that time he had bent over her, and I could not see past his bulk. I could, however, hear his voice.

"He was found dead on the landing, there. I do not know who he is. None of us know, for he was not a guest at the hotel. I am just going to call the police. This man with me found him."

He turned to me: "My wife can go and telephone for the police, since you insist."

The red-haired woman, then, was Madame Lovschiem. I could see her now as she rose. A rather handsome woman, she was, or would have been except for her shocked face, which made her look old, though she couldn't have been past forty. She clutched the yellow shawl about her. The tight folds hugged her full breast and narrow waist and curving hips; even at the moment I was conscious, as a man is, of a kind of attraction about her. It wasn't charm; it wasn't anything you can put a word to; yet at that first moment I must have been conscious of it, for I remembered it later.

In the very act of rising she had caught sight of the dagger with its ominous wet stain. Her shining eyes fastened on it, and widened, and held their gaze so fixedly that both Lovschiem and I looked at it, too. But she did not scream. She did not make any motion of fright. She said finally:

"He was killed with that." It was a statement, but Lovschiem nodded, and I suppose I made some motion, for she looked swiftly at me. "Who killed him?"

"He was killed with this dagger," replied Lovschiem obliquely. "And it is the sword from the clock in this man's room. This man says he found him on the landing there and doesn't know anything about it. He insists on my calling the police. He says —" finished Lovschiem, with the effect of dubious afterthought — "he says that his name's Sundean. That's how he registered. Sundean."

There was certainly a meaning in the afterthought which Madame Lovschiem caught and I did not. She looked at me again. Studied me with the same intentness her husband had shown. The wind shrieked, and the window beside us rattled. Her eyes were gleaming; her face had lost its white look of shock and had become firm and thoughtful, and her mouth was tight.

She said briskly:

"Lovschiem, you're a fool."

And as the fat man sagged a little and blustered something to cover it, she cut through his mumble.

"You're a fool," she repeated, and I felt that she'd have liked to amplify the remark, for her eyes were not too pleasant. "Of course the man's name is Sundean. And if he says he hasn't anything to do with this murder, why should we think he has? That clock sword — there are a dozen explanations. But the thing is — the police won't believe any of them. Now then, the best plan is simply to forget the clock sword. Here, give it to me."

The man made a protestant gesture, but nevertheless handed her the sword, and she took it coolly. If the stains shocked or repelled her, her blunt fingers gave no evidence of it, and she eyed it with a sangfroid that would have done credit to a bluebeard.

"I'll just wash this off and replace it and nobody need know anything about it."

Lovschiem looked blank.

"That won't do at all," he said. "I don't know what you —"

"Lovschiem," she said sharply. Her eyes quelled his, and he stood there looking at her and looking at me for all the world as if he were trying to receive some wordless message concerning me and failing. As indeed must have been actually the case. There was no reason that I could see for Madame Lovschiem's suddenly championing me.

Moreover, I didn't know that I wanted her championship. This thing of the dagger cut two ways.

In the first place, if I let her do as she proposed there was no danger of the girl, Sue Tally, getting involved in the affair. There was also, which was an important enough view, not much danger of Jim Sundean's being accused of murder. At the same time, if the truth eventually came out, as it readily might, things would look much blacker for me or for Sue Tally (you see, I was being very cool about it and not proposing to sacrifice myself for a girl I had seen just twice) than if I had told the truth and showed thus that I was unafraid of it at the outset. And finally, if I let Madame Lovschiem carry through her scheme, I should give the Lovschiems a most detestable hold over me.

So it was not so much daring that led to my quick decision as it was that I couldn't let the Lovschiems do this thing which she proposed. She was walking toward the bathroom, the dagger held nonchalantly in her fingers, when I stopped her.

"No," I said. "We'll call the police and let them know the whole thing, dagger and all. I didn't kill him. I'm not afraid."

She stopped and looked at me incredulously. I saw then that her eyes were green, limpid, and clear, and yet with that look of secret reflection that a cat's have. She looked me up and down and smiled a little and moved nearer me.

"Not afraid?" she said rather softly. "American, aren't you? Not bad-looking, either. Tall, hard-looking, brown hair, nice head, blue-gray eyes — how many of your type I have seen! Why, your face is made on planes, isn't it? Eyebrows, eyes, and mouth straight across one way and nose and chin as straight the other way. Accustomed to having your own way, I suppose, with men — and women?"

"You are too kind, madame. You'll leave the dagger exactly as it is, please, and your husband and I will wait together while you phone for the police."

"I'll do nothing of the kind," she said and turned to the bathroom, but I caught her wrist and led her back to the dead man and to where her husband stood staring at us with his face still blank and only his small eyes active. She did not protest or even pull back when I told her to place the dagger on the dead man's chest, but I did not release her wrist until she had done so, and her eyes shone like a cat's when the light strikes them.

She said nothing to me, however. She gave her husband a glance of scorn and fury but said in a smooth voice that was under perfect control that, since Mr. Sundean so wished, they might as well call the police.

"Very well," said Lovschiem sluggishly, as if his thoughts were sunk in some dark mire. "Call them."

She looked at him again in a kind of impatient scorn, shrugged lightly, and then glanced all about.

"Father Robart!" she said suddenly. "Of course. Father Robart. I'll get him at once. This — this dead man must have prayers said for his soul immediately." And as I looked at her, wondering what her scheme was now, her green eyes met mine, and there was actually a flash of wicked laughter in them while she said: "He must have prayers immediately. A violent death, without absolution. And he may have been a very, very evil man. Who knows? Besides, it is not bad to give a more

57

pious atmosphere, eh?"

The fringes of her yellow scarf swirled and vanished in the gloom of the long corridor. Shadows followed her, and the wind whispered, and the whisper rose to a gust, and the whole place rattled like a dead man's dry bones.

I said to myself: It's a nightmare. The whole thing's a nightmare. Things like this don't happen. It began to be a nightmare when the wind sobbed at me, at the door above that dead man's feet, and then it was not the wind, it was Sue. That's when it began to be a dream, when Sue flew in from the dark. I said: I'll shut my eyes and then open them and look directly at the mantel clock. The sword will still be there, and it will all have been a dream.

The clock sword was, of course, not on the mantel: it was lying bloodstained there below me, and the dead man's face was real enough.

Lovschiem was standing quiet beside me, his gaze too upon the dead man, and his fat face only vaguely frightened now, for he was still sunk deep in his thoughts and looked more troubled and perplexed than he looked frightened.

And I had been set thinking of Sue. Sue Tally. For the first time the things she had told me sounded improbable. You couldn't evade the fact. She had not told me why she was abducted, and she must have known. She hadn't told me why it would make things difficult for her if I insisted on going after the man who had followed her into the courtyard. She had told me, made me promise in effect to tell no one about the affair, "especially the Lovschiems," and she'd said — or at least strongly implied — that the Lovschiems were her very good friends. It was unreasonable to think that her abductor would simply drive about the country for hours and then wind up at the hotel again. With an effect of frankness she had really told me very little. And what she did tell me was full of holes. Yes, the whole thing was improbable.

Ordinary common sense told me that.

The curious thing about it was that I believed her. And it had certainly been extraordinarily pleasant to have her sitting there before the fire with her bright hair and black coat and little scarlet slippers with their silver heels. I could see again her beautiful hands and her dark eyes with their vivid, compelling way of looking at me.

I was thinking of her eyes when I remembered suddenly the matter of the key. It was rather a jolt.

She had sent me for a key that wasn't where she said it would be.

And I rushed irresistibly on: while I was gone for that key a murder had been done.

Sue had been left in the room where the clock sword was, she had been looking at it and had said how sharp it was and that it was like a dagger; and I had seen her figure flash across the light from my room, and the door had been open and she was gone and the clock sword was in the breast of the murdered man.

The ridiculous thing was that I still believed her. There were all those things against her. And it was quite possible that this lumpish, grotesque thing at our feet had been pursuing her, had reached her during my absence from the room, and in fear and desperation she had snatched the clock sword and struck at him. Which would have been justifiable, I thought. But I felt rather sickish and wished the wind wouldn't surge things about so wildly, and that the thing's head didn't loll so carelessly and limply there, and that its eyes and its mouth were shut.

I started to say something — anything — to Lovschiem, for the silence of all things in that narrow black passage, except the creaking of the windows, and the hurling shadows and wind outside, was growing oppressive, when we heard a sound down the corridor, and Madame Lovschiem's yellow shawl emerged, followed by the black skirts of the priest. From the corner of my eye I saw Lovschiem wipe his forehead, and I suddenly knew that the waiting and the dead man and the feeling of things had not been pleasant to him, either.

Madame Lovschiem led the priest directly to the man at our feet. We both moved back a little when the priest's red beard loomed up into the light. He bent over, as we all had, and stared at the dead man. But he looked puzzled and clumsy and did not seem to know exactly what Madame Lovschiem expected of him. He got down, however, on his knees and got out his crucifix and rosary and began passing his fingers over the beads.

I couldn't see his face, only his bent head and rather thin and narrow shoulders in their tightly buttoned soutane, and his feet, which projected from the black folds of the skirt of the garment he wore and looked very large. He was younger than he had seemed on my first glimpse of him; there was an unwrinkled look about the back of his neck, there seemed to be no gray in his mouse-colored hair, and his figure was rather lean. It was strange, I thought, that he was wearing American-made shoes. It was so strange that I looked closely at the soles and heels and stitching. They had undoubtedly been made in America.

He was mumbling then, and Lovschiem was staring blankly across the shadow-swept court, and Madame was looking very devout except for her eyes, which were shining and were looking at me with an expression that came very close to a kind of wicked amusement.

All the same, amused or not, I suspected that she was thinking furiously back of her devout face and glittering eyes.

The priest kept on muttering. To my approval he had asked no questions about the murder, which was self-evident, to be sure; and he offered no churchly admonitions or advice. It occurred to me that he might be, in his youth, a little uncertain in what was likely an unprecedented experience with him.

Lovschiem drew back a little, and Madame and I moved also.

I was tired and would have done with the thing; I said:

"And now, madame, the police."

"You go, Grethe," said Lovschiem stupidly. "Tell them what you think best."

This time she consented, and after giving one quick glance about which lingered with a certain satisfaction on the kneeling figure of the priest, she went. Again Lovschiem and I were left waiting — Lovschiem still sunk in some morass of worried thoughts while I stood by wishing the thing were done with and dreading the commotion and the questions. I was suddenly frightfully weary. And I knew that I must have my story ready. My story in which there must be no holes, for

I should have to stick to it and tell it at the later and formal inquiry which would undoubtedly take place. The weakest point was my trip to the lobby.

How could I explain that without telling about Sue?

Through the glass windows I looked out over the shadows of the court. If the wind would stop, perhaps things would be better. But instead of stopping or even lulling a bit, there was a terrific onslaught which fell upon the court and the old house with cold and raging fury. The shadows flew, and the small light above the great iron gate waved madly. It made such a wide arc that suddenly its flickering rays fell upon a window across the court and above. The shutters of that window were thrown back, and a face was watching us. The room beyond was black, so the watcher must have been able to see us all quite clearly against the light behind us. The face looked white in that flash of light upon it, and dreadfully haggard.

You felt at once that whatever watched had some strong and dreadful interest in the scene it looked upon.

But the thing was, it was a girl's face — and it was framed in hair parted in the middle of a white forehead and long around her cheeks after the fashion of a medieval page.

CHAPTER IV

It was Sue Tally. It was not Sue Tally. It was Sue Tally.

I told myself that I was mistaken. I told myself that the light upon it had been too brief, too sudden and swift a flash, to permit me to recognize any face. I told myself that I couldn't have sworn, even, that it was a woman's face, for the more I thought of it the less I was able to recall any feature at all and therefore I could not reasonably believe that it was Sue Tally's face. But I stared and stared at that unshuttered window and wondered what was back of those winking black panes, and that strange, haunting resemblance to Sue Tally's face would not leave me.

But even if it had been Sue Tally, what of it? The weird flash of light would have made anyone's face look distorted and white and strange.

Suddenly I was conscious that Lovschiem had roused from his distraction sufficiently to note my gaze and follow it. When I glanced at him he too was looking at that unshuttered window, and his fat face looked more acutely uneasy; I had the impression that with all his somber delving into the depths the problem of the murder had presented to him, still he had overlooked some pressing and urgent aspect of it. This impression was confirmed when he caught his breath sharply, slid a quick glance at me, and said suddenly:

"But I must go. There are things — Grethe will want — you and Father Robart can stay with the — with this." His eyes indicated the thing at our feet.

"Wait," I said. "What room is that across there? What number is it? The one with the shutters open."

His eyes were veiled and yet intensely aware of me and my question.

"You mean across the court there? The number of that room? That is about thirty-four or thirty-five. Why?"

Not nineteen, then.

"Is it unoccupied?"

"Yes." He replied directly, without a shadow of hesitation.

"I saw a face just now in the window."

"No, no. You are mistaken. There is no one there." He moistened his lips and said: "Unless, of course, someone strayed into the room.

65

Madame Byng, perhaps, or one of the servants."

"There certainly was a face there, Lovschiem."

It seemed to me he looked faintly relieved at the implication that I did not know the face. But he said a word or two to the priest, who did not look around or reply, and waddled hurriedly away. At the end of the passage he met the little porter and stopped for a few words with him before he disappeared around the corner, and the porter hurried toward us.

Apparently the porter had already been told something of the affair, for he stared at the dead man and crossed himself but asked no questions, although his bright eyes snapped with excitement and he shot nervous glances into the shadows about us.

Madame had called him, he said breathlessly, and he was to remain with us while Monsieur went to her assistance.

Went, I thought, to connive with her, and I wondered what they were scheming down there in the blackness of the draft-swept rooms of the old hotel. Probably methods and means to keep themselves out of danger. And it ill behooved me to stand there waiting while the police were on their way and the likeliest man to arrest for the murder was certainly me. Yet there was little to be done. I might take a look at the landing where I'd stumbled upon that grisly heap, however; and it would do no harm to take another look about that shadowy courtyard.

Turning into my room, I threw my coat over my shoulders and took a flashlight from my bag. The little porter watched me anxiously, and I said as I returned to the corridor:

"I'm going to look about the court. Back in a moment."

He did not seem reassured, but, of course, had nothing to say. The priest continued his rapid low stream of what I took to be prayers and did not look around even when I opened the door to the landing and the wind swooped through the passage and upon them, lifting the thin black strands of the little porter's hair and stirring the skirt of the priest's soutane and moving the open coat of the murdered man so that for an instant it gave him a gruesome semblance of half-life.

Then I closed the door, saw the porter's bright eyes watching it and what he could see of me, stepped out of their range of vision, and snapped the button on my flashlight. It made a darting circle of thin light on the stone floor of the landing.

There were no signs of a struggle, but I could have expected none. There were no muddy footprints, for there was no mud;

everything in A— was dry and cold and wind-swept. There were no cigar ashes. There were no coat buttons. There was nothing but a dark blotch, quite small, where the dead man had huddled.

I bent close to the worn stone and looked and looked, turning my flashlight here and there, and eventually I did discover a small red piece of what looked like hard rubber or very hard wax. It was rough and irregularly semicircular and about the size of half a two-franc piece. It bore no faint resemblance to any kind of clue. I put it in my pocket merely because it was the only thing except the dark patch on the stone and a dry brown leaf that the landing held. It was just at that second that there was a sudden lull in the wind; everything, shadows and shrubbery and rattling windows, fell into dead quiet, and I heard an unguarded step on the stairway below me.

It wasn't any sound but a step; I knew that perfectly, and I daresay if the wind had not lulled just at that instant I should not be alive now. But I heard it and moved to one side in order to look over the curve of the railing. And at that very instant there were two sharp cracks of a revolver, my flashlight spun out of my hand and thudded somewhere below, the wind swooped down upon the courtyard with a crash, and every light in the hotel went out.

My hand tingled but wasn't hurt.

The wind hurled furiously in my ears, but there were no longer flying shadows, for everything was dark, the hotel itself merely a huge blacker shape against the darkness above, and the courtyard was a well, dense and black and mysterious. There was not even a light in the corridor near me, where the dead man lay and the priest prayed over him.

There was no sound but the hurling of the wind, and I found myself running down the stairway, holding to the railing. It was not prudence, Heaven knows, that impelled me; it was in fact extraordinary stupidity. I had no revolver, the place was black as a cellar, and I didn't know its ins and outs. There is no excuse for it, but that is what I did.

I encountered nothing on the stairway. At its foot I clutched something that brushed against my hand, discovered it was a leafy shrub, and stepped nearer it while I waited for another lull. It was a noisy place; I strained my ears to hear through the tumult of the wind another sound of a step or a motion, but did not. Finally, as the gusts continued I started cautiously away from the shelter of the shrub and toward the wall of the court. If it was Lovschiem who had shot at me — and I thought it possible — he would probably either follow me to finish the job or seek to reënter the hotel himself. He certainly was not apt to reënter the hotel by way of the winding stairway and the corridor where the priest and the porter waited; if I followed the wall cautiously past the great iron gate below the entrance arch and then around the corner opposite, I might catch him at the door to the lobby.

By this time I had cooled a trifle, and my progress was slower and more careful, and I wished I had some kind of weapon. Lovschiem was fat, however, and out of condition. If I could get him before he had time to use his revolver — Again something brushed my hand. This time it was not a shrub. It was rough fabric and an arm, and it moved quickly away, and I hurled myself in its direction, tackling low as in football.

I caught only the flying end of some kind of garment which wrenched itself out of my clutch, my knees scraped the pavement, and there were three flashes of light from somewhere off at my left and three revolver shots that spat viciously through the tumult. Vaguely I thought it was lucky I was flat on the pavement and waited. There were no more shots, and the wind shrieked, and it was black as pitch everywhere.

Suddenly I became convinced that my assailant was stalking me. And simultaneously

I realized what a fool I'd been.

He had a gun and I hadn't: that was the sum and substance of the thing.

At any second the light above the entrance might flash on, and I would be outlined, an excellent target. Or, which was somehow worse, at any second he might brush against me or I against him, and he had the revolver: it always came back to that.

I wished I had had the good sense to retreat before it was too late, and got cautiously to my knees, then swiftly to my feet and ran to my right a few steps. The sound made by the wind covered my own footsteps, but it also covered the sound of any movement he had made.

The shots had come from my left, which was then toward the door of the lobby. I felt, however (without reason, for I could hear and see nothing), that he had moved toward the entrance arch. It was only a kind of feeling that told me that; an instinct that I dared not rely upon. The thing for me to do was find a corner of the wall and hope for luck.

Cautiously, straining my ears to hear, I edged toward the wall of the north wing, not, however, toward the corner of the stairway. That, I thought, was where he would expect me to go; it would be natural for me to attempt to escape by the way in which I had entered the courtyard — an entrance which, I realized rather chillingly, had been entirely too precipitate. When someone starts shooting at you in the dark and you have no weapon at all, you can't help wishing vehemently that you were elsewhere.

Against the wall, with some kind of small tree in a tub at one side of me, I waited. If he approached from the side of the shrub I would hear him or feel him and have some warning; then, since you'd rather take a chance than stand still and be shot, I could take him perhaps unexpectedly and have a better chance in a fight.

I waited and listened. The wind came in gusts, and once in a while there were brief lulls, but I could not hear a sound of anyone near me.

Presently I began to work quietly toward the door to the lobby. The entrance gates were locked, Sue had said; he would not deliberately enter the hotel by the north-wing corridor above, and the only place left was the lobby door.

I encountered no one and heard nothing but the wind. And I had not more than arrived at the lobby door when the lights suddenly flashed up: the light swaying above the entrance, throwing the court into shadows and empty white spaces again; the light from my door above; and now a light in the lobby beside me. I stepped aside from the door into the shadow and waited again. There was nothing to be seen but the shadows and the bending shrubs and trees in the courtyard.

The whole thing had seemed probably much longer than it actually was, and, I don't know when or exactly why, I became convinced that there was no one in the courtyard. Perhaps it was because, had he still been there, he would certainly have started to look for me. The entrance gates, I could see, were locked with a solid-looking padlock: he had not then escaped that way.

Feeling defeated and inwardly raging, I finally turned to the lobby and opened the door. Madame, whose red hair shone under the desk light, looked up at me with a quick flash of her green eyes, and the cockatoo on her shoulder gave a startled cluck.

"Your husband just came in by this door," I said. "Where is he?"

She frowned.

"No one has entered by that door," she said crisply. The cockatoo chattered, and she said: "Hush, Pucci," and I closed the door sharply behind me.

I could clearly see, silhouetted in the light from my room, the little porter waiting in the corridor above. Except for the witches and the wind and myself, the courtyard was empty. I crossed it again and had the good sense to find and put the discoverable pieces of my flashlight into my pocket against the search the police would make, before I ascended the little iron stairway.

The porter looked up with relief as I opened the door and stepped again into the corridor. I wondered if he had heard the revolver shots, but he said nothing, and I thought it possible that the violent night had drowned all sounds other than its own tumult. The revolver had been, too, of a small caliber; I could tell that from the sharp spitting sounds of its shots.

The priest had gone, and the little porter wore an anxious look, and Sue Tally was standing there beside him.

She looked at me, and I closed the door and shut out some of the wind, and she said, "Oh," in a gasping way. She looked stricken. The toe of her scarlet slipper was near the dead man's hand, and I got the impression that she had been leaning over him.

I said to the porter: "Where is Father Robart?"

"I don't know. He went away. As soon as you left us he went away too."

"You were alone here?"

"Yes." His wiry little shoulders moved in a kind of shudder, and I believed him, al-

74

though that left the porter and the priest each to his own devices at a time when I was pursuing and being pursued in the courtyard below. I paused to consider whether the priest or the porter could have got by way of the corridor into the courtyard in time to discover me still on the landing with my flashlight and fired up at me, and decided that neither of the two had had time to do so. Still, there it was: the priest or the porter or Lovschiem; I inclined toward Lovschiem.

The porter repeated: "But yes, monsieur. Until Miss Tally arrived."

There were things I wanted to ask Miss Tally. I said to the porter:

"What was the matter with the lights?"

He shrugged and spread out his hands. "I do not know. It is very bad here without lights. There was one that moved, I think. I think *he* move — but it is only that I have fear." Sue Tally caught her breath, and the little porter added quickly with an anxious glance at her: "There was only the wind. Me, I am not afraid."

"Go and —" And what? I sought for an excuse. "Go and bring some wood, please. The fire in my room is down. The police will soon be here and will question us all."

He gave me a sharp and rather dubious look but went.

"Do you know this man?" I asked Sue across the thing on the floor.

She shrank back a little at my tone. "No."

"Don't look frightened. I'll help you. Tell me if you've seen him before."

She leaned forward then and looked at him. She did not, as I expected, seem so affected by the horror of it as by a driving need to know; her look was peculiarly earnest and searching. It took in every feature of that shocking face. It seemed even to seek some familiar line. Then she looked at me.

"To the best of my belief," she said slowly and so gravely that at the moment I did not note the curious wording of her reply, "I have never seen him before."

"Then he wasn't the man who — abducted you?"

At that she looked troubled.

"I don't know," she said. "I don't know. How could I know? I didn't see him."

She was white and tired and frightened and lovely. I turned my eyes resolutely away from her and said:

"Why did you leave my room? Why didn't you wait?"

"I was — afraid," she said in a small voice. "When you left, I was afraid. I followed you almost at once, thinking to meet you in the corridor. But when I reached my room the key was in the door. I can't think why I was so stupid — it still seems that I left it on the key board."

I did not like her explaining the matter of the key before it had been asked about. It savored somehow of duplicity, though I knew if I looked at her I would believe her, and it was better to stick to reason rather than permit myself to be swayed by instinct or desire.

"I couldn't wait," she said again.

"How long *did* you wait?" I asked, despising myself and staring through the shadows at the lighted lobby.

"Only a moment or two."

"Long enough for me to reach the lobby?"

"Oh, no," she said. "Not even that long." She hesitated and then added, as if ashamed of the confession, "As a matter of fact, I was counting. I thought I would count up to a hundred and then another hundred and then another, and I could begin to expect you back again. But I got to my first hundred, and the wind was rattling things, and I — ran out and along the corridor." Her voice broke, and she added more steadily: "Silly of me. To be so absurdly afraid. I'm not as a rule. I thought of locking the door of your room, but the key wasn't in the lock, and it had no bolt, and I kept thinking the knob was turning."

Terribly I wanted to believe her. But something inside me kept saying coldly: Circumstantial. "Counting" and "afraid." Too circumstantial by far. And, anyway, you saw her leave your room. You saw her leave with your own eyes, and it had been far longer than she says.

There were other things I had to ask, but I looked at her, and our eyes met, and I was silent again with all my doubts and half-certainties and fears crowding and seething inside me. My hand went out toward her, and with a kind of quiet directness that made the gesture the most natural thing in the world, she slipped her own in it, and I loathed myself for doubting her, and then the courtyard was alive with short-caped figures and stiff little caps, all so active that there seemed many more of them than there actually were, and the policemen were tumbling up the winding stairs.

They were attended by Lovschiem and Madame Lovschiem; Sue Tally and I stepped back into my room, and there were talking and exclamations and furious questioning and rapid orders which sent the short blue capes in every direction, and the whole place was suddenly quick with voices and lights and gendarmes.

Their examination of the body was brief,

and I could not see it for the blue capes. It was only a few moments before the Lovschiems and two of the police followed us into the light and comparative warmth of my room where we stood in an agitated group.

From the first I was at a disadvantage owing to my inability to recall any but a word or two of the French language. I cursed the reluctance with which I had approached verbs in far-away prep-school days, and the speed with which, once the examinations were got through, I cast the few things I'd been obliged to learn out of my head. It was a disadvantage of which Madame Grethe took the fullest opportunity; or at least, so I've always suspected.

That night the police let me almost entirely alone beyond a few painstaking questions as to how and when I had found the murdered man. The queries were made by a slender young man whose eyes were remarkably bright and quick, and who spoke very slow and distinct and remarkably idiomatic English to me and then relayed my replies to an older man with a gray imperial and mustache, who was the commissaire de police and in charge of the affair, and who was unnecessarily pompous about it.

Madame Grethe's green eyes were very clear and bright and knowing during the brief questions, but they looked less knowing when

I began to tell of the man who had shot at me in the courtyard. She looked for the first time at a loss, and Lovschiem, who had let her do most of the talking thus far, suddenly became possessed of an active tongue.

"But you are mistaken, Mr. Sundean!" he cried. "The wind deceived you. There could have been no one in the courtyard. The gate was locked still when the police arrived. There is no one in the hotel but Father Robart, Marcel, here —" he indicated the porter, who had returned with the wood and was heaping it on the fire — "Marcel and — and me! There was no one in the court just now. It was the wind."

"Hell, don't I know when I've been shot at?" I took the flashlight out of my pocket and showed them how it was shattered. "The wind cannot do this. There was someone in the court not fifteen minutes ago. He had a revolver and shot at me twice on the stairway — that's when he got the flashlight — and three times in the courtyard." I heard Sue Tally give a little cry, and the young policeman looked impressed. "If the gates were still locked when you arrived, then he must be somewhere in the hotel." I still felt it might have been Lovschiem; still, it would do no harm to give their search an impetus.

The young officer turned to the pompous

commissaire de police, there was an excited sputtering of French, the older man gave a quick order which sent one of the men in the background hurrying away, and Madame Grethe sent me a most unpleasant look from her green eyes.

"Père Robart, où est-il?" she said to Marcel.

"Il s'en alla, madame. Tandis-que Monsieur était en-bas. I remained alone with — *him."*

"He went away?" Her narrow eyebrows were straight and her eyes wary. The priest's defection plus my obstinacy apparently irritated her, and I expected her to tell the damaging story of the dagger then and there out of sheer spite. She went, however, into rapid French, telling, as near as I could make out from the occasional word that I caught out of the mêlée, that she had sent at once for the priest, *"Oh, at once!"* and that he had said prayers over the dead man.

Following her example, Lovschiem plunged into the stream of conversation, and Sue and I were momentarily forgotten. She was standing quite near me, and I said in an undertone:

"What are they saying?"

She gave me a startled look.

"Oh — you do not understand them — Lovschiem is saying that he does not know the man. He says that the man is an entire stranger, that they never saw him before." She spoke in a very low but clear tone, so I heard every word under the torrent of French that, to my alien ears, fairly crackled with excitement and turbulent exclamations; and it is a fact that more than once the bearded French officer, the young one, Madame Grethe, and Lovschiem himself were all talking at once, with a kind of spasmodic shrill obbligato from Marcel. "Lovschiem is saying that the man was killed outside, away from the hotel, and brought here and left to throw suspicion from the murderer. They are considering it. But you and your shattered flashlight are troubling the younger man: he says the murderer must be here in the hotel. Lovschiem says you —" she looked faintly indignant — "that you were frightened by the wind and dropped it. He says no one could have got into the hotel. The commissaire — that is, the older one — says in case you are telling the truth they will discover him."

"What do they say of the dagger?"

She did not reply at once; it was strange that where I had felt a kind of friendliness about her, now I felt as distinctly a withdrawal.

She did not look at me; she was watching the excited group near us. Madame's hair was shining red under the garish light from the crystal chandelier. The two blue capes of the officers cut off the view into the corridor so I could no longer see the dead man, although I could see the small box-like cap of the policeman guarding him. Lovschiem's face was dark and glistening, and he was gesticulating with his fat hands, and the jewels on them glittered. And little Marcel in the background watched with snapping eyes and did not know that his bald spot was ruthlessly exposed and his thin dark hair wild. The wind outside still howled, but it seemed farther away, as if the violence of contending emotions in the old hotel had at last outdone the fury of the night.

"They say nothing of the dagger," said Sue warily, her eyes on Madame Grethe, as if to be sure she was not overheard.

And at that the young officer whirled to me and said very, very politely:

"Will Monsieur be kind to tell me why he was in the lobby of the hotel so late in the night?"

Why was I? How could I avoid telling of Sue Tally? Her own words returned to me in the very nick of time. She had said something about wanting to lock the door of my room while waiting for me but that the key was gone. I said, not daring to look at the door to be sure there was no key in it: "I went to the lobby for a key. There was no

83

key in my door."

The young officer's eyebrows went up a little, but he repeated my reply to the commissaire. I added no further word, though I longed to do so; explanations can be more damaging than silence.

"Monsieur prefers that the door is locked at night?" offered the young officer.

"Why, of course," I said. "Certainly."

They looked at me dubiously. The young officer suggested: "Monsieur has perhaps enemies?"

I smiled. "No. It is the custom in America."

That cleared the air. There was an unspoken implication that anything could be expected of Americans, and the four launched into discussion again the more fervent, it seemed to me, for the momentary bottling up. All at once Sue spoke; it was almost a whisper:

"They are talking of how the murder was done," she said. "They are going to look at it again." She looked frightened.

"Will Monsieur approach himself this way?" asked the young officer politely. "Will he be kind to regard the one that is dead?"

I followed them into the corridor. Lovschiem stepped back to let me pass, and I caught a flicker of Madame Grethe's eyes.

"Approach near, monsieur," said the young officer. "Now." He motioned the others back, and we were all crowded into the corridor, but the full light fell on the murdered man. "Now, monsieur. Is this the way you found him? Was he like this exactly? No passport? Nothing in his pockets? Was there no weapon?"

CHAPTER V

There was no weapon. The dagger I had forced Madame Grethe to drop there on the dead man's chest, the dagger I had so carefully refrained from touching myself in order not to leave fingerprints, was certainly not there. Had not been there evidently when the police came upon the scene. Had it been there on my return from the courtyard? I could not recall more than glancing at the body. Who then had taken it? The priest? Marcel? Sue Tally? — Was that why I had felt so definitely her sudden withdrawal from the subject of the dagger? And if so, was it because her own frightened hand had snatched that thing and plunged it? Because she knew its grim significance? Because she knew its urgent importance as a clue? It was an inconceivably ugly thought, but it was not one that could easily be thrust aside. And it was one that, naturally, had its own influence upon what was to come.

I straightened up.

"Of course there was a weapon," I said. "It was a small steel dagger. Very slender and short, but long enough. It had a small hilt which protruded. Lovschiem, here, withdrew it to look at it, and we discovered that it was the sword from the clock in there on the mantel. We left it on the dead man. Someone has taken it."

"The clock in your room there!" cried the young officer without waiting to translate to the older one.

"Yes."

"And you knew nothing of it?"

"Nothing. Except that it was here on the dead man's body when I went down into the courtyard, and now it is not here."

He turned then, and French crackled between himself and his superior while the others listened anxiously.

"Who was with the body while you were gone?"

"The porter and the priest."

"Where is this priest?"

Madame intervened.

"Probably in his room. Your men will find him."

The young officer whirled to Marcel, whose black eyes were snapping. There was a rapid exchange of questions, and he turned back to me.

"The porter says he knows nothing of it. That he saw no one take the dagger; did not of a truth know that it was not here. But he says there was no light for perhaps ten minutes."

"That is right."

Sue had turned toward the door to my room. Suddenly she said:

"It is there! The sword is on the clock again."

Everyone else looked at once. I shot one look at Sue. It was a very brief look, but it was enough. I knew suddenly that I was right. Sue herself had cleaned that dagger and replaced it. And then, when it was inevitable, she had called attention to it again. Her eyelids flickered toward me, and I turned hurriedly so I would not meet her gaze just then. There was something singing in my ears, and I stared at the elaborate mantel clock.

The little bronze soldier again held his steel sword — a sword that had at last been dipped in blood. Madame Grethe's face told nothing, Lovschiem's was a fat glistening mask, Marcel's eyes sparkled. A torrent of French broke out, and I watched the faces and strained my ears for words that I knew.

Finally the young officer turned again to me.

"Monsieur will remain here, please, and

hold himself at the disposition of the police. There will be investigation."

The commissaire knew and liked the word. He caught it and repeated rather sinisterly: "Ha! Investigations! *Oui,* monsieur. Investigations!" and eyed me with a look that expected the worst. He knew another word and said it in case there should be any doubt in my mind. "Inquiry. *Est-ce-que c'est compris?* Inquiry."

I said shortly that I understood. After all, they didn't mean to clap me into jail on suspicion, as I've been given to understand is the prerogative of the French police.

It was just as the young officer was detaching the tiny sword from the soldier's grasp and wrapping it carefully in a handkerchief that a commotion arose in the corridor. It grew louder, the young officer and Marcel darted to the door to look and then stepped back, and the commotion resolved itself into several policemen, the dark little maid weeping, Father Robart, and a bundle of shawls topped by what appeared to be a large white cabbage in a stage of imminent dissolution.

I said: "My God, do you intend to hold a court of inquiry here in my bedroom? Has a man no privacy in France? First a murder at my door, then an attack on my life, and now a —"

"Sh!" said Sue Tally. "Don't antagonize them." Voices and the commotion covered her whisper. "They are inclined to look favorably upon you because you told of the clock sword, although one of them thinks it may have been a very clever ruse on your part to induce that very effect. But they are still doubtful. You must be careful. I know France better than you."

". . . torn from my bed and dragged along icy corridors. I want an explanation of this remarkable conduct. Madame, what does this mean?" The bundle of shawls was Mrs. Byng, and the cabbage proved to be a large lace cap, pulled over her hair, which had grown curiously knobby, and down to her thick black eyebrows. Her nose looked more than ordinarily bellicose, her voice dominated and drowned all other speech, and she was clearly in a frame of mind that brooked no liberties. The dark little maid half strangled on a sob, Father Robart was a tall, noncommittal black clothespin with a flaming red beard, and Mrs. Byng shouted: "In my night clothes. Torn from my bed in my night clothes. What are these men doing here?"

I wondered fleetingly whether she made it a habit to sleep in five or six brown woolen shawls and thought it possible, and Madame Lovschiem said sharply:

"It is the police, madame."

The young officer who spoke English was at her side, taking her by the arm. He turned her around facing the corridor. Inexplicably she had failed to see the huddle that still lay there — perhaps her be-caped escort had shielded it from her eyes. Now, however, the light fell strongly upon it.

Well, it was bad enough. I felt a little sick when I looked at it myself, and wondered why they didn't remove it. But it had a startling effect upon Mrs. Byng.

I could not see her face. I only saw her shawls seem to shrink inward, heard her beginning speech stop as if it had been choked. Then suddenly she gave a choking shriek, turned, two long white flannel arms shot out from the shawls and clasped the commissaire tightly around the neck, and she collapsed on his reluctant chest.

I rather liked it. I had an idiotic desire to look at him sternly and say: "Ha! There will be inquiry. Investigations."

The man was purple, his beard was agitated, one hand clasped the shawls with all the fervor with which one clasps a red-hot stove, he waved the other helplessly, and his eyes shot rage above the agitated white cabbage. The young officer was purple, too, but not with rage, and I heard a distinct giggle from some-

91

where near me, though when I glanced at him Marcel's face was rigidly sober.

"You'd better get her to lie down," said Sue.

"Not on my bed!" I interjected, and Sue walked over to the shawls.

The young officer, who looked dangerously near to bursting, helped her disengage the flannel-clad arms, and somehow they got Mrs. Byng into the corridor with Marcel and the young officer (less amused with one of the white flannel arms around his own neck) assisting her progress, and Madame Lovschiem and Sue bringing up the rear, and the little maid running for hot water, and Mrs. Byng herself emitting faint shrieks.

The commissaire touched his forehead with his handkerchief, looked decidedly less pompous, and to me, at least, Mrs. Byng justified her existence, for he seemed in a sudden mood to cut the present inquiry short. He asked the priest a number of short questions, to which Father Robart replied imperturbably and with apparent satisfaction to everyone, and a small man in civilian clothes (a doctor evidently) appeared from somewhere and made a brief examination of the body. It was then removed, and before I could quite credit my good luck they were all leaving. It is true that, from the corridor, the commissaire turned to look threateningly at me and say again: "Investigations. Inquiry," but that was very mild to what I had begun to expect. Then — astonishingly the corridor was empty. In the court below were several caped figures; lights shone from the lobby and in slits from several shuttered windows facing the court, but my room and the corridor were empty.

No, not quite empty, for as I turned into my room with a sigh Marcel, who had appeared from somewhere while the others were leaving, rose from poking the fire.

"I will go now," he said. "Is there anything Monsieur wishes?"

"No, Marcel. Only sleep and the rest of the night in peace. But wait — who took the dagger from the dead man's chest and put it up there on the clock again?"

His shining black eyes were a bright impenetrable shield to the knowledge I knew he must have.

"I do not know, monsieur," he said in his politest manner.

But as he reached the door he turned and looked soberly at me.

"Monsieur," he said slowly, "is a brave but a very foolish man."

With which comforting reflection he left me alone.

Alone, I thought wearily, at last. I hoped

most heartily there would be no more intruders. To make sure of it I went to the door. But Sue had been right; there was no key and no bolt, and I looked at the empty hand of the soldier on the mantel and wished there were both. I moved the table against the door in such a manner that anyone trying to enter would immediately wake me.

Presently I went to bed. I remember thinking vaguely that it must be nearly morning and looking at my watch and discovering that it was only past three, which was entirely incredible. I did not expect to sleep. I expected the crazy, ugly business of the night to circle madly through my thoughts and that I should inevitably try to sort out the various threads and seek out my own somewhat precarious position and course of conduct. But I must have gone straight to sleep from very weariness. Once I woke with an immediate recollection of where I was and what had happened, and the impression that there was a sound like sobbing somewhere in that deserted wing. It was low and muffled but had been continuing for some time. But I must have sunk back into sleep at once, for in the morning it was only a faint recollection.

The morning was cold and the wind was still blowing. I woke late, and when I rang for coffee and Marcel brought it I asked him what had been done.

"Nothing, monsieur," he said. He looked tired and hollow-eyed but his eyes were still excited. "The police were here again but have gone. They are making inquiry."

"Have they discovered who the fellow was?"

"No, monsieur. Not yet. It is a very bad affair, this."

"Look here, Marcel, who locks the entrance gate at night?"

"Me, I attend to it."

"When?"

"At the same hour, eleven o'clock each night."

"And you locked it last night? You are very sure?"

"But yes, monsieur. I remember perfectly."

"Is there any other way into the hotel?"

He shrugged. "The back door, from the kitchens. But it, too, is locked. There is a bolt inside. I lock it when the cook leaves. Paul, that is: he goes to his home at night."

"Windows?" I suggested.

"All with bolted shutters — does Monsieur wish a fire?"

That was a curious day.

Only Lovschiem was about when I went downstairs — Lovschiem and his white cockatoo. The cockatoo greeted me with a cluck and looked with interest at the cigarette in my hand, and Lovschiem said good morning unctuously and was I going for a walk. He made it clear at once that, to him at least, our somewhat strained relation of the previous night was a thing forgotten.

"A little fresh air," I said. "Is there any news?"

There was, he said, no news. He looked bad in the clear morning light: dark and liverish; but he was still suave.

"Did you have a good sleep?" he asked too pleasantly and with an oily effect of rubbing his hands together which in actuality he was not doing at all, one hand being engaged in stroking the white neck of the cockatoo.

Pucci was watching my hand with his head on one side and appeared to be meditating as to the taste and biteable qualities of cigarettes. I drew my hand away and replied shortly and honestly that I had slept very well, upon which Lovschiem looked inconsistently disappointed.

"Americans," he said, forgetting for the moment his own claims, "are like the British. You are phlegmatic. You have no nerves. No sensibilities. I — now — though you would not think it to look at me — am a mass of sensibility. You would not believe how nervous I become. I did not sleep at all. I could not."

I thought but did not say that bad consciences had been known to have that effect and walked out into the courtyard.

Daylight did not better it. It still looked bare and cold, and the shrubs and potted trees and vines were still so harried by the wind that you wondered that they were not in shreds. The tall grilled-iron gates were open and fastened back, the small stairway wound upward through concealing vines, and Father Robart huddled in a corner. The wind swept his red beard sideways and flapped his shovel hat, and he turned queer light eyes upon me. I said good-morning, and he muttered something in reply, and I walked out through the gate and on to a white paved road that twisted narrowly between old stone houses.

The little town was strange to me, but I did not feel like exploring it. Instead I followed the road to the bridge, walked half across it, found a spot sheltered from the wind and stood there, leaning against the railing and watching the water flowing below, or looking at the white, clean-swept old place, with its stretch of white wall that the Romans had built, and its close-huddled peaks and red roofs, and I smoked and tried to think out the grisly puzzle of the night.

I do not remember that I came to any particular conclusions. I knew I had found a murdered man, that someone had shot at me and that most persistently, and that I was not in an enviable position with regard to the police.

Anything else was pure surmise. But I spent considerable time on the part that was surmise.

After a while I walked some, but thoughtfully and without noting anything in particular, and it was not until about lunch time when I turned again into the hotel that I happened to look around and discover a blue-caped figure at a discreet distance. I did not know or care how long he had been following me, but I must say it gave me a rather chilly sensation up my spine.

And the edge of my appetite was a little dulled when I discovered that during my absence my room and my bags had been thoroughly searched, and that with no attempt at concealment, which could only mean the police.

I ate alone in the chilly dining room with Marcel serving me a really excellent lunch. Father Robart had apparently eaten early, for his table had been cleared, Mrs. Byng must have been still quite literally *hors de combat,* and Sue Tally did not appear. I lingered for some time in a not unnatural wish to see her again. She played so large and important a part in the train of surmise and supposition that had set itself going in my mind that I wanted very much to see her, and that in the cool and logical and unemotional light of day.

It was not, however, until toward evening that I saw her again, and then she was with David Lorn, and they were talking.

David Lorn arrived during the afternoon. Because I was tired of sitting smoking in the empty lounge, holding a three-months-old magazine in my hand, and thinking still in weary circles of the affair in which I had got entangled and of the police (who had made another extended visit immediately after lunch) — because, as I say, I felt restless and tired of the enforced inactivity, I watched Lorn's entrance and registration and his subsequent progress through the lounge in Marcel's active convoy with more interest than I should have otherwise given him. I had, of course, no premonition that he was to become such an active and important figure in the really hideous affair which, had we but known it, had only begun.

He was, however, not a man who would have commanded ordinarily any attention. He was medium tall, medium slender, his hair was medium brown, his face just a face, and his clothes ordinary traveling tweeds. His bags had no distinguishing marks; there was, in fact, nothing at all about the man that was of much interest. His chin was perhaps a little smaller than his nose and forehead promised. And it seemed to me that his darkish eyes were rather guarded, seeing more than they appeared to see. Then he disappeared into the tiny lift, and I rose and strolled to the lobby and looked at the register to see the name of this stranger who dared enter a hotel where murder had been at large and which even then seemed to be silently holding its breath.

Madame Lovschiem, imperturbable and rather nice-looking in a tight-fitting green gown with swaying gold hoops at her ears, was at the desk and watched me look at the register.

The cockatoo watched too, and I was as conscious of his knowing eyes as of Madame's, which were as wise.

The newcomer's name was below mine on the otherwise clean page. It was David Lorn, and the place of residence was New York, which told me exactly nothing except that, presumably, here was another American. It is strange, now that it is over, to think of that handful of Americans, synthetic and real, set down in the old hotel in A—, all of us drawn into the mad and dreadful struggle that centered around Sue Tally and was until the very last so ruthless in its terrible advance and yet so grimly inexplicable.

My own part in it was sheer accident. So

was Marcel's — poor little Marcel. Yet none of us could escape.

Madame, I think, would have talked, but I had no wish to. I went up the stairs again and past the gallery — I glanced down and saw Madame Grethe in the door of the lounge watching me, and her green eyes were smiling a little, and the white cockatoo was on her shoulder — and through the corridor toward my own room. My day's thought had come to very little except the bare conclusion that I could do nothing then but await developments; the police had not approached me during their visits, except to search my room, and the whole rambling place seemed to have entered upon a conspiracy of silence and secrecy. I saw no one in the corridors, I heard no one. I knew that Mrs. Byng and the red-bearded priest and Marcel and the cook and the maid were about somewhere, but for all I saw of anyone but Marcel they might have been dead and buried. Even Lovschiem had inexplicably vanished.

Passing a door numbered nineteen, I walked more slowly, but I heard and saw nothing of Sue Tally then.

I tried to sleep, there in my own room, but succeeded only in staring into the fire, which Marcel had thoughtfully kept going, and smoking innumerable cigarettes.

The silence and the inactivity and the feeling of things going on about me, things of which I knew nothing and was perhaps purposely kept in ignorance, had got a little on my nerves, I think. I was conscious of growing impatience and restlessness and a kind of increasing apprehension. It is probable that with time for thought I had come to a fuller realization of the seriousness of the thing and of the things I knew but could not explain, and of my own danger.

Cursing myself for getting into the affair — although I don't know just how I could have kept out of it — for coming to A— at all, for staying at the hotel, for having promised to meet Jack there, for being early at the place, for planning a holiday in Spain, and for a number of other equally irrelevant affairs, I roused at last to the fact that I was letting the silence and the growing dusk and the sigh of the wind and the stubborn memory of that dead face and of stumbling over that dead body make me, as Lovschiem would say, become nervous.

A walk in the wind would clear my head.

It was as I turned from the north corridor into the main hall of the middle part of the hotel that I finally saw Sue Tally.

She was standing in a sort of recess. The man Lorn was with her, and they were talking very low and so earnestly that they did not appear to see me at all. Yet, in spite of their being so unguarded as not to see my passing, I had an impression that they did not wish be seen together. It was only an impression; I suppose their low voices and the way Lorn was leaning toward her and their meeting in a niche of the deserted and rather dark corridor, instead of openly in the lounge or parlor downstairs, gave it to me. It was undoubtedly Sue; and her hair was as soft and bright and her face as sweet as I remembered it from the previous night.

I went on. I felt savage and wished I had never seen the place. I hated its rambling dark corridors and its blank and silent doors and that air of waiting and of secrecy.

I got to the lounge. In the lobby there were two policemen, again. Madame Grethe was there, and Lovschiem, looking, somehow, smug.

One of the policemen approached me and tapped my shoulder, and then suddenly another one was at my elbow and was gripping it rather firmly. They were saying something in French to me, and then Lovschiem undertook to interpret.

He actually did rub his hands together this time, and his commiserating manner did not disguise his oily satisfaction.

"What a misfortune! What a misfortune!" he said. "They wish — oh, most mistakenly — but they insist upon arresting Monsieur. They are taking you away at once."

"There isn't enough evidence," I cried sharply. "You can't arrest me. This is absurd."

The police tightened their grip, and Lovschiem, rubbing his hands, said softly:

"Ah, *quel malheur!* You see, monsieur, there is new evidence against you."

CHAPTER VI

My reception in a French jail was not at all what I might have expected. I was inclined to suspect that, it being at the hour when the Frenchman feels a need to repair to a café, the entire machinery necessary properly and formally to enter a prisoner was not, for the moment, on hand. This suspicion, however, would lead one to think that the French jails have a rather casual form of organization, and that is decidedly not true. So I've no doubt the other explanation, namely that they were not too sure I was guilty but thought it discreet to hold me for a time, was the true one. Owing to my hazy knowledge of French and to the unexpected turn the situation was so soon to take, I never did discover what the real and formal procedure constituted.

As it was, I was simply searched, finger-printed, and led to a cold little room, locked in, and then through the grating asked politely to remain there, which seemed a redundancy.

Lovschiem had blandly refused to tell me what the new evidence was, and while the gendarmes who arrested me did enough talking, the only word I was sure I understood was *oui,* which is unmistakable and which was repeated among them many times, thus arguing a degree of mutual satisfaction which was not exactly pleasing to me.

I did manage to drag up the words *papier* and *encre* from some faint schoolday memory, both of which they brought me after considerable excited discussion.

Thus I spent my first hour in a French jail composing somewhat feverish telegrams to the American consul in Paris — I couldn't for the life of me think of a nearer one — and to Jack, although I knew only that Jack had left Shanghai ten days before and hadn't the faintest notion as to his probable present address. And I might say here that by the time he did turn up the whole thing had reached its swift and terrible climax.

The telegrams, however, were never sent.

And I wanted first of all a lawyer; I felt rather cold as I suddenly recalled that in France there is no writ of habeas corpus. It is true that I was an American citizen, a fact clearly set forth in my passport, but this had not appeared to relieve the situation in the least. It didn't seem at all legal that they should simply throw me into jail and keep me there, but everything I had ever heard about the remarkable freedom of the French police in such matters returned to my memory, and I began to feel a degree of anxiety which, I was to discover, was quite justifiable. I was, too, seething with rage, the worse because there was no outlet for it. I did manage to keep fairly cool outwardly, but I could scarcely have done otherwise; the policemen who arrested me were obviously only acting under orders, and there was nothing to do but wait until I could get hold of someone in authority and discover exactly what their case against me consisted of and what they proposed to do about it.

Night comes early in the winter at A——, and the room was quite dark, and no one had appeared to light it, and I was smoking my last cigarette and wishing I had the pompous old commissaire by the beard when I heard footsteps and voices and a key turning in the lock. The cold, dark little room was flooded with light, and a visitor, a man, was ushered in to see me.

I got to my feet and was blinking in the unexpected light as he insinuated something that rattled gently into the hand of the man who had opened the door and whose countenance became very blank indeed as his hand went to his pocket and he closed the door again. Then my visitor turned, and I saw the man who had arrived at the hotel during the afternoon.

He said briskly:

"I'm sorry to see you here, Mr. Sundean. My name is Lorn — David Lorn." He paused and then added: "Miss Tally asked me to see you."

His words were neither promising nor exactly explanatory; still, things looked suddenly better. I was not, after all, entirely without a friend.

"Sit down?"

He drew up the small straight chair, and I sat down on the cot. He put his hat on the floor, opened his coat, and drew out a folded paper. While his chin was no larger than it had been in the afternoon and his eyes actually did seem to see the whole room, the door, the gratings, the cot, the note he held, and every single item of my own clothing at one and the same time, and yet did not openly focus on anything — still I'm bound to admit that the sight of his countenance was very welcome. He handed me the paper, and it was a note from Sue Tally. It was brief but nice.

She had written: *"Your being thrust into jail is absurd and intolerable. This is Mr. Lorn. He knows the whole affair and thinks he can do something about it."*

She had written hurriedly and, I thought, agitatedly, and her signature was a spirited S. Tally. I liked the quick, vigorous strokes of her pen and the feeling of heated indignation and impatience the note breathed, and I liked the prompt way she had come, or tried to come, to my defense. I was conscious, however, of the man Lorn's observation, which so far as appearances went was focused on the grating over the window but which yet, I was sure, was taking in any change of expression in my face.

"Miss Tally is very good," I said. I put the note in my pocket.

He cleared his throat and looked at the floor by my feet.

"She thinks you didn't do this."

"She's right," I said with some heat.

"In fact," he went on rather cautiously, "after hearing her story of the whole affair, I am inclined to agree with her. At least," he continued before I could speak, "there appear to be a number of rather interesting points of which she has told me which may — mind, I only say may — prove to be evidence."

"Evidence?"

"Evidence in your favor, I mean to say. Circumstances that upon investigation may tend to prove your complete — er — innocence of the crime. However, you — er —" I thought he looked directly at me and he said unexpectedly: "It's just as well to start with a clean slate, however. I take it you really didn't murder the man."

I rose.

"You're damned right, I didn't murder him. I never even saw him before —"

"Never mind, never mind. I didn't think so. Sit down, Mr. Sundean, sit down." He looked up at me doubtfully and went on: "Do sit down and let's talk this over calmly. I may as well say at once that after hearing Miss Tally's story of the affair I felt that something might be done. She asked me to come to see you. She asked me to do what I could. And I really believe something can be done." I sat down, and he said: "There, now, that's better, Mr. Sundean. Let's be calm about this. First, however, do you feel like — er — accepting my help?"

"Hell, man, am I in a position to refuse help?"

He smiled faintly.

"No," he said as if I had expected a reply. "Nice that you can keep your spirits up. You aren't in a very nice position, you know."

Reminding me was not needed.

I said more graciously:

"It's very good of you to offer to help. I need help. But what exactly is there to do?"

"You know Miss Tally well?"

"Why, no," I said. "Surely she told you we met last night and under what circumstances."

"Oh, yes, of course," he agreed. "She told me of the attempted abduction. However — she was rather hurried in her story, of course, and I — it doesn't matter. First, Mr. Sundean, you told the police that there were five revolver shots last night while you were in the court with some person whom you did not see?"

"Yes, five."

"You are sure of that?"

"Positive."

"H'mm. Then I may be right in my surmise. It's a possibility at least —"

"What is a possibility?"

"That the other revolver shot, the sixth —"

"But there was no sixth; there were only five."

"He fired twice at your flashlight, three times over your head. You still remained in the courtyard —"

"I couldn't get away," I said.

"Exactly. Therefore it is reasonable to suppose that if the sixth shot had still remained in his revolver he would have again tried to — er — shoot you."

"I don't see," I said, "that that has anything to do with getting me out of here. The man was murdered by stabbing. Look here, perhaps you can tell me just why I'm here. What's this new evidence Lovschiem was so afraid he'd tell me about?"

"You don't know?"

"Of course not. No one has even questioned me here yet."

"H'mm. Well, it's rather bad, Mr. Sundean. But still not at all convincing. There's the matter of the clock sword being from your room: they are divided in opinion at the moment regarding your seemingly frank bringing the thing to their attention. At the moment I fear the weight of opinion is that it was only a clever ruse on your part."

"How do you know that?"

"I've been talking to the officer in charge. I took the liberty of telling him, Mr. Sundean, that I was your legal representative. And owing to a matter which I brought before him he was inclined to talk to me at some length."

"That's very good of you," I said warmly.

"Then there's your shattered flashlight."

"But it was shot out of my hand."

"Yes, of course. But unfortunately it is so completely shattered that it is difficult to tell just what did happen to it. Pieces were found just below the landing on which there was a patch of blood from the murdered man; those pieces might be taken to mean that you simply dropped your flashlight in a struggle with him."

"But that's — why, that's no evidence."

"Perhaps not; still, it proves you were there."

"But of course I was there. That's where I stumbled over the body. I told it openly. Of course I was there."

"The police are apt to take a different view from what we expect. But there are two other things, Mr. Sundean. There's a matter of a soiled towel; a towel which bears traces of blood. They say you dried your hands on it."

"Yes. I did."

He looked quickly at me. I could feel rather than see the tightening of his face.

"Why, of course, I washed my hands! Remember, I stumbled and went down on the body. And then when I discovered what it was I dragged him through the door and into the corridor."

"That's what you say."

"It's the truth."

"Oh, certainly, Mr. Sundean. But there's the other way of looking at it. — And the conclusive thing to their mind is this: Letters were found among your things, as well as various articles of clothing and papers, that proved you have been in Russia, near and in Moscow for the last two years. Yet your *bulletin d'arrivée*, on file here with the police, makes no mention at all of Moscow. In it you claim your home is in New York. Is your home New York?"

"Yes. That is, no. That is — I have no home, exactly. New York does as well as any place. And I've been on a construction job in Russia. I'm an engineer."

"So Miss Tally told me," he said. He was at last looking directly at me, but I could not measure the look in his dull deep-set eyes. He added expressionlessly: "Perhaps I'd better tell you that I cannot possibly help you unless you give me your confidence."

"Hang it, man, I am telling the truth. I've told the truth all along. There was no reason not to. I didn't murder that man. And I'll make it hot for somebody, once I get out of here." Realizing that I was making rather a fool of myself I said more calmly: "I've been in Moscow, certainly, but what of it? Many people have been in Moscow; the city's full of people."

"Well, you see," said Lorn slowly. "The murdered man — they have reason to think that he's a Russian, too."

"Well?"

"Why, don't you see, my friend, that there's

114

an obvious connection? A connection, at least, in the eye of the police. And you can't blame them much; they've had some trouble with Communistic feuds lately."

"Oh, good God! It's —" I was futile and raging at my futility. "Of all the damned, dumb, asinine — why, it's preposterous! It's stark raving crazy! It's —"

"No doubt," he said, watching me. "But that's what they think."

"Have you got a cigarette?"

He had, and gave me one, and even offered me a light from a square little lighter that worked immediately.

I said:

"You say you think there is something you can do? What is it?"

"I don't know how it's going to come out. Don't expect too much. But I suggested that they hold a post-mortem."

"A post-mortem? Don't they always?"

He smiled again, faintly.

"This is not Paris, Mr. Sundean. It is a very small place. Besides, the cause of the death appeared to be obvious. The police doctor is, mainly, a private practitioner, and he's been very busy. And, as I say, the cause of death was so very obvious."

"What do you mean?"

"I'm not sure I mean anything; I'm pinning

my faith to the sixth bullet. Why wasn't it fired at you? Had it already been fired?"

"You mean — you think the fellow was not killed by stabbing? That he was shot?"

"Perhaps."

"But that's — why, that's out of the question, Lorn! The doctor and the police would see that at once. There'd be no possible way of hiding it."

"Yes," he agreed. "You are right. Still, it's well not to overlook any possibility —"

"But there's no possibility there."

"Only one. I've looked at the dagger: it's barely possible that it made a jagged wound. One that might conceal —"

"A bullet hole?" My private opinion was that the man was mad. His intentions might be good, but he was undoubtedly poor-witted. "Do you mean to say that it is possible that the murderer first shot the man through the heart and then — That's preposterous!"

"And then inserted the dagger exactly through the bullet hole. You look incredulous, Mr. Sundean. Believe me, stranger things than that have been done in the hope of averting suspicion. And some of them succeed."

"But the clothing — the bullet hole in the clothing."

"I think that might be successfully concealed. Mind you, I'm not saying it was done.

I am saying that there's a slim possibility that some such thing was attempted, and thus there may be a chance of getting you out of here. For a while, at least. Do you want to stay here until they manage to discover the exact identity of the murdered man and whether or not your path and his had ever crossed before?"

"No!" I said with some fervor. "But I can't think there's been any such hocus-pocus with the body."

"We may be dealing with an exceptional criminal, Mr. Sundean. One never knows. The murderer may be one who calculates every chance; one who has made the fullest use of any advantages that present themselves; in this case, obviously, one of the advantages would be the fact that he is not in a city. The police organization in a small place is often very good, but still it would be unreasonable to suppose that they had the trained men and the scientific equipment of the police organization in a city. Also all papers of identification were removed from the dead man. Thus, naturally, the pressure of effort to discover the murderer is not as great as it would be if the murdered man were known to be, for instance, a person of importance."

"It's great enough," I said bitterly. "Do you mean that the removal of his passport and papers and all would indicate that he was an important person?"

"That would be impossible to say. I know, however, that the pressure of public opinion is never as urgent regarding the murder of an unidentified stranger as it is about the murder of — say, John Smith or Tom Jones."

"Are you a lawyer?"

"No," he said flatly, and then continued briefly: "I arrived this afternoon, early. Miss Tally told me of the murder and of the attempt to abduct her last night. She urged me to come to see you and insisted that I put forth every energy to assist you. Otherwise I should not have thrust myself upon you in this manner."

"It's very good of you," I murmured, rather taken aback by his stateliness. "Very good, indeed," I repeated more heartily, although I didn't see that he was apt to improve the situation if all his notions were as harebrained as the one he had proposed.

He looked at his watch and picked up his hat and rose.

"The doctor should have arrived by this time, and I think I can manage to see something of the post-mortem. I shall return as soon as I discover the result."

I said some kind of thanks; the man in the corridor outside let Lorn out and locked the door again but left the light on.

My hopes were very faint. But he'd given me something to think of; and I felt rather better to think that someone — anyone — was working on my side of the affair. It's true, too, that while I didn't know just what to think of the man himself, still he did seem to know something of the ins and outs of police courts. There was a slim chance that he could do something for me. And Sue Tally had sent him. I got out her note and read it again.

Lorn had said merely that he had just arrived and that she had told him of the murder and of the attempt to abduct her. This presupposed an acquaintance between them. Well, from my point of view, his arrival had been most opportune. But I wondered what his relation was with Sue Tally, and it increased the mystery that surrounded her.

Again I fell to wishing that she had told me the truth about her leaving my room last night; then I read her note again and discovered a number of excuses for her. None of them, however, completely answered, and once, indeed, I wondered if she was so anxious to get me out of jail because of what she knew herself about the crime. There was the dagger. If she had struck in self-defense and terror —

I got up and walked back and forth from one wall to another until I was warmer. After all, I told myself, it was too crazy and nightmarish a situation to endure for long. I hadn't murdered the man, and it was ridiculous to be cooped up in a French jail for something I hadn't done, and it couldn't last long. They couldn't prove I had done it, because I hadn't.

And all the time I was arguing thus to myself the words "Circumstantial evidence" were repeating themselves coldly in the back of my mind. And I wanted to be out of jail.

In an hour or so the warder brought me a tray with a very sparse meal on it, consisting of thick and greasy soup, a chunk of bread, and a boiled potato. I was still looking at the stuff and thinking that if I didn't manage to eat it I should be very hungry indeed by morning and that, after all, there'd been times when I'd been obliged to eat much worse food and like it, when there were sudden and many footsteps in the corridor.

Men were coming hurriedly along it, and from the sounds every one of them was talking furiously. The commotion reached my door, and I was standing waiting, for I knew they were coming to me. It was, of course, impossible that Lorn's crazy hypothesis had turned out to be correct; still, they must be coming at last to make some inquiry and to give me a chance to defend myself as best I could.

The first man through the door was the

commissaire of the previous night; he was puffing and not at all pompous and looked, in fact, rather like an outraged billy-goat. After him was Lorn, looking, I thought, a little surprised, but that was all. And after him, the young officer of the night before and several others, all highly excited.

The commissaire, his mustaches and imperial quivering, talked to me for a long time in French, speaking very rapidly. He finally paused with a question, and was suddenly purple and baffled when it became apparent that I hadn't understood a word and his efforts had been wasted.

Lorn stepped quietly into the breach.

"He says they are releasing you for the time being, but that you must remain at hand," he said. "At least, that's the gist of what he said. I'll explain later. At present you'd better leave."

"Releasing me now? Immediately?"

"Yes."

"No doubt about it?"

"No."

I took a long breath. I believe I picked up my hat. Then I turned to the commissaire.

"See here," I said earnestly. "You were entirely wrong to arrest me. I didn't murder the man. I had nothing at all to do with it. I never saw him before. I am an American citizen traveling through your city. This is preposterous. You are crazy. You've arrested an innocent man and you'll suffer for it." I had started calmly enough but was growing enraged all over again as I proceeded with the injustice that had been done me. "You can't arrest me and throw me into jail and just leave me there without even telling me why. Without making any inquiry of me. Without giving me any chance at all to defend myself. You are a pompous old ass of a billy-goat anyhow, and —"

"Monsieur, monsieur!" The young officer who understood English was shaking my arm. He looked pink and friendly. "You must stop, monsieur. There is danger he will comprehend a word or two."

"Oh, my God!" I said, disgusted. "How do you say what I want to say in French?"

"Monsieur must leave it to me," said the young officer rapidly. His face was pinker, and he held his mouth very tight. "Monsieur is not out of danger. He must take care. I will tell for him that he wishes to thank Monsieur le commissaire for his kindness."

"You tell Monsieur le commissaire for me he can go to —" Lorn cleared his throat warningly, and I stopped. After all, there is only one thing to say to police in a foreign land, and that is, thank you.

The commissaire shot out several sharp and suspicious questions just then, and I don't know what the young officer said. He did not, however, interpret literally for me, for the commissaire became gradually calm and soothed and was actually smiling a little when the young officer concluded. Lorn's face was without expression, and the other policemen looked, I thought, faintly disappointed.

At any rate, I was free. Fifteen minutes later Lorn and I were walking along the dark narrow streets toward the old hotel, bending against the furious wind which hurled any few words out of our mouths and prohibited my eager inquiries. He would tell me the story, I promised myself, over dinner.

At the entrance to the courtyard he paused and drew me into a corner that was a little out of the wind.

"It is as well," he said in my ear, "for us not to be seen together. It is not wise at the moment. Will you precede me into the hotel?"

"But I want to see you at once. Why did they let me out? Were you right? There are things — to be done."

"Yes and no; it's a longish story. I'll come to your room tonight," he said. "Go on. I'll come later."

He turned away to let me enter the hotel ahead of him, but I seized his arm.

"Wait," I said. "What do you mean 'yes and no'?"

I was obliged to shriek against a furious gust of wind, and he looked at me in sharp disapproval.

"Wind is tricky," he said. "We may be overheard."

"I don't care who hears. What killed him?"

He jerked his arm away.

"He was poisoned," he said. "If I am to help you, Mr. Sundean, you must let me do it my own way. I shall come to your room after I've had dinner. We can talk then. Not here." He vanished into the darkness.

CHAPTER VII

He was right, of course. It was neither the place nor the time for the talk we must have. And, anyway, he had told me the main fact, although his reply was so unexpected that it left me stunned and incredulous.

Poisoned. But the murdered man had been stabbed. I had found him, and I had seen the ugliness of the wound. I'd been obliged to wash my hands of the blood from it.

Mechanically I crossed the courtyard, passed under the swaying light, and entered the lobby. Lovschiem was bending over the desk.

The cockatoo clucked, and Lovschiem looked up, and it was curious to see how his eyes leaped when he saw me and how flabby his cheeks looked all at once and how his fat hands moved aimlessly about the desk. He stared at me, and I stared back, and the cockatoo took a sidling step toward me and clutched at my sleeve with a long claw. Finally

Lovschiem said:

"How did you — get out?" His voice was husky.

I lifted my eyebrows.

"Walked, Lovschiem. Walked. I'll have some dinner at once, please."

His flabby hands moved helplessly, and the cockatoo, attracted by some glint of jewels, cocked his head knowingly on one side, made a kissing sound with his tongue, and sidled toward the hand nearer him.

"You can have it served in my room," I added airily. "And see that there's a good fire."

With that I left him, still staring and flabby, with the cockatoo examining the ring suspiciously and clicking his tongue in an experimental fashion.

The place looked, as usual, completely empty, although someone had had coffee in the lounge, for a cup and small coffee service stood on one of the tables. The dining room was empty and very cold-looking, and I was glad I'd had the forethought to order a fire in my own room and dinner beside it.

The corridors were empty and darkish and long. But there was a gleam of light below the door labeled nineteen, and I paused beside it and hesitated and finally knocked lightly.

It opened in a moment, and Sue, her bright

hair aureoled against the light behind her, stood on the threshold.

"It's you!" she cried softly and happily and stretched out both her hands, and as I took them she said with a little catch in her voice, "Oh, I'm glad."

Her hands were warm and small and soft in mine, and yet they had a kind of firmness. I liked their touch.

"Your Mr. Lorn managed to get me out," I said. "It was good of you to send him."

"The whole thing was absurd," she said vigorously. "They had no right to arrest you like that. But he isn't my Mr. Lorn. And what did he do?"

"The Mr. Lorn, then. Whoever he is, he managed it very cleverly. Although I don't know exactly what happened yet. See here, isn't there some place where we can talk? Come downstairs to the lounge."

She hesitated and after a moment said, as if she'd come to a decision:

"I do want to talk to you. There are things I want to know. But — I think it is as well if we aren't seen together."

"What do you mean?" I said, puzzled. "Who is there to see us? The Lovschiems? The priest? Mrs. Byng? And anyway, suppose they do! What does it matter?"

She looked confused and embarrassed. I was

suddenly aware that I was still holding her hands rather tightly and that she was trying to withdraw them. I released them and said quickly:

"I didn't mean to say — I didn't — mean —" I floundered and finished abruptly: "I don't understand you."

"All this seems silly and purposefully mysterious. But it isn't intentional. I — you see, I'm in an awfully queer sort of affair and can't help myself. And I think — oh, I shall tell you about it. It would be best, of course. I've been warned not to tell anyone of it, but I —"

"See here," I said. "Lorn is coming to my room right after dinner. I've ordered a fire, and it will be warm. Can't you come there, too?"

She didn't say anything for a moment, and I added:

"We'll hold a council of war. I'll have them open the salon next my room, if you like; the Pope's piano ought to offer a measure of propriety."

She smiled.

"It wasn't thoughts of propriety that made me hesitate," she said. "Though that sounds rather abandoned. The trouble is —" she stopped again and when she continued her voice was very sober — "the trouble is, I don't like involving you in any — danger."

Her voice rather than her words carried conviction.

"You don't mean to say you are in actual danger?"

"I hope not," she said quietly. "But I'm rather — after that affair of last night, I'm rather doubtful. I'm being mysterious again! Yes, I'll come to your room in an hour."

"Good, then. But I want to tell you —"

"Someone is coming," she said. "You must go."

"I liked your note," I said hurriedly, and she closed the door, and I went on. At the corner of the passage I glanced over my shoulder. Mrs. Byng was standing in the hall. Her tall figure was unmistakable even in the dimness of the corridor. She had one hand outstretched toward a door leading to a room not far from Sue's, and she was watching me. I felt an impulse to wave cheerfully in her direction but restrained it and turned the corner.

Marcel brought me dinner and hovered over me while I ate. With the soup he said that he was glad I had returned; with the fish he said he had feared I should be arrested, and by the time I had reached a liqueur he was talking quite frankly and openly of the murder in a way which strongly suggested that he considered his ears were for use and treated them accordingly. He was telling me of how the police had searched my things during the morning, when I interrupted:

"But how do you know all this, Marcel?"

"There are ways to hear," he said cheerily. "Me, I like to know what goes on." He stopped, and his face darkened a little. "I know what I know," he said. "But sometimes one does not at once understand what one hears. Or sees."

I sat up at that.

"Do you mean you know something about this murder?" I asked directly.

At once I realized that if, which I doubted, he actually did know something, I had made a mistake in questioning him so promptly and so directly. His face tightened.

"Ah, no, no, no, no, no, monsieur," he said torrentially. "Nothing. Nothing. *Pas du tout!*"

But he remained thoughtful, and though I said one or two casual things with a view to encouraging his former cheerily conversational mood — usually altogether too easy with the vivacious little porter — he did not rise to the temptation. He looked, even, vaguely uneasy, as if he wished he had talked less, and left me as soon as I had finished.

It wasn't long after he'd gone that there was a knock on the door. I sprang up, thinking it was Sue Tally. But it was Madame Grethe.

She entered as I held the door open. She

130

looked rather nice; she wore again the clinging, coppery-green silk gown, and her red hair
shone under the light. Gold hoops swung at
her ears; her face was white and soft and her
lips heavily rouged. The white cockatoo sat
on her shoulder; his crest was flared handsomely upward, and he was twisting his head
this way and that in an inquisitive but faintly
reproving manner. I shouldn't have been at
all surprised if he'd said to me conversation-
ally, "So this is where the murder was. Tut,
tut!"

"Am I disturbing you?" said Madame
Grethe. Her green eyes were shining, and her
manner was very pleasant.

"Not at all," I said and then, as she gave
every indication of having come merely to pay
a social call, I added: "Won't you sit down?"

She moved in a graceful, leisurely manner
to the chair opposite me and sat down; the
cockatoo clung to her shoulder and made an
admonitory remark which was aimed apparently at me.

"Pucci, Pucci," she said in a caressing voice.
"I am sorry about your being arrested, Mr.
Sundean. My husband and I regret it very
much."

There was a shade of mockery in her shining
eyes.

"At any rate," I said, "it didn't last long."

131

"No. Apparently not. I hope that is all you will hear of the affair."

"Your hope is shared, madame."

A short silence fell; the flames sputtered a little, Pucci scratched vigorously under one wing and looked dissatisfied with the result, we could hear gusts of wind rattling the place, and Grethe watched me musingly. I was sure she wanted to know exactly how I had got out of jail but preferred not to ask directly.

"Did you have any particular trouble about it?" she said presently in a soft and sympathetic way.

"Oh — no," I said lightly. "Really very polite they were. The police, I mean."

"Ah, yes." She nodded. "Perhaps." Her eyes lost their caressing look for an instant. "But do not count on that too much, Mr. Sundean."

For the instant I employed the ghost of Marcel's shrug, a useful gesture which I was growing to admire very much. It irritated her. Her eyes lit for a moment, then she dropped smooth lids over them, lifted one rather large but soft and white hand to Pucci's neck, caressed him for a moment, and then glanced about the room.

"How the wind blows!" she said. "I didn't realize that it blows so dreadfully upon this north wing. We usually keep it closed during the winter months. Doesn't the wind annoy you at night? Surely there is a loose shutter somewhere near."

"One of those on the window, there."

"I must tell Marcel to repair the catch. Although — shouldn't you like another room, Mr. Sundean? This room is never warm in the winter without a hearth fire. We do have central heating but —" her shoulders rippled under the silk — "it isn't too good. Especially in this far-off wing."

"I'm quite all right here, thank you." I wondered what time it was.

"We are making you comfortable, then?" she asked, smiling. I smiled too, but said nothing, and she added: "Come, come, Mr. Sundean, admit that you'd be happier in another room. One not so far from the rest of us. One not so near —" She did not finish her sentence in words but moved one supple hand in a quick gesture toward the corridor in a suggestive way which left words unneeded.

But I was firm, mainly because she insisted, for I had no reason to like my present room, heaven knew! And I was beginning to wish she would leave. It would soon be time for Sue's promised arrival.

"Oh, very well, then," said Madame at last rather sharply. "On your own head be it. If you wish to remain here in this room, I suppose you must. Mr. Sundean —" she leaned suddenly forward, and Pucci toppled, caught his balance, and gave a hoarse cluck of disapproval — "*why* are you here?" she asked almost in a whisper, her green eyes shining into mine.

"I came to meet a friend," I said. "Will you have a cigarette?"

She brushed aside the offered case in an impatient way.

"You don't mind —" I said, pausing with the light in my fingers.

She shook her head.

"You are evasive, Mr. Sundean," she said in a less caressing way than she had previously employed.

I lifted my eyebrows.

"Evasive? You ask me why I have come to A— and why I have come to this hotel. I tell you, to meet a friend, which is the truth." I smiled at her. Her green eyes were sparkling angrily through the little veil of smoke that drifted between us.

"At such a time, Mr. Sundean, one must ask questions of unidentified strangers."

"No doubt," I said pleasantly. "And I suppose it would be well for unidentified strangers to look more closely into matters which possibly do not concern them. What's it all about, madame? An attempt on my life and a murder at my threshold. That's more than coincidence. Are you so determined to make me leave?"

I had spoken experimentally, more than from conviction, and I was a little astonished to see how my words affected her — astonished and yet, somehow, put on my guard. She leaned quietly back in the chair again, but her face had gone rather sharp and set, and the red paste stood out on her lips, and I did not like the look of her eyes back of their darkened eyelashes. It was a good sixty seconds before she spoke, and in the little interval a log crackled sharply in the fire, and Pucci cast it a reproving glance and then pushed his wide bill against Grethe's red hair and flared his yellow crest.

"I don't understand you, Mr. Sundean," she said at last. "Surely you don't think the murder of last night had connection with you?"

It was clear, of course, that there was something evil going on in the old hotel: abductions, murders, shots in the night, all those things had to have some kind of hub, and the hub must be contained somewhere about that secretive place with its deserted corridors and rooms and its rattling shutters. That had been clear from the first. But I think that, until that very moment, I had not felt so definitely the presence of widening and entangling currents. It was as if something very dark and very strong were swirling about, and I knew of the threat of its presence but not where and how to avoid it.

She did not, I think, detect the course of my thoughts, although her green gaze was very sharp. I said quietly but more cautiously:

"No, I don't think anything of the kind. I never saw the murdered man before, so his death could have no possible connection with me. While I may not be a particularly welcome guest, still I don't think — anyone — would go to the trouble of murdering a man in order to get rid of me. By the way — *who* was the murdered man?"

"I don't know," she said in a tight voice; narrowed eyes watched my face. "Do you?"

"I? Absurd! You know that. But another question, madame." In my turn I leaned toward her. "Why were you anxious to keep me from arrest last night?"

Her smooth lids went down again, but not before I'd caught a look that warned me. She rose, and I rose too, naturally, and the move brought her very close to me. So near that I could feel the warmth of her body. Her lips were parted a little, and her eyes, lifted again to mine, were very bright and shining.

"It should not be difficult to find the answer for that," she said softly.

She would be pliant and warm and exciting

in my arms. I wondered fleetingly how soon I could replace the faintly triumphant look I'd caught in her eyes with something quite different.

I tossed my cigarette into the fire. I took the cockatoo from her shoulder and set him on the chair near and bent over her mouth.

But it waited for me, and I straightened suddenly without touching it or her.

"Madame," I said pleasantly, "is more than kind. Madame is also beautiful. The cockatoo is eating fringe off the chair."

He was actually doing just that, in a heaven-inspired moment but with a very dubious look. He took another bite without eagerness but philosophically, as if in scientific pursuit one must put up with a poor-tasting bite now and then, and Madame Grethe looked at me. I was rather interested to note that there was nothing but a kind of faintly surprised curiosity in her gaze. Then she laughed a little, turned and picked up the cockatoo — he resisted out of pure deviltry, stretching out his neck for more fringe and squalling, but her hands were firm about him — and she faced me again, still smiling.

"And Monsieur," she said, "is a very reckless young man. Good-night."

I opened the door for her. She held out her hand to me, still smiling, and I think genuinely amused and not in the least angry. I bowed very low over her hand, and she turned gracefully into the corridor, and I closed the door behind her and took a long breath and hoped she wouldn't meet Sue. At least until she was at a considerable distance from my room.

I was thinking of Sue when I heard her knock on the door. As I opened it she was looking rather fixedly at the spot on the corridor floor where the dead man had huddled. She looked small and quiet and frightened, and I took her hand and pulled her quickly into the room and closed the door.

"Were the corridors creepy?" I said. "Come over to the fire."

She shivered and said yes rather breathlessly and sat down in the chair I had just left.

"It's very queer," said Sue. "But for the last week or two I've been ridiculously nervous about going through these half-dark corridors. I keep feeling that there's someone coming along behind me. Or looking out of closed doors."

"It's probably the wind. It has a way of shrieking through them and rattling doors and windows." She looked very beautiful; the flames sent glancing highlights to touch her bright hair to gold here and there, and I liked the fine sweep of her slender black eyebrows and the look of pride and spirit about her arrogant little nose and her mouth. My glance lingered on her mouth; it was lovely and delicately curved; it had intelligence and firmness. Still, it made you think of a very fresh cool rose.

"I suppose so," she was saying rather dubiously. She was looking at me; her eyes were dark blue and were remarkably steady between their extravagant dark eyelashes. I wondered whether she was actually so lovely to look upon or whether she just seemed so to me because I had forgotten how beautiful a woman can be. In all likelihood she was just an ordinarily pretty American girl.

Then I found that I was losing myself again in her eyes; odd that I seemed to forget myself and what I wanted to think or say whenever I caught that deep, inward look in her eyes. It was as if something very strong in her had touched and then held something in me that rushed to meet it, and that the two things met and merged irresistibly while Sue Tally and Jim Sundean waited.

Then I wrenched myself away from such fancy and forced myself to hear what she was saying.

". . . and it's quite apt to blow like this for weeks at a time. Mr. Lorn hasn't arrived yet?"

"No."

She took a long breath. Her hands had met

and were faintly pink against the black velvet of the coat she wore — the same coat she'd worn the previous night, and the same slender scarlet slippers with their shining silver heels were there on the rug with the flickering lights on them, too.

"I've come to say this," she said with an air of decision. "You helped me last night. I was obliged to thrust myself and my troubles upon you, and you were — you helped me. Now it seems that whether you like it or not you can hardly escape being involved in this dreadful affair. I mean the — the murder — all that. And I think it's only fair to warn you. To let you know — what I know. Because you see —" she hesitated — "you see, I'm afraid that the man was killed —" she hesitated again, and then the words came out in a little rush — "because of me!" she said amazingly and looked at me again.

"Because of you!"

She nodded.

"It's — terrible, isn't it?" she said. "Are you sure you want to hear?"

"Of course I want to hear," I said. "But don't be frightened. Don't look as if you are blaming yourself. Let's talk about it coolly and sensibly."

Her cheeks grew pink.

"I'm being sensible," she said indignantly.

"But it *is* dreadful. I shall never forget how he —" She stopped herself abruptly and went on: "I'm not frightened. And I'm not silly and nervous over nothing."

"I know that," I said hastily. And I did know it. There was courage in the very lift of her head on her slender white neck. Besides, I didn't like to think myself of the way the dead man had looked. After all, it had been only the night before, and the wind had been blowing and the shutters rattling as they were doing at that very moment, and I had no doubt the witches were out again in full force in the courtyard.

"Tell me anything you wish, and don't feel that you are burdening me with your troubles. As a matter of fact, I'm in a rather unpleasant sort of fix myself, and I've got to get myself out of it. And while I've got notions in plenty about all this business there are few things I know definitely. And I thought, of course, that your — experience of last night —"

"Abduction," she said firmly.

"Yes. That it was likely the murder somehow concerned it. Otherwise one would be expecting too much of coincidence."

"Very well," she said. "I'll have no more scruples, then. But it's a rather difficult story, and it has to do with things that one does not ordinarily tell — strangers —" she paused over the word and chose another — "that one does not ordinarily tell friends. I don't know where to begin."

"Tell me why you were abducted," I said, liking the word friends. "Do you know why?"

"Oh, yes," she said at once. "I was abducted because of something I possess." She laughed rather sadly and continued: "I haven't any money. I've so little that I don't know how I'd have managed during the last year if the Lovschiems had not been very good to me. And to my mother. But I've got something that's worth, roughly, about five millions." She looked at me doubtfully and added: "Dollars, I mean."

I believed her. I was a little stunned, but I believed every word she'd said. The amazing thing about it was that I believed it in spite of a voice which was saying inside me: That's right. Believe her. She'll say next that she's got some of the Russian Crown jewels and that a gang of Bolshevists are after her and them. And you'll believe that, too.

"In that case," I said, "you'd better put it in a safe place."

"You don't believe me," she said quietly.

"Yes, I do. I don't want to, but I do. I know that every word you've said is the truth."

"And after I've gone," she said very quietly, "after I've gone, you'll wonder how you came to credit it for a moment. Well, I can quite understand it."

"You don't understand in the least," I said brusquely.

I offered her a cigarette, lighted one myself at her nod, and threw the match toward the fire and said: "All right. What next? As I say, you'd better put it in a safe place, whatever it is."

"Oh, it's in a safe place," she said. "And actually I've only got half of it — what I have isn't worth a cent all by itself. But you see — this is the way of it, Mr. Sundean; I'm going to start really at the beginning. I'll make it as brief as I can make it, for it isn't a pleasant story. My mother, as I told you, died here last year. My father, in America, died some months ago, too. They had been estranged for years — since I was three years old. Mother had lived here and there, and I've always been with my mother. That was one of the — agreements. My brother remained with my father. He was four years older than I when our parents separated. My mother —" she paused and took a long breath as if she'd reached the most difficult part of the story — "my mother was an extraordinary person, Mr. Sundean. I didn't know — and it doesn't concern this, why they separated, but whatever the reason was, my mother held it more important than anything else in the world. More important even than that I should ever see my father."

"You mean to say you never saw him again?"

She nodded her head. She was looking at the fire.

"Yes," she said quietly. "I never saw him again. I should not have known him if I passed him in the street. And I should not have known my brother."

I said: "Don't tell me all this if it distresses you."

She made a quick gesture with her hand.

"Oh, but I must, Mr. Sundean. It's the explanation for all this. My mother was very bitter and remained so. My brother was to stay with my father, I with my mother. My mother had a small income, but during her illness we were obliged to use up most of the capital. She refused to the last to hold any communication with my father or brother; it was not easy for her to do that — but she was — she had extraordinary command over herself." She paused thoughtfully and then continued in a brisker tone:

"At any rate, my father was a wealthy man when he died. He wanted me to have half his estate — to share it with Francis, that's my brother. And — and this, of course, is the kernel of the affair — when my mother went away he gave me a — a small —" She hesitated and glanced at me and said: "I'm not to tell anyone what it was exactly. And, anyway, it doesn't matter, because it has no intrinsic value, it's only its significance that counts. I had part and my brother had part, and probably there are no others identical with those we have in the world. You see, of course, what it was for."

"Identification," I said.

"Yes. My mother being what she was, my father knew that she would take steps to loose us from any possible connection with him. And that's just what she did. We went under various names, I think, for a while, though I don't remember much of that; all I remember about those days is the continual going here and there. Well — the point is that my father didn't keep in touch with us — my mother was determined that he should not. After I reached an age to notice things we used our own name, of course, and I knew the whole story. Mother had not been well, and I felt closer to her than to my father. Then she — died."

She paused again, and I put another small log on the fire and bent over its arrangement and gave her a little time.

"She gave me, of course, an envelope with her marriage certificate and my birth certificate and various things of that sort in it. And at the last she told me to find my father. After a time I wrote: he was dying. Francis, my brother, replied. He said there would be the matter of identification. It seems that my father, trying to discover me again before his death, as he must have tried many, many times during those years, had finally advertised, and the story had leaked out a bit, and they'd had a number of letters from girls who said they were Sue Tally. He said that birth and marriage certificates could be faked, but that if I were really his sister there would be one means of identification. I knew, of course, what he meant. But I wrote in as guarded a fashion as he had written, saying only that I had it and not what it was. The exchange of letters," she said rather dryly, "didn't make me feel exactly welcome. Yet I saw exactly what had happened. Then my father died; there was business for Francis to see to. Francis sent Mr. Lorn — the detective, you know — to see me. He evidently reported that I appeared to be actually Sue Tally. And Francis —" She smiled a little wryly. "Perhaps I'd better read you the letter Mr. Lorn brought to me from Francis."

She unbuttoned her velvet coat. Under it was some kind of black lace frock through which there were glimpses of white. She

146

reached under the laces and brought out a letter.

"I've grown very cautious," she said, smiling a little. "I did not wish to leave the letter in my room or carry it openly about in a bag. I want you to read it." She leaned over and held the letter toward me.

CHAPTER VIII

It began rather coolly: *"My dear Madam:"*

I glanced at Sue. She smiled into my eyes, but there was a determined look about her face and a spark of anger in her eyes; I guessed that brother Francis's reluctance had had its share in molding her determination to prove herself. I went back to the letter, reading it slowly.

"MY DEAR MADAM: *Mr. Lorn's report has been favorable. However, I think it advisable that I and my lawyer visit you in order to make further inquiries. You will kindly await our arrival in A—, which may be somewhat delayed owing to pressing business matters. Of course, you understand that our projected trip to see you does not bind me in any way to grant your claim. While, as I say, my detective's report has been favorable, still there is one matter in particular to be satisfactorily proved.*

"You will understand that my sister's portion of the estate, if she is still alive and can prove her identity beyond a shadow of a doubt, is considerable, and since the whole matter has been left in my hands to act at my discretion, I feel deeply responsible.

"I must add a word to the effect that, if you actually prove to be Sue Tally, having in your possession every means of proving this to my complete satisfaction — in this case I must warn you to take no one into your confidence. Owing to my father's indiscreet action we have been troubled with several impostors, and it is not out of the question that you are in danger yourself.

"With this in mind, I am sending Mr. Lorn again to A—. He will remain there and is under orders from me to give you every possible protection, which under the circumstances is, I think, really more than you can expect from me. I trust that you will reciprocate by following my wishes in the matter. Which are, I repeat, to await our arrival at A— and to take no one into your confidence."

It was all typed, even to the *"Yours truly, Francis Tally,"* although he had placed very intricately interwoven initials below the typed signature.

She was watching me thoughtfully.

"Your brother Francis," I said slowly, "appears to be a somewhat canny sort of person. Not overeager, perhaps, to welcome his sister."

Her eyes lit.

"Then you do believe I'm what I say I am."

"Why — see here, do I look as if I doubted it?"

She shook her head slowly. "No," she said smiling, and her eyes shining. "No, you look as if you believed it." Her voice trembled a little. "It hasn't been very pleasant for me, you know. But I quite understand why he — writes like that. He's got to be — cautious."

"He's cautious enough," I said briefly. "One might even call him overcautious."

She nodded, still looking happy; her pleasure over the small fact of my own faith in her story and in herself gave me a rather shocked glimpse into the long period of unhappiness she had experienced. Why didn't her brother drop everything and come at her first letter? "Important business matters" would delay him; more important it seemed than to come immediately to this beautiful sister of his, who certainly needed a brother and his protection. I wondered if Francis had exactly pleasurable anticipation of giving up half his fortune to his sister. I didn't, of course, say all this, but Sue read my look. She said:

"You must remember that he's been troubled with impostors, and that he has not even seen me since I was a baby. We have practically no recollections of each other. It would be natural, too, for him to be a little prejudiced against me. And then, besides, he did send the detective. That's something."

"That's something," I agreed dryly. I rose to give her the letter. Her hand approached mine, and I took it and the other in mine, as I had there in the corridor only an hour or so before. I said clumsily:

"You must let me help you." The words were trite, but she understood what I'd meant and not managed to say.

She said, "Thank you," and looked at me, and the something leaped from our eyes and communicated and merged while I stood there looking down at her. It lasted only a few seconds, but it seemed a long time before I dropped her hands and turned abruptly to the mantel and stood leaning against it.

"And now," said Sue, slipping the letter under the laces again — I thought it too lovely and sweet a place for such a thing, and she must have read something in my eyes, for she flushed a little and buttoned her black coat tightly again. "And now you understand. At least, you understand most of it."

I looked away from her and considered the matter.

"Your mother kept the token for you?" I asked.

"Yes. I didn't know, of course, what it meant. I think I've got a vague memory of my father calling Francis and me to him and putting it — and giving a —" she hesitated and used my word — "token — to each of us. But my mother took mine and kept it for me and later told me why my father had given it to me. She was fair according to her views."

"Is it possible that your mother, before her death, told anyone else of it?"

She frowned.

"That's something, of course, that I've wondered about. Especially since, for the last two or three weeks, I've felt — apprehensive. Oh — except for the abduction, I've nothing definite to go on. I've been a little nervous — once or twice I've thought my room was searched — at least, things seemed to have moved themselves mysteriously about — and then I told you that the corridors had got on my nerves a little. The whole hotel has, for that matter. And then — the attempted abduction. That was rather — bad, you know."

"It was," I said grimly. "Look here, why don't you go to Paris? I'll go with — that is, I'll go at the same time. Go to a good hotel and wait for your brother there."

"I'd thought of that," she said quietly. "But there are reasons against it. The chief one is that Francis would never believe that I'm Sue Tally if I turned up in another place." She'd spoken rather lightly, but there was underlying truth in her words; from the one letter of Francis's writing that I'd seen I thought she was probably quite right. "I don't intend," she added more soberly, "to give him the least further chance to dispute my identity. He seems — unduly suspicious already. And I — please understand me. I don't need millions to get along, but I do need money. And my father wanted me to have it. And I'm Sue Tally. I *am* Sue Tally. I won't let him say I'm not!"

"You are right," I said admiringly, watching her eyes darken and her mouth set itself with determination. At the same time and for the first time I felt a kind of chill at the thought of those millions. I hadn't a doubt that she was what she said she was; that being true, the time might come when she would be quite literally surrounded by millions. It would be like a wall — an enormous, insurmountable wall of gold. And she was so very sweet.

I wrenched myself back to the business at hand. After all, she was nothing to me. Noth-

153

ing to me. Nothing to me. A girl I liked and admired, and a girl in such danger that any decent man would have given her what help he could give — but that was all.

"What about these records — marriage and birth and all that — are they, too, in a safe place?"

"Oh, quite," she said at once. "They are in the safe in Lovschiem's office."

"In Lovschiem's safe?" I cried incredulously.

"Why, yes," she said, looking at me in a puzzled way. "Why not? They — Grethe and Marcus Lovschiem have been very kind to me. They have been almost my only friends. They and — well, Marcel. The porter, you know. He's been kind in many, many small ways. And the Lovschiems did everything they could for my mother."

"Do they know anything of all this?"

She looked at me doubtfully; she was always very swift to catch any implications.

"Lovschiem isn't prepossessing," she said, "but I think he means well. However, I have told them very little about it."

"What have you told them?"

"Only that I was waiting for my brother to come."

She met my look and flushed again.

"I know it seems — unusual — that I should tell them nothing and you — so much," she

154

said. "But you — you are —" She stopped as if seeking words, and I said:

"It shows that you must have had some faint distrust of them. You haven't wanted to admit it, perhaps, but it's there."

"No, no," she said. "They are my friends. But I wanted to tell someone, and you — you were here." She stopped, looking rather puzzled. Then her face cleared. "It was a question of your protecting yourself," she said, and I felt, unreasonably, a distinct sense of disappointment.

"You haven't given this — token — into the Lovschiems' care?"

"Oh, no. They know nothing about it at all. I will show it to no one until I see my brother Francis and match his own with it. He must be convinced."

"Of course," I said slowly. "If anyone has got wind of the affair, as your brother suggests, you may be in considerable danger. Are you sure it's wise to stick it out here rather than go to Paris — or some other place? It might be better even for you to go directly to America and find your brother."

"Perhaps, but I intend to stay here. My brother ought to come to me. At least I shall do as he wishes — that seems fair. He wants me to stay here until he and his lawyer come. So I will do that."

"But — that abduction last night. I don't like dragging up the subject, but it's a very serious matter."

"I know," she said. "It frightened me awfully. It frightens me to think of it now. You need not tell me it is serious." She paused and looked at me meditatively, her slim fingers across one black velvet knee. "I wonder what you thought of me last night. You must have thought I was quite mad."

Her eyes met mine, and we looked for a long moment. A log crackled behind me, and it was somehow significant, the small sound in the stillness, full of some mysterious but important meaning.

"Do you want to know what I thought?" I said slowly. "I thought you were very sweet."

I had spoken gravely, and she had listened as gravely. For an instant the air between us was alive and trembling and aware, and our glances clung together. Then there was a knock on the door.

It was Lorn, of course. He was unexcited, matter-of-fact; he entered, gave one look at Sue, said "Good-evening," and took the chair I offered.

"I've been telling Mr. Sundean why I fear that my affairs have had some connection with the murder last night," Sue told him thought-

156

fully. "I felt it only fair to do so, since he was unfortunate enough to become rather involved in the affair. I'm sorry to go against my brother's wishes in the matter, but I felt obliged to do so in this case."

Lorn made an inexpressive gesture.

"Your brother merely expressed his wishes, as I understand it, Miss Tally. I don't know that you are obliged to comply with them."

"I prefer to do so," she said rather stiffly, "in all other respects. However, it would have been most unfair to Mr. Sundean to give him no means to defend himself."

The detective took the cigarette I offered, thanked me absently, and frowned at Sue.

"Defend himself?" he questioned. "How can your affair provide a defense for Sundean?"

Her eyes flashed a quickly controlled impatience.

"I've already told you about the murder coming right on the heels of someone's attempting to carry me off. Heaven knows, I hope it was only a dreadful coincidence. But — " She paused gravely and added: "Perhaps I'm only growing nervous. It has been a rather long strain, and I hoped Francis would be here and the thing settled long before this."

Lorn said more pleasantly: "Well, at any rate, we managed to get Mr. Sundean out of jail."

"What about the poison, Lorn?" I asked.

"Poison!" cried Sue.

"The man there in the corridor last night actually died of poison," said Lorn. "I was able to suggest something which hurried up their post-mortem a bit — made it perhaps a little more searching than it would have been otherwise — so far it seemed to have been a rather cursory affair. Although the cause of death was very obvious —"

"But the poison," I interrupted. "How on earth was the man poisoned? And if poisoned why was he also stabbed?"

"They are having the traces analyzed," Lorn said precisely. "I don't know just what kind of poison it was — not definitely, that is. But the point is that he wasn't shot at all. And as to the little clock sword —" Lorn's curiously hazy gaze seemed to be fastened on the clock — "they are inclined to think that death had actually occurred before the clock sword was driven into his heart."

Sue cried out something, and Lorn continued dryly: "They are rather uncertain about the poison and how it could have been administered — the man might even have been a suicide, you know. It will take some time to prove all this, and some expert opinion. Which is why you were released for the time being, Mr. Sundean."

158

I did not like his expression "for the time being." But since he'd done me a very good turn indeed I ignored it and said:

"Curious that you should have hit upon the method but not the means."

"Well," he said without an undue effect of modesty, "it struck me that the little clock sword was an odd weapon to use. It argued an amount of impulse in the matter that was out of the ordinary. But I didn't expect it to be poison."

"Poison — that implies deliberation, doesn't it?" said Sue.

"A certain preparedness, at least," said Lorn dryly.

"I was surprised," he added grudgingly. "It wasn't at all what I expected." He paused thoughtfully and continued in a disgruntled way: "Poison *and* stabbing. It isn't reasonable. But, as I say, we may be dealing with an exceptional criminal. Do you want to hear the details of the inquest? I was fortunate to get on fairly friendly terms with the police, and I can tell you —"

"*No,*" said Sue sharply.

"Very well," said the detective imperturbably. "Now then, Mr. Sundean, Miss Tally suggests that your man in the courtyard and her abductor and the murderer are one and the same man. What's your opinion?"

159

"It's entirely possible," I said. "Anything's possible. But of course there's no way to be sure of that. I couldn't possibly identify the man in the courtyard; Miss Tally didn't even get a look at her abductor, and neither of us saw the murderer."

"There isn't any way in which you could arrive at some means of identifying the man in the courtyard?"

"No. He was only footsteps and a revolver and once a bit of cloth. I did manage to touch his coat or cloak or whatever he wore once. It was roughish material, and that's all I know. Nothing to identify him there. But I feel, I don't know why, that it's possible that the murdered man was the man who carried Miss Tally off earlier in the evening."

"Ah," said Lorn. "How about it, Miss Tally?"

"I don't know," she said. Her face was white and pinched-looking at the recollection. "I thought of that, too. But I couldn't tell. If he were the same man, though," she said doubtfully, "why should he have been killed? Who killed him?"

I remembered the flying figure against the light from my opened door; I remembered her slim fingers holding the little dagger. I remembered its being replaced on the clock.

"There are a dozen answers to that," said

160

Lorn quietly. "The most obvious one is that, in that case, he was murdered by a second person who would like to get possession of your means of identifying yourself to your brother and who thought your abductor had succeeded: you remember the murdered man had been searched. That theory would complicate things further. I take it," he added rather hurriedly, "that you've told Mr. Sundean everything about the affair."

"Yes," said Sue briefly.

I said thoughtfully:

"Look here, if we presuppose that that's the reason for the murder — or better, if we simply assume that there is a conspiracy or a plot to rob Miss Tally —"

"I think we can scarcely escape assuming that," murmured Lorn.

"Well, then, what would the plan be, do you suppose? Miss Tally says the token she has isn't worth anything in itself."

"You can answer that yourself, Mr. Sundean," said Lorn. He leaned back in his chair, put the tips of his fingers together, and half closed his eyes. It was, I guessed, the kind of question he liked.

"Oh, the obvious thing is to substitute someone for Miss Tally."

"Certainly," said Lorn. "Substitution is the essential part of the scheme. We must keep that in mind. There could be no other way of doing. And that implies two people at least knowing the secret — the fellow who tried to abduct Miss Tally, and the girl he intends to substitute — providing he already had a girl ready. You see, he would have to discover one near Miss Tally's height and general description, coach her a bit on what he could discover of Miss Tally's and her mother's life, secure the papers you gave — unwisely, I fear, Miss Tally — to Lovschiem for safe keeping —" there was a faintly ironic emphasis in his last two words, as if he shared my own doubts as to Lovschiem's integrity — "and — which is most important — he must secure the token by which you are to prove yourself to your brother. His abducting you argues either that your room was to be thoroughly searched at a given time, and thus you were to be out of the way during that time, or —" he paused, looking at the fire with half-shut eyes for so long that Sue's fingers began to clasp and unclasp on her knee, and I moved restlessly — "Or," he continued presently, "that he had some reason to believe you carried the token with you — somewhere about your clothing — and intended to search you —"

"It's all right now," I said quickly to Sue. "You are perfectly safe now."

"Oh —" she said faintly. "Don't mind me.

It's only that I keep remembering — Do go on, Mr. Lorn."

"I was only going to say," continued Lorn rather disapprovingly, "that there might be an alternative plan. Even two alternatives. One would be that there would be an attempt to gain your confidence and thus discover the whereabouts of the token. Another might be the posing of some man as your brother."

"As my brother —" said Sue.

"Of course." Lorn looked impatient. "Some young man with an American accent and knowledge of America and of your home and affairs — enough to convince you that he was your brother."

"Upon which I would presumably turn over the token to him! Well, I won't do that. Francis shall not see my token until he shows me his own. No one shall see it."

"But see here, Lorn," I offered. "There's a flaw in all three of your alternatives. You know the real Sue. And you know the real Francis."

He nodded. "Unfortunately it's the same flaw, and I am it. But there's a simple solution. You forget, Mr. Sundean, the existence of someone in the affair who's rapid and ready with his revolver. And dead men tell no tales."

"Oh!" cried Sue with horror. "You don't mean that, Mr. Lorn!"

He shrugged.

"Why, yes. It is obvious. However, I'm not unused to danger."

"And what," said Sue, "do they expect to do with me?" Her eyes had widened with horror, and her face was white and rigid.

I started toward her: it was a ghastly suggestion she'd put into words. But Lorn intercepted me.

"Oh, don't think of that, Miss Tally," he said easily. "The token protects you so long as they don't discover it: perhaps I should say the secret of the whereabouts of the thing protects you in a measure."

She looked faintly less rigid under the easy assurance of his words. But I was thinking: abduction, search, threat, unspeakable! — Torture, even — then when it is discovered she'll have to be got out of the way forever. Five million — if it were only smaller — but five million — and they would be unscrupulous — the previous night had proved that. But I couldn't say all that: I couldn't brutally add to her shock and terror. And she was like a rock in her determination not to go to her brother.

"Can't you cable something to Francis to bring him here sooner?" I suggested.

"No," cried Sue spiritedly. "I won't beg —"

"Nonsense," I said. "This is too serious for petty pride —"

"Petty pride! —" She was on her feet again, her eyes flashing dangerously.

"Come, come, Miss Tally," murmured Lorn quietly. "We understand your position. But I'll cable to Mr. Tally."

"I won't have it —"

"Then I'll do it myself," I said grimly, and meant it, though I have the average man's dislike for meddling in someone else's affairs.

"You won't," said Sue, sitting down again.

"Then you'll tell the police about it and get their permission to leave —"

"I won't," said Sue quite sweetly.

Lorn cleared his throat in, somehow, a placative fashion.

"The question of cabling your brother can wait," he said quietly. "It wouldn't help us now, anyway. It would take Mr. Tally some time to get here, and this business will be, probably, cleared up and done with long before he can arrive. As soon as we are permitted we can go to meet him. Or wait here. Whatever Miss Tally prefers. But there is no use talking of leaving now. The police will not let her go. Will not let any of us leave. Not under any circumstances. It is out of the question. You can call that settled."

He looked thoughtfully from Sue to me and back.

"And as to telling them of what we know,"

he added gravely, "I am strongly of the opinion that that would be most unwise."

Well, it was all true.

He paused again and then continued in a brisker fashion:

"Have you any reason at all to suspect that the Lovschiems are at the bottom of this, Miss Tally? There's a very obvious implication of a sort of conspiracy of at least two people — possibly more. One person alone could not possibly swing it, any way you look at it."

"The Lovschiems! No," cried Sue stubbornly. "I told you I'd been nervous about it. That my room had been searched a time or two. That I'd had a jittery sort of feeling about the corridors — as if someone were just behind me or just around the corner — that kind of silly, stupid thing. But nothing definite — except that abduction. And nothing at all to involve the Lovschiems."

"But there's no one else in the hotel," said Lorn.

"No," agreed Sue at once. "Except the servants, and they couldn't be the offenders — Marcel is too loyal, Marianne too honest, and the cook has no brains at all and besides is a shocking coward."

"Well," said Lorn, "there's the priest and Mrs. Byng."

"And do you seriously suspect either of

them?" asked Sue scornfully. "No — if there actually is a — conspiracy, as you call it — against me, it comes from outside the hotel."

"But ways and means?" hinted Lorn dryly.

"Pouf! There are plenty of ways and means. People could easily get in and out of the place, and without being seen. It stands open all day. It's practically deserted in the winter. And it's a great rambling affair with a hundred hiding places."

"Do you know any of them?" asked Lorn sharply.

She looked at him in a perplexed way.

"Oh, I see," she said after a moment. "You mean really secret hiding places. Isn't that a little absurd, Mr. Lorn?"

"Perhaps," he said. "Still — it's a very old place, you know."

"The gates were locked," I said. "The police found no one hiding here when they arrived. That leaves only Lovschiem, Marcel, the priest, and me. There were no other men about the place."

"You are sure it was a man in the courtyard, Mr. Sundean?" asked the detective.

"Why, yes, of course. That is, well — no. I didn't actually see him, and I suppose a woman can fire a revolver as easily as a man. But I felt that it was a man."

She said quickly: "You've forgotten, Mr.

Sundean. I told you there is a way into the hotel after the doors and gates have been locked for the night. I know it. Lovschiem and his wife know it. Marcel knows it. But otherwise it is supposed to be kept a secret. For no reason," she added hastily, forestalling Lorn's question, "except that there wouldn't be much use in locking up if everyone knew the other way into the court."

I remembered her words at once.

"And you said the man who followed you last night knew the way into the hotel? That limits it further, then, if the way is supposed to be kept a secret. If we can discover just who knows of that way — providing of course it has actually been kept a secret —" Sue nodded vigorously, though I thought it unlikely — "then among those people must be —"

I checked myself, as I saw I was getting nowhere, and Lorn said a little maliciously: "Must be whom, Mr. Sundean? The murderer or the murdered man?"

"That depends on the identity of the murdered man," I said rather glumly. "At any rate, it proves that the man who tried to abduct Miss Tally had some connection with the hotel — or with the Lovschiems. The fact that, after driving about for so long a time, he finally brought her back to the immediate vicinity of the hotel indicates that, too."

Lorn nodded. "Possibly," he said.

"Then," I said, "there's the car she was carried off in. If the murdered man was her abductor, then the car must be standing about near the hotel."

"True," said Lorn, giving me a faintly respectful look. "I'll see what I can find out about that. Fortunately, as I said, the police here are inclined to be friendly to me. I wonder how soon we'll know the exact poison: we can't consider its hypothetical relation to the few facts we have until we know what the poison was, how it might be administered, and when. It was evidently a poison whose presence does not stare one in the face even some hours after death. Some poisons affect the body in a very short time — I beg your pardon, Miss Tally." She had put out one hand in a pleading way, and Lorn continued, "Of course, it's been a shock to you. I'd forgotten what a bad night it must have been. However," he said to me, "he, the abductor, may have had accomplices."

"There was only one man," said Sue with a small shudder. I glanced at her white face and said quickly:

"Well, there seem to be several things that will bear investigation. I want to know, first, about this business of the dagger; who took it off the dead man and washed it and then put it back on the clock. Then I want to know why the lights went out just as they did while I was in the court. It was a most opportune accident — if accident it was — for the man in the court with me; otherwise I should certainly have caught a glimpse of him. My only surmise about that is that, if it was Lovschiem in the court, then Madame Lovschiem could easily have pulled the main switch. She might have been watching the affair and have come to her husband's assistance, in that way. Where were you, Miss Tally, when the lights in the hotel went out?"

"I was still in my room," she said at once.

"That was," I asked, hating myself but remembering too vividly the face in the third-floor window, "your own room — nineteen? On this floor?"

"Why, yes, of course," she said.

"Do you mind if I ask how you knew of the murder?"

"Not at all. I was opening my window; I could not see through the shutters, and I unlatched one in order to glance out into the court. I saw light streaming from your room and several figures — yours, I thought, and Marcel's — and I could see Father Robart bending as if he were kneeling. It was clear, of course, that something unusual had happened, and I was — curious, I suppose. I know

I felt apprehensive and alarmed and couldn't possibly have gone to sleep without knowing. Finally I closed the shutter and started to dress again. While I was dressing the light in my room went out. That has happened before, so I just waited till it came on again and thought nothing of it. As soon as I got my coat on I came out into the corridor and hurried along it and into the north corridor and saw Marcel. You and the priest weren't there any more. Marcel told me what had happened, and then you came."

"You met no one in the corridors?"

"No," she said promptly. "No one."

Clear, direct, reasonable sounding; and her eyes were as clear and direct in their steady gaze into mine. Yet there was the vivid recollection of the face looking from the third-floor window; the face so white and strange in that glancing light — and so dreadfully interested in the scene it was watching.

I couldn't say: But I saw you looking from a third-floor window and you looked white and terrible. I couldn't say: Why was your story about the key so strangely apt? I couldn't say: Why did you replace the dagger? I couldn't say: Why, oh, why didn't you tell me the truth about the time when you left my room?

171

CHAPTER IX

The wind hurled about the hotel and banged the loose shutter, and I said instead, rather heavily:

"Then, again, there's the identity of the murdered man. His knowing the secret way into the hotel —"

"But you aren't certain of that, Mr. Sundean," said Lorn dryly. "He may have been brought here. You can't be sure he, himself, knew the secret way in. By the way, Miss Tally, what is this tremendously important way into the hotel?"

Her cheeks went a little pink.

"Of course, it sounds silly," she said indignantly. "But in view of what has happened it isn't so silly. It's nothing at all complicated. The oval in the middle of one of the doors is a sort of gate in itself; the hinges are concealed in the fancy ironwork and it opens with a catch. It's very simple. It's been there since the place was built, I suppose, many, many years ago. But it had been forgotten in late years. Marcel rediscovered it accidentally last year, while he was cleaning the thing."

"And you say that only the Lovschiems, Marcel, and yourself know about it?" asked Lorn.

"So far as I know," she said. "It pleased Lovschiem to keep it a secret."

"But," I said, "your abductor seems to have known it."

"If you mean that the Lovschiems had something to do with — my — with that affair, you are quite wrong," said Sue warmly, with an air of defence. "It's true that, so far as I know, the entrance through the gate has been kept a secret. But at the same time that doesn't mean that I think the Lovschiems could connive at abduction. They have been very kind to me. They were kind to my mother. I — I feel sure it was not the Lovschiems."

"Very well," I said. "But there's another curious point about the Lovschiems — I'm sorry, Miss Tally, since you say they've been your friends — but — well, I saw Madame Lovschiem, remember, at the moment when she first saw the murdered man. And she said something to Lovschiem that was rather strange. Strange, that is, if they actually knew nothing of the murdered man. She said: 'So, you've killed him.' "

There was a little silence. Both Lorn and Sue were looking at me; Lorn thoughtfully, Sue with a look of curiously mixed uncertainty and indignation and doubt. But she had a ready suggestion.

"That really means nothing, however. She might have thought it was some robber he'd killed. Some intruder. Lovschiem, for all his smiles, hasn't too nice a temper. She would of course be alarmed if he had acted so impulsively."

"Impulsively?" I murmured.

"It usually is an impulse," offered Lorn tonelessly.

"You may be right, of course," I continued, meeting Sue's eyes. "But it looks to me more as if she knew the murdered man and Lovschiem knew him. It even hints, to my way of thinking, that the murder wasn't entirely a surprise to her."

"Oh — no!" cried Sue parenthetically and I went on: "And while we are talking of the Lovschiems —"

"While you are talking of them," interrupted Sue again and rather pointedly.

"Very well, while I am talking of them. Why did Madame Lovschiem try to replace the dagger in the clock under my very eyes and suggest that we keep any knowledge of it from the police?"

"Did she do that?" said Lorn.

"She did," I said, and told him at length of the incident. I did not, however, tell of the very recent sequel to it, and during the telling I avoided Sue's eyes. And I said nothing of the dagger's reappearance. That was one thing Lorn might discover for himself. Lorn made no comment when I'd finished, and Sue finally said thoughtfully, but very stubbornly, it seemed to me:

"Perhaps Madame only wanted to keep the hotel out of as much scandal as was possible. It is bad enough, with the murder and all. And she thinks you didn't do it, Mr. Sundean."

"Nice of her, I'm sure," I said, exasperated. "But I think you are carrying your loyalty to your — friends — a little too far."

Her eyes flared darker again, but Lorn intervened.

"You evidently don't know, Mr. Sundean, that the police have gone quite thoroughly into the matter of alibis, for the time just preceding your discovery of the murder. The Lovschiems say they were together; that Lovschiem was going over his accounts in his own room, and that Madame was in the adjoining room, but they were within sight of each other and were actually talking when the bell rang and Lovschiem heard it. Marianne, the maid, says she was sound asleep, and the police had to bang on the door of her room —"

"Where is her room?" I interrupted to ask, and Lorn, looking a little put out, replied:

"On the second floor back toward the service stairway. As I was saying, the police think she is telling the truth because they had to bang on the door to wake her and wait until she got some clothes on. It was the same with Mrs. Byng, and I'm given to understand that, in her case at least, the police feel quite convinced that she had no previous knowledge of the affair. The priest says Marcel had been with him up to a moment or two before Madame Lovschiem knocked on the door of his room and begged him to come to the dead man. Marcel agrees. It seems that the priest had a — er — touch of —"

"Stomach-ache," said Sue rapidly. "And rang for Marcel and Marcel brought him hot water and brandy and stayed with him an hour."

"Exactly," said the detective.

"And further," said Sue, "I let your story of why you had gone to the lobby and thus, returning by way of the courtyard, stumbled upon the murdered man — I let that pass last night because I honestly didn't know what to do, and I could see they believed you at the moment. It's true I shrank from telling about that attempted abduction and about how I — how you helped me and all. The French have — awfully curious notions about such things: it's a matter of psychology with them. The police would never believe the thing as it stands, and one needn't expect them to do so. And — it does sound a little — improbable. But I can see now that I made a mistake, and I'm going to tell them the truth about it at once. That is the least I can do. I didn't realize that I was placing you in such a position. I can give you a complete alibi, Mr. Sundean, and I intend to do so."

"It's wholly unnecessary," I said. "And anyway, I won't hear of it. I'm not being silly and chivalrous. Don't think that. But I simply won't let you."

"How," said Sue, "are you going to stop me?"

"You know," said Lorn in a bored way, "there's no need for this discussion. I was about to remind you that those alibis are of practically no importance. In view of the recent discovery, I mean. The poison."

He was right, of course.

After a moment Sue rose. The clinging black velvet fell into soft folds about her slim, pretty figure. She pushed one hand over her bright hair and sighed.

"It's late," she said wearily. "And we seem to be getting nowhere. It was a dreadful night, and it's been a crazy day, and if the wind doesn't stop blowing for a while tonight I shall go quite out of my head. But at any rate I'm going to try to get some rest." She paused and smiled a little wryly and said: "When shall we three meet again?"

The wind howled and rattled a window in the corridor.

"When the hurly-burly's done," I said absently.

"Tomorrow," said Lorn prosaically. "I don't wish to be over-encouraging, Mr. Sundean, and there are a number of questions I shall still want to ask you, but I really think you've given me something to go on. You are sure you've forgotten nothing? Even the smallest thing that might be a clue?"

"There was on the landing a broken bit of something that looks like wax or rubber, and a brown leaf," I said thoughtfully. "I've got them here. And the man in the courtyard wore a longish coat or cape of some rough material. That's all."

We all looked at the shriveled leaf and the bit of hard wax in the palm of my hand, but they were only a leaf and a scrap of reddish brown.

Lorn finally shrugged and dismissed them.

178

"Nothing, probably," he said. "I'll keep them in mind, however."

He turned suggestively toward the door. It is strange now to think how little significance we gave that small burden in the palm of my hand — the small burden that so nearly meant my death. But that was later.

"Then," I said slowly, "I believe Marcel knows something. I'm not sure. I may be all wrong. It's only an impression."

Lorn looked faint scorn but said dryly:

"We shall see. Going, Miss Tally?"

"Yes," said Sue abruptly. "Good-night."

"Wait. I don't like your going through the corridors. Let me —"

"Oh, I'm going now, too," said Lorn. "I'll see that she gets to her room all right."

It occurred to me that this fellow Lorn might prove to be something of a nuisance. And I could not let Sue leave without making certain of one thing. I should have preferred asking her without Lorn's being there, although I didn't know exactly why; anyway, I must ask her.

"Look here, Miss Tally," I said. "You had a very terrible experience last night. I want you to assure me that you —" strange that I stumbled over my trite words and wished Lorn were back in New York — "will take no risks."

179

"Thank you," she said slowly. "I — no — I can't think I'm in danger now." She put out her hand, and I held it a moment, and Lorn said briefly:

"I shall try to see that Miss Tally is in no danger. Good-night, Mr. Sundean."

Definitely and positively now I resented his arrival. I saw them go — they went quietly and quickly, and there was no one to see them — with mingled feelings, but the chief one was a wish that Lorn had never turned up. Although, I reminded myself, in that case I should still be in jail, with a very dubious future. Not that my future at the moment was any too bright.

The whole thing, in all its contradictory aspects, whirled and whirled through my mind. The wind howled outside, the place rattled in all its bones, and the flames in the fireplace gradually died to a red glow. Just as the glow fell into ashes I think I went to sleep.

I woke suddenly.

I did not know what had wakened me.

It was entirely dark in the room, and cold, and very still. Painfully still, for the tumult of the wind had died.

And yet in the stillness and the darkness and the cold of that deserted wing there was some sort of life awakened. I heard it again. A slight noise of some motion somewhere.

180

I got up on my elbow and peered toward the door, and finally rose silently and went to it. The table which I had again placed before it was undisturbed.

"Mice," I told myself. "In the walls. The place is full of them, probably." And went back to bed. But not this time to sleep. Among several other things I determined to get a few quiet words with Marcel in the morning.

I should also remember to ask Lovschiem for a key to my room. After all, keys existed, and while they seemed to be regarded in the same light and casual spirit with which they, in that hotel, looked upon the matter of central heating, still I myself intended to make no casual matter of it.

There was something decidedly unpleasant about that deserted wing: the ceilings were too high, the curtains and thick carpets too secretive and muffling, the spaces too dark, the corridor too long and empty and wind-swept. And now that the wind had gone down I particularly disliked the way various creaks and small mysterious rustles came to life. It was as if all the tormented spirits that had slept in that room were returning to visit it and walk lightly about and sigh.

With dawn I fell asleep again and woke late to a gray and troublous day.

It was easy to have a quiet moment with

Marcel, and during the night I had discovered, I thought, the way to approach him. When he brought my coffee and some very hard rolls and had given me a good morning and the news that it made bad times out today, I began:

"Marcel," I said directly, "you know, of course, that I'm in rather a bad fix about this murder?"

Oh, yes, he knew.

"Well, it develops that the murder — I'm trusting you not to tell this, Marcel — may affect Miss Tally's safety."

His bright eyes sparkled, and he nodded a great many times. I wondered just how much he knew about it, and continued:

"It is of the utmost importance to both Miss Tally and me to discover everything possible about the murder. I myself —" I was speaking with complete candor, and I must say I didn't quite like the sound of my own words — "I myself am in some danger of being hanged for it — or guillotined or whatever they do — and Miss Tally —"

"Miss Tally is in danger, also," finished Marcel quickly, his eyes snapping. "Me, I know that."

"Well, then," I said slowly, "I won't press you, Marcel, but I want you to think it over. Miss Tally says you have been very kind to her — perhaps when you consider the matter for a time you may — er — recall something you've seen or heard that will help us discover the real murderer."

He nodded soberly.

"It is very bad, this," he said, with the sparkle gone from his eyes. "It is bad to feel that a murderer is about somewhere. He may be anywhere — one does not know —" He paused thoughtfully, looking very somber, and added: "Marianne, she has fear that every shadow, every corner, every closed room may conceal the murderer. And there are many closed rooms."

"You know, then, that I didn't do it?"

I had gone too far.

"Monsieur is not a criminal," said Marcel. "I cannot say more. — But I will think. Yes, I will think. It may be — I do not say I know, you understand — but it may be that I can remember something — something —" He stared at the figures on the wall for a long moment, while I scarcely dared breathe for fear of turning his decision one way or the other. I felt more certain now that he knew something — something perhaps of not much importance, still, something, and I was in a mood, and rightly, to catch at straws. However, he sighed presently and repeated, his eyes still clouded and morose: "It is possible —

perhaps. Monsieur would like his bath now?"

And after running the tub full of almost lukewarm water he left abruptly. There was about his departure a suggestion of escape, and I could only hope that his liking for Sue Tally would work in our favor. I wanted to help Sue, of course, but at the same time there's no use denying that I wanted quite as much to help myself.

That morning, long and gray and dull, was an unpleasant replica of the preceding one, except that I saw nothing of the police. Nothing, that is, except a blue-caped figure which followed me unobtrusively during my solitary and very chilly walk through wind-swept streets and one or two others who lurked about, shielding themselves in corners from the wind but nevertheless keeping, I thought, an unpleasantly sharp eye upon the hotel.

The place had been deserted when I first came down in the morning; only Pucci cocked a suspicious eye toward me as I went through the lobby. But when I returned, Madame Grethe was at the desk — her eyes looked very green and knowing, and she smiled secretively as she spoke to me — and Mrs. Byng and the priest were sitting in the lounge. Mrs. Byng was knitting furiously on some enormous garment and had her back to a radiator and her feet on a cushion, and the priest was in the corner by the lift; he looked long and black and morose with his red beard hidden by the newspaper. The place was silent except for the newspaper rustling now and then and Mrs. Byng's needles clicking. I looked up; the skylight was gray and the encircling galleries were empty and bare and the doors blank. It was not, to say the least, a cheerful spot, and it was rather appalling to think that we'd all got to stay there until the police gave us permission to leave.

Sue Tally was not to be seen, Lorn was invisible too, and I thought it probable he was off on some clue, perhaps, or even hobnobbing with the police. After all, the shape and quantity of a man's chin are scarcely his own fault, and certainly Lorn had proved himself a friend — a rather dry and detached sort of friend, but still a friend — in time of need.

I sat down fairly near the priest. The cockatoo had sidled along the floor after me and paid me the dubious compliment of promptly taking hold of a fold of my coat and pulling himself upward to perch on my arm and stare at me with his head cocked on one side and his shining black eyes looking like lacquered shoe buttons. I got out my cigarettes; Pucci transferred his attention to the watch on my wrist.

"I'm sorry," I said, across the very obvious barrier of the newspaper. "But — may I have a match?"

Mrs. Byng's needles clicked, and she gave me a sharp look, and her equine nose lifted a little as if it sniffed battle. The priest's newspaper rustled reluctantly as he shifted it to one hand. The flaming radiance of his beard came into view, he reached for the box of matches lying before him on the small table and passed it over to me.

"Thanks," I murmured, lit my cigarette, and as he immersed himself in the newspaper at once, I persisted: "You speak English, then?"

He gave me a morose look from the edge of the newspaper.

"Yes," he said flatly, and disappeared again. Mrs. Byng's needles clicked violently.

I kept on; I was in no frame of mind to consider the amenities.

"Traveling?" I remarked in a touristy approach.

"No." This time he did not even glance around the newspaper.

"English, are you?"

He looked at me fully this time. His face was not old, but it was lined; his eyes were a light yellow-gray, and around his mouth the hairs of his red beard grew thin, and you felt a sort of distaste looking at it.

"No," he said sharply. "French." He stared at me a moment and then added: "If you must know, I've spent two years in America and I'm here for my health. I also speak French and Italian. And I can read Latin."

With which he disappeared again, and Mrs. Byng sniffed quite audibly.

I said blandly: "Funny place to come to for your health. Have you been here long?"

The newspaper quivered for a moment, then his light eyes and flaming soft beard reappeared.

"If," he said coldly, "you want my full history, go to the police. They've just acquired it, owing to the very strange affair which accompanied your arrival here. There was," he added, driving the point further home, "no murder before you arrived." He continued to stare coldly and blandly at me. It was unfortunate that Pucci, who had been exploring silently in the vicinity of my pocket, drew forth at that moment a box of matches, laid it carefully upon my knee, and uttered a triumphant cluck. The priest looked at it, and Mrs. Byng looked at it, and the cockatoo looked at it and preened himself and clucked again happily.

The second cluck was too much for Father Robart, who himself uttered a sound not too faintly resembling it, shoved his paper together with an angry motion, rose, and stalked toward the lift. The little iron gate banged, the two narrow doors dipped together, and the small lift, looking not unlike a very tall coffin, murmured dully and started to crawl upward.

"Pucci," I said softly, "some day someone's going to wring your neck."

Mrs. Byng sniffed again.

"Exactly," she observed with harsh complaisance. "What I've often thought myself."

She did something to her long needles which whirled the whole garment about and gave an effect of tremendous decision to her words.

"If there ever was a bird in league with a devil, it is that one." She eyed the bird with asperity, and Pucci, eyeing her brightly, uttered a kind of squawky gurgle which certainly suggested a hoarsely diabolic laugh.

Mrs. Byng's thick eyebrows flew upward in a startled manner, and the needles paused for just an instant; then, recovering herself nobly, she nodded to me in an "I-told-you-so" way and resumed her knitting. Pucci returned to the matches quite as if sulphur had a natural attraction for him, and I said to Mrs. Byng:

"I'm glad to see you've recovered from the shock of the other night."

"I may look better," she said, knitting rapidly. "But I still feel the shock. I feel anything for a long time, Mr. Sundean, and feel it deeply. I have temperament. I have temperament. And I might say right here —" she glanced quickly all around, and, though there was no one else to be seen, she leaned forward and finished in a harsh whisper — "there's things going on here that don't just meet the eye. Things I don't like." She nodded sternly at me and added in her natural voice, which was one of a general surveying the field: "And I have good eyes, Mr. Sundean. *And* temperament."

"No doubt," I said warmly under the compulsion of her waiting gaze, and just then the gong for lunch arose with a sharp and sudden clamor which always impelled me to leap for the water buckets or the fire hose, an impulse which, I might add, I always conquered. Mrs. Byng nodded sternly at me again — a nod which mysteriously managed to convey the possibility that I too had temperament and thus we understood each other — gathered up her knitting and descended upon the dining room.

I lured Pucci onto the table by holding a lighted match before him — humanely out of biting distance, though it was a nice question as to whether flames would affect him adversely — and followed.

The priest turned up late, looking rather like an enraged exclamation mark, and finally Sue and Lorn: Sue quiet and rather pale, and Lorn fully as obtrusive and lively as the blank wall back of him. It was a strained and silent meal — silent because even a word to little Marcel reverberated in the empty space in a curiously embarrassing way, and strained because we all were intensely aware, I think, of one another's presence. Sue left first, giving me only a smile and a formal good-morning as she passed.

The meal over, I returned to the lounge and settled in a corner at the far end with coffee and a cigarette and an old *Punch*, hoping either Sue or Lorn would find me there. But Lorn slipped quietly out again (though I got some small satisfaction from a barely encouraging nod he gave me as he passed). Sue had disappeared, as had Mrs. Byng and the priest, and only Pucci, sitting on an armchair opposite, kept me company. And even Pucci looked a little depressed, rousing only to a kind of morose, preoccupied scratching now and then.

Gradually the faint clatter from regions back of the dining room died away.

The day had grown darker, and the well of the lounge, lighted only by the gray and sullen skylight, was shadowy and dim and very

190

silent. The whole place in fact had sunk into as complete a silence as if there were no one living about; at the same time it was a kind of sentient, brooding silence which reminded you that, beyond those twisting dark corridors and blank doors, there was, actually — well, who? — Mrs. Byng, the priest, Sue — the Lovschiems — the same small circle that had been in the hotel that wind-ridden night when a man was murdered.

The thought was not a pleasant one, and the silence and the shadows and the deserted lounge with its spaces going up and up past empty shadowy railings and blank doors were not pleasant either. I felt uneasy and restless, and was oddly relieved to hear quick light footsteps cross the dining room back of me.

It was Marcel. His long white apron loomed up ghost-like from the dimness, and he closed the dining-room door carefully behind him and crossed the lounge toward me. At the first glimpse of his face I guessed that he had come to some decision, and I sat up, tingling and alert.

He came closer to me. His eyes darted quickly about the lounge.

"I have decided myself. I will tell you," he said then, soberly and in a low voice. "No one can hear. No one is about at this hour," he added as I suppose I made some warning gesture.

"It is not much, perhaps," he went on. "It is at best only three things that I know. One is about the towels. And one is about Father Robart. And the third one —" He paused, his bright eyes looking alert and speculative. He nodded quickly and said: "I have fear that the third one is of importance. Perhaps it is of too much importance for me to keep secret. My silence may mean a life."

I was standing, facing him, and my heart was thudding.

"You won't regret it," I said. "What is it? Whose life?"

"First," he said — he would not be hurried, and I thought he had rehearsed the whole telling of his tale, and his bright eyes were sparkling — "first, the towels. There were used towels in an unused room the morning after the murder. There was also a round —" he described it with his lively little hands — "hollow on the eiderdown as if someone had sat there for a moment. I ask you — who was that?" I started to speak and checked myself for fear he would stop if I interrupted.

"Then," he held up two fingers. "Second. Father Robart was not sick during the night. I was not with him. I slept. Wait — you will ask why I permit the police to think I was with him. But what would you? He, a holy father, to ask such a small favor of me and me refuse. *Jamais!* And for the police —" He shrugged his shoulders in a manner which left little doubt as to the opinion he held of the police.

"Then, third —" He paused and then went on slowly: "It is of Miss Tally, and you will know what to do. That is why I tell you, for I have fear. Me, I do not like dead men. But there is danger. Danger of the gravest."

Afterward it seemed to me I had been faintly conscious of some sort of murmuring sound, but I actually heard only the words coming from the little porter's mouth.

"Third," he said, "I saw that night —"And then it happened.

Though I didn't know at once what had happened. I was only conscious of a sharply spitting sound and a smell, and of Marcel's face, which sagged and was surprised and held wide black eyes and an open mouth. Both his hands went to his back, and he tried to speak, and moaned and fell forward against me.

I caught him. He'd been shot. There was no one in the lounge — no one on the galleries, no one anywhere.

I eased him downward onto a chair; he was huddled and dying, and I tried to do something and couldn't, and then I knew that the murmur was the lift. The shot had come from there, and the lift was crawling upward toward the first gallery.

It was only a step or two that I ran forward. That was what was expected of me — to run forward and up the stairs and lose him somewhere about those dark corridors. Instead I stepped backward until I could see the entrance from the lift to the first gallery, and the entrance to the second gallery, and the entrance to the lounge where I stood, and there were no other means of exit from the lift.

The thing crawled upward. I could see the top of its doors above the narrow gallery floor before I lost sight of the doors below the intervening stretch of gallery.

The cage was dark. The two little doors blank.

It neared the first gallery. Would it stop there or go on?

There was no possible way for the murderer to escape. In another moment I should see him. He would open those blank little doors; I should see him. I would wreak a bitter vengeance on him who had wrenched the sparkling life from the little huddle that had been Marcel.

The lift slowly came to a stop there at the first floor. There was for a moment nothing but silence; then the doors trembled.

CHAPTER X

The narrow black space between the doors widened almost imperceptibly.

I can't remember that I had any definite plan. I only knew I must see who emerged from that slowly widening black slit.

Curiously, I heard the shot and felt the hot sting in my shoulder before I saw the muzzle of the revolver. Then things happened all at once.

I saw the short nose of a revolver poking out from behind one of the little doors, I was conscious of a furiously sharp pain in my shoulder somewhere, I was dodging instinctively, and there was the sound of another shot. The door to the lobby was just behind me, and I had leaped to shelter behind the wall and, using the key board for a shield, was peering around it, determined to see who was in the lift.

I saw the gleam of the revolver flying through the air downward, but not the arm that had thrown it. It fell with a clatter on the floor of the lounge, and at the very instant that I was leaning forward, sure now of seeing the murderer, someone seized me from behind; I struggled, twisting, straining my eyes toward the doors of the lift.

But I was jerked aside.

There were two policemen hanging to my arms and my waist, and the more furiously I struggled and shouted at them and tried to make them understand that the murderer was in the lift and that he was even now escaping, the more energetically they pulled me away from where I could see, and the more they shouted, and the tighter they held me, and I could not even point with my hands.

My shoulder hurt like hell, I was cursing with rage and pain and baffled fury, another policeman was running into the lobby from outside, and a woman was screaming from somewhere in the well of the lounge, and the screams rose thin and sharp and in dreadful horror above the tumult we were making in the lobby.

It was the screaming that drew one of the policemen into the lounge; at his shout the two holding me dragged me after them to the door again and then into the lounge, Mrs. Byng, hanging over the gallery rail, stopped screaming to stare, and then suddenly people were coming. Lovschiem and Grethe and little Sue with her face like chalk were running along the gallery and down the stairs and into the floor of the lounge.

All at once the lounge was crowded. Even the priest had turned up, panting, his red beard agitated, and Lorn, breathless, was hurrying through the lobby and was at my side, and the little maid, Marianne, was kneeling and sobbing, and the center of it all was the small white-aproned figure sprawling in the frivolous wicker chair. Sprawled so strangely still because we had seen it always so lively. The very flap and whisk of the white apron had savored of gayety and life.

In all the commotion and hubbub and torrents of French and Marianne's sobs, it was Lorn who remained fairly cool, and I'm sure it was Lorn who kept them from dragging me immediately to jail. I don't know what he said, though I guessed, from the way he pointed at my shoulder, and the blood that was soaking my coat, and the lack of powder burns, the direction of his argument. One of the policemen had picked up the gun and was holding it gingerly by the tips of his fingers when Lorn suddenly turned toward me.

"Have you touched the gun?" he barked sharply. He was, under fire, like another man, quick, sharp, decisive, his eyes no longer dull.

197

"No." That much I was sure of. "Whoever was in the lift threw it on the floor."

"In the lift? What do you mean? Tell me quickly."

I told him quickly. The others listened breathlessly, all but Marianne, who understood only one thing. Lorn translated with equal brevity and speed, and one of the policemen ran upstairs to the lift. The two remaining still held me tightly, as if that were the only thing they understood must be done. One of them, however, snapped suddenly a few words to Lovschiem, who was standing there, green with fright and looking quivery like an unwholesome sort of jelly, at which Lovschiem ran heavily into the lobby to the telephone.

Madame, standing near me, had a tense, sharp white face, but she said nothing, though her green eyes took in everything. And just then Sue perceived my wounded shoulder (she'd been stooping over Marianne, and there were tears on her white face when she turned). She came swiftly to me and put her hands on my arms and said something quickly to the police and I thought pleadingly. But they would not relinquish their hold.

I was beginning by that time to feel a little giddy and sick. Lorn said:

"Leave it to me. I may be able to get you

off. Your fingerprints can't be on the revolver, and there are no powder burns so you couldn't have done it yourself. Your being wounded may help."

I remember that very clearly. And I remember the crazy confusion. And I remember Sue's bringing me something to drink and holding it to my mouth because the police wouldn't release my arms, and how it brought tears to my eyes and stung my throat, and suddenly I felt revived and strong again and things were less dizzy and much clearer.

It must have been only a few moments before more policemen arrived, and all at once the commissaire with the billy-goat beard and the young officer who understood English were there, French was pouring out excitedly, and policemen were searching the hotel, and I was being questioned at length with Lorn and the young French officer (all friendliness gone now and only suspicion and excitement remaining in his glances toward me) translating for me. Sue managed somehow to stand near me, and she listened to every word, and it was extraordinary how strongly I felt her unspoken defense of me.

Gradually things became more orderly. Lorn, I could see, was making a convincing case of my wound and the lack of fingerprints on the revolver and powder burns on my coat.

For it developed there were no fingerprints to be found on the revolver at all. Thus it argued that the murderer had worn gloves. It was at this point that I and my clothes and the lobby and the lounge and finally even the lift were thoroughly searched for gloves, and to my great relief no gloves were found. It was not, of course, a conclusive proof of my innocence, but it helped.

They seemed to be talking of it heatedly when the doctor arrived. He examined the little huddle on the chair first and very swiftly; ordered Marianne to a chair in the corner, where she sat sobbing helplessly while the slender body of the little porter was carried away. Then at Sue's request he turned his attention toward me. The two policemen still holding me were inclined to resist his interference, but he said something in a very sharp and scornful tone, and then the commissaire gave some kind of order, and the police released me reluctantly, and I sat down on a chair.

The doctor dressed my wound then and there. Sue helped him; I remember the set look about her white face and the darkness of her eyes and the firm touch of her fingers. It proved to be, she told me, a not very serious wound. I think she was relieved at the doctor's muttered comments; and I'm sure I felt better when she said that the doctor had said it would be painful and I had lost a lot of blood but that there was no reason why it should not heal perfectly. I felt a little weak by that time, for there'd been a bad moment or two before he held the bullet triumphantly between his fingers.

"What have they decided to do?" I asked her, glancing toward the police.

"I don't know," she said. "You see they were outside — the two who held you — they had heard the sound of the first shot but were not sure it was a revolver shot, as they had not heard it distinctly. However, one of them felt certain it was inside the hotel. So they were in the court when they heard the other two shots. They ran to the door of the lobby and caught you apparently escaping. They both launched themselves at you."

"And kept me from discovering the murderer," I said bitterly.

The police were coming toward me again. I said rapidly:

"Sue, you must take no chances. Marcel was telling me that you were in danger. He was telling me when he was shot." Then before she could speak they were questioning me again.

Well, it was a long-drawn-out affair — long and dreadful, somehow, and terribly tiring, for I still felt a little sick and dizzy, and it was difficult not to trip in my answers to their carefully worded questions. I stuck, however, to the main facts. I had been talking to Marcel. He had admitted that he knew something that was of importance about the murder of the unknown man. He had been about to tell me when he was shot.

I felt instinctively that I must not bring Sue into it; afterward I knew that something inside me had reasoned that with the murderer at large and Sue in the danger Marcel had told me of, telling it to them all would only increase her danger. Would bring things to perhaps an unspeakable climax. I must think, first.

Once during the proceedings the police searching the hotel returned, dragging a fat and volubly protesting man with a long egg-like head and a tiny black mustache who turned out to be the cook, Paul, just returning from the markets with his basket of carrots and turnips under his arm.

Otherwise they found no one.

And once the commissaire questioned Mrs. Byng at some length, since it developed that she was the first on the scene. The commissaire kept, however, at a discreet distance from her and held the young officer by the arm, as if it might become necessary at any moment to interpose him as a barrier.

Mrs. Byng insisted even at that moment in

replying in French which seemed to be almost unintelligible to them; at length they got her into English, and the upshot of the thing was that she had seen no one. She had heard the shots, and the noise had wakened her from her after lunch nap and she had put on a shawl and hurried out into the corridor and toward the gallery running along the well of the lounge. She had come, in other words, directly along the path which the escaping murderer must have taken. And she had seen nothing.

My heart went down at that, for she was my only hope of the murderer having been seen. Lorn pointed out at once, Sue told me, that the murderer might have seen her coming and hidden in a vacant room until she passed. Or that he might even have gone up the remaining flight of stairs.

Mrs. Byng said "Perhaps" in a dubious voice, her eyebrows traveling up and down at a great rate, although she was looking sympathetically at me, and I think would have preferred helping me. As it was, her story made things worse.

At the last I began to think they were going to drag us all to the police court; and I felt so dizzy that I didn't much care. But they did finally leave without taking me along, which was incredible.

It was true, of course, that they left a guard

of several policemen and warned us all against trying to escape in a manner that was, as Sue remarked later, almost as conclusive as arrest. And it was true, too, that I was their principal suspect; was, indeed, their only suspect, and the doctor told them flatly that there was no need of taking me to jail just then. He added, and the young French officer translated in a way that left no doubt in my mind, that I was too weak from loss of blood to go very far that night, and that, moreover, if my wound didn't get attention there was every chance of its causing me considerable trouble.

"He makes not, you understand, of necessity a fatal," said the young officer precisely, but he added in a rather sinister way: "But he makes of a seriousness to keep you prisoner here. That and our police. I am ordered to say that you must consider yourself entirely at the disposition of the police."

"And lucky you are at that," said Lorn soberly.

Later that night, in my room, with a fire going, and the remains of a scrambled meal which had been prepared by the hysterical cook, whom Madame Grethe scolded and threatened and browbeat into submission (it seemed, Lorn said, that he'd wanted to leave immediately and never come back. "I don't blame him," I interjected with feeling) —

later, I say, I agreed with him. At the time things were rather hazy.

The doctor had stayed a few moments after the others left to give me some pills to take if the pain became very bad during the night and to tell me he would call again in the morning. He went to my room with me and was altogether rather kind, and I thought he believed in my innocence of both murders.

Madame Grethe had brought me a dinner tray, which surprised me a little, set it down beside my chair, and hurried away.

"Mrs. Byng wants her dinner in her room, too," she had said briefly. "She has chills and won't unlock her door until she looks through the keyhole. Miss Tally is with Marianne, who's nearly out of her wits. I've got to go down and threaten that fat cook into serving Father Robart's dinner. I'll bring you a tray, because you're half sick, but I won't serve tables in the dining room, and that's flat."

"Make Lovschiem do it."

"Lovschiem!" She had given me a glance that held a kind of derisive scorn and shrugged her shoulders and repeated: "Lovschiem! Here, I'll cut the meat for you."

She did, and was gone. But she had been still and white and shaken under her cool words, and there was something cold and secretive back of her shining green eyes. It was a look that left me uneasy; it occurred to me that Madame Grethe herself was quite capable of undertaking and executing just such a cold-blooded murder as I had witnessed. Lovschiem's fat hand would tremble; hers on a revolver would be steady and diabolically sure. She had plenty of cold nerve and was, I suspected, fundamentally an actress. Added to that, she had more brains in her little finger than Lovschiem had in his whole great hulking body.

But there was no clue leading to her. And as to that, there was only Lovschiem's presence and the fact that I suspected him of knowing the unidentified murdered man that led to him.

There was only one thing to base an inquiry upon, and that was the fact that the crimes certainly seemed to be limited to the people in the hotel. But even that offered loopholes, and did not approach certainty.

And in the meantime, I, Jim Sundean, had been thrown headlong into the fantastic yet dreadfully real and horrible affair. My shoulder was already beginning to throb — that was real enough. And I found I was staring at the little sign beside the door: It said:

Sonnez: Une fois pour la femme de chambre
Deux fois pour le valet
Trois fois pour le portier.

Three times for the porter. Ring three times for little Marcel.

I think I must have been a little feverish, for I felt hot and cold, and something crazy inside me kept saying: Ring. Press the bell: Ring three times.

It was just then that Lorn arrived. I was glad to see him. My head cleared, and things were better.

He was very quiet. The fiery, quick-spoken, glittering-eyed man of the excited moments following the murder had again lapsed into this unobtrusive, toneless nonentity of a man.

"Now then," said Lorn. "Let's hear the whole story. Had Marcel managed to tell you anything?"

"Yes. But not enough. He only told me that some towels had been found the morning after the murder, and that the towels had been used, but were in a supposedly empty room. That Father Robart's alibi was false. And at the last that Sue Tally was in danger. I think it was her danger that made him talk at all. It was just then that he was shot."

"Do you mean to say it was before he'd managed to tell you what the danger was?"

"Yes."

"Not even a word? Not a hint? Think — don't get excited."

"I'm not excited," I said wearily. "That's

207

all. It was right there — the very words were on his lips when he was shot."

"Look here," said Lorn, looking curiously at me. "Maybe I'd better not stay now. You look feverish — maybe that wound is worse than they think."

"I'm all right. But we've got to do something about Sue. She's wandering about the hotel any place — she's with the maid now. There's no telling what might happen to her. We've got to watch her. We've got to plan —"

"Did you have a chance to tell her what Marcel had said?"

"Oh, yes, I warned her. But she — the hotel is like home to her. She isn't apt to be as careful as she would be in a strange place. And she's got too much courage for her own good."

"You don't do credit to Miss Tally's intelligence," said Lorn dryly. He was still watching me rather curiously, and I remembered that I'd called her Sue and had probably shown a degree of anxiety about her which he considered out of proportion.

But it didn't matter. The thing that mattered was that some arrangement should be made to protect Sue. Two murders had already occurred in that hotel. And there was no doubt now, after Marcel's warning and his shocking death, that Sue was linked to the murders. It was like a thread going straight from Sue to Marcel's murder.

"Get her," I insisted. "Or I will. I've been sitting here thinking horrors, and I don't like her to go about the place alone."

"A road is never safer than after an accident has occurred," said Lorn sententiously. "However, if you insist —"

Talking of it made it more definite. I got up and went with him; I was still a little weak, but the hot dinner made me feel more like a man.

We found her in Marianne's room, whither Lorn led me at once. He smiled a little as I exclaimed over his knowledge of the topography of the rambling old place.

"That's my business, Sundean," he said.

Marianne by that time had sobbed herself to quiet, and Sue came with us without hesitancy. I remember that, as she left the room and closed the door, we heard the maid's heels bounce suddenly on the floor and tap across it and the rasp of the key in the lock.

It was very quiet there in that back corridor, and Sue shivered. Her eyes met mine, and she said:

"Well — come along."

She went with us back to my room. We chose that room without thinking about it. I suppose because we had met and talked there before and because it was warm and the wing was deserted and thus we would be apt to have no observers. The police, Lorn said dryly, were stationed at various places around the hotel.

"We're like rats in a trap," said Sue suddenly and caught her breath.

And so began another strange conference in that old-fashioned room in the cold, deserted wing, with the fire crackling now and then, and the wind blowing in the court below and outside the windows. The loose shutter no longer banged, and I wondered when Marcel had fixed the thing, and I felt cold and wanted my hands on the throat of the man who'd killed him.

Lorn and I did most of the talking. Sue was very quiet and pale, and there had been tears on her cheeks. Our talk was not long, for we were all desperately weary and shaken with the ugly affair of the afternoon. It was, however, important; particularly important in view of what happened later.

"See here," I said abruptly. "I know you consider the Lovschiems your friends. But I want to suggest something. Why don't you tell Madame that you've put the token in a bank? A bank in Paris or London or somewhere. Don't tell me where you have it — perhaps that's exactly what you did — at any rate,

I think you're wise to keep its whereabouts a secret. But that will put them off —"

"Always providing," interrupted Sue dangerously, "that my friends who have been my only friends for a long and hard year are planning to murder me for an inheritance that they don't even know I've got."

"Always providing that," I said, wishing I could shake her. It was curious how easily a little flame of queer antagonism could leap up between us; it was as if for a flash each resented something in the other. I resented her not agreeing with me, and then I knew that somehow she had a kind of hold upon me or I shouldn't have hated her disagreeing with me, and so then something in me resented that hold upon me. And in another second there was no feeling of resentment at all, only a warm kind of pleasure because she was there, sitting quietly before me, her bright head bent, and the fine angle of her chin faintly pink against the black velvet of her tightly buttoned coat, her slender feet on the rug, her whole lovely body slim and fine and yet beautifully rounded.

I said in a matter-of-fact way:

"We can scarcely help wondering about the Lovschiems. You admitted that your mother might have told them something. They are here — managing the hotel. Who else is there to suspect?"

"We've been over all this before," said Sue. "And, anyway, you have no evidence against either of them."

"That's quite true," said Lorn dryly. "There's not one definite thing we've got against Lovschiem."

"Unless we can prove he knew the man who was first murdered. As for Marcel's murder — anyone — everyone in the hotel is open to suspicion."

"Do you still feel it may be limited to the hotel?" asked Sue. "That — surely that can't be true. I can't believe that the Lovschiems are involved. You and Mr. Lorn and Father Robart are self-explanatory. The cook is just a fat and rather stupid cook — and anyway, he wasn't here the night of the first murder. Marianne — that's absurd. Mrs. Byng — equally absurd. And I didn't do it. And there's no one else. — No, it can't be limited to us in the hotel. After all, someone could easily have got into the place this afternoon — no reason at all why he shouldn't have walked boldly in, either front or kitchen entrance, shot Marcel, and escaped without being seen." Her voice trembled over Marcel, and I experienced a strange little surge of tenderness toward her.

"And as to the night of the first murder?" I said.

"Oh," — she spread out her hands in a hopeless gesture — "I don't know. Anything could have been done that night. Perhaps that way through the hotel gate was known to more people than I thought. At any rate it's not to be thought of that the murderer is here, now, in this hotel. But I promise you, Mr. Sundean, that I shall be very careful." Her breath caught in what was very near a sob. "How could I help being careful after what I've seen?"

Her face was tired and white. There were slender blue marks under her eyes. I said:

"See here. We'll cut this talk short. We can finish it tomorrow. The main thing is for you to keep your door locked and bolted tonight. And the first thing in the morning —" I hesitated, for after all what I was about to say was Lorn's business, not mine. But I continued: "The first thing in the morning it might not be a bad idea to get the papers that you gave to Lovschiem out of his safe and take them to the bank."

"That's what Mr. Lorn advised," said Sue wearily. "Very well. I'll do it. But the Lovschiems —" She broke off abruptly and said instead, "I'm going now."

We both went with her to her room. Lorn stood with her at the door while I searched her room; there was, of course, no one hiding in the great wardrobe or behind the curtains or in the bathtub, and there was little other place in which to hide. But I wanted to be certain, and I waited in the corridor until she had whispered "Good-night" and vanished and I heard the key turning and then immediately the bolt slipping into place.

The corridors were deserted, and there had been no one to see us. Lorn turned in another direction. I walked toward the north-wing corridor again. The halls were half dark, as usual. It was just as I turned suddenly around the angle above the steps that I thought I saw a darker shadow down the length of the corridor ahead of me which moved quickly out of sight beyond the angle of the intersecting corridor. I ran lightly and rapidly toward where it had been, but when I reached the angle there was nothing but blank doors and narrow hall leading back to a window at its end.

Probably, I told myself, turning finally into the long bare corridor of the north wing with its cold shining windows all along the court side and its bitter draft — probably a mere optical illusion composed of nothing but shadow.

The court was crazy again that night; though the wind was not as strong as it had been, and the gusts were not as wild with their flying shadows. Still, it did not look inviting;

neither did the little iron stairway descending into darkness.

In the turmoil of the day I had again neglected to ask Lovschiem for a key, and I again, with a kind of grim amusement at myself, propped the table against the door. I was determined to stay in that room, but I never liked it. Neither did I like the cold, deserted wing with its mysterious creaks and rustles. And neither, I confessed to myself, had I liked that flying shadow. It had had, somehow, a substantiality one does not associate with mere shadows.

My shoulder was aching and throbbing damnably, and I took one of the pills the doctor had left me and finally went to sleep.

I awoke with a start. I'd been dreaming wildly of Father Robart's black soutane with its full black skirt and of Sue's red slippers and the wind. The wind had lulled again into such quiet that probably the mice in the old walls were noisy again. I listened, but if a noise had awakened me I heard no further sound. And if a prowling ghost had come to visit me, awakening me with a passing touch or sigh, then it was a lively ghost indeed, for I smelled very definitely the odor of tobacco.

I sniffed again and sat up.

There was no ghost about it.

Someone, somewhere near me, was smoking.

CHAPTER XI

It was very cold, and the glow from the red ashes still lighted the room sufficiently for me to see that there was no one about and the table before the door was undisturbed. My shoulder throbbed as I pulled a dressing gown around me and went to the window. One casement was already a little open, and I pulled it wider and opened the shutters and looked down into the street.

It was dark and gray and deserted. The night was dark, but there was a light near the bridge and I could see fairly clearly the narrow old street and the walls opposite. There was no one about, and I closed the shutters and, partially, the window again.

That had been, of course, on the side of the narrow wing directly on the street.

There was the courtyard.

Cautiously I moved the table away and opened the door.

No one was in the long, half-dark corridor.

Across the shadowy court the window and glass-paned door of the lobby made bright rectangles of light, and I could see two policemen; they sat at a small table directly under the light and were placidly playing some kind of card game.

As I watched from the corridor (whence I could command, as from a seat in a theater, the whole stretch of court and entrance and shuttered, encircling hotel), another policeman, on the street outside, passed with a measured step under the light of the entrance arch. I could see his figure through the spaces of grilled iron gates which had been closed. They were, then, taking no chances of any of us leaving. I thought that was the explanation of their assiduous attention, rather than that they were offering it as a protection to us. But, whatever motive was uppermost in the commissaire's mind, still both purposes were achieved.

The man was not smoking, although, if he had been, the odor would never have reached my room.

But behind me the whole north wing was deserted and silent. I walked carefully along its length. There was no betraying slit of light from under any door, no tiny beam from any keyhole, and it was silent except for the creaks of windows and old walls and old floors and old furniture. I even opened, very cautiously, a door or two near my own room. But the rooms were black cavities, and the air that rushed to meet me was cold and stale and had that peculiarly musty, dank smell of rooms that are very old and have been empty for a long time. Moreover, the smell of tobacco smoke was much fainter here — was indeed so faint that I was not sure it was there at all. It was only when I returned to my own room that it was definite and strong again. I closed the door, puzzled, and snapped on the light.

It was not the scent of my own tobacco; it was a different and rather harsh brand. And none of us had smoked during the brief little talk in the night.

It puzzled me so much that I examined the room and adjoining bathroom. There was no one there, of course, and no evidence that anyone had been there. I even looked for hidden entrances to my room — feeling a little silly and melodramatic about it, but thinking still that there might be some such thing in that old place, built in the days when secret stairways and hidden doors were not a strange and absurd thing but were the most matter-of-fact and commonplace of arrangements, suited admirably and sensibly to that lively and somewhat complicated day. But there was nothing;

indeed, there was no place for anything except behind the enormous wardrobe, and if I moved that I should rouse the whole hotel in the process, for it was very heavy and large.

The odor, too, was either growing fainter, or I had grown very suddenly accustomed to it. I went back to bed; my face was hot, and my shoulder was throbbing miserably, worse in every position to which I shifted it.

However, I did drift into uneasy dreams again, and by morning the odor of tobacco smoke — a silly and trivial thing at its clearest — had merged into those dreams and no longer seemed important, although I told Lorn about it when I saw him.

That was when we met in the lounge after breakfast.

Marianne, red-eyed and dark and somehow sullen, had brought in the breakfast tray and bounced out again. As I was going downstairs, having made a miserable botch of my tie and getting on my coat and shirt only with an astonishing amount of pain, I met the girl again. She was carrying another tray, and when I asked her if anyone was about she shook her head as if she did not understand and went on. All her giggles were gone, poor child. I wondered what little Marcel had been to her.

Lorn was, as I said, in the lounge. He listened politely but without much interest to my story of the tobacco smoke — which did in fact sound extremely trivial and fanciful by the light of day — said in a listless way that it was probably a policeman somewhere but that he would try to make sure; asked how my shoulder was and said he was off to try to discover what the police were doing.

"They're busy, that's sure," he said. "And if I work it right I may be able to find out just what progress they've made and what line they plan to take. They wouldn't guard the hotel so carefully if they hadn't something quite definite up their sleeves. And the French police, Mr. Sundean, are nothing to be sneezed at. They are extremely efficient."

"Then perhaps they'll discover the real murderer and get me out of this."

"Perhaps," said Lorn gloomily, in the manner of one who says, "Think that way if it makes you any happier," and left.

The matter of Father Robart's alibi would, I thought, await more important investigations, though I felt that the sooner we came to a conclusion about the information little Marcel had given me the better.

I followed Lorn through the small lobby and into the court. No one was in the lobby, but Father Robart was sitting outside in the court; he was smoking and hastily put up a newspaper as he saw me and began to read assiduously. Pucci was sitting disconsolately on a chair back near the priest, and I took another chair. It was rather disconcerting to see a policeman's head and blue cap pop out from around the wall by the entrance arch, survey me unwinkingly and leisurely, and then pop back again in a way that left no doubt in the world that I had actually the closest of company.

Suspiciously I sniffed at the tobacco the priest was smoking, could not trace in it the fragrance of the tobacco smoke that had inexplicably drifted into my room during the night, and fell to speculating regarding that enigmatical figure. Why had he taken so much trouble about an alibi?

Had he had none at all, there would have been no reason to suspect him or to question his good faith — none, that is, beyond the feeling that persisted in me that somewhere there, in the depths of the old hotel, existed the hub and secret of the whole grisly affair and that thus everybody in the hotel was suspect.

But the fact that he had so carefully arranged a needless alibi was in itself suspicious. Highly suspicious, I told myself, looking at his long black legs and American shoes. He'd explained the shoes, when he'd said casually that he'd spent two years in America. And doubtless his papers were in order, for the police had left no stone unturned in discovering the exact identity and history of the rest of us, and they would not make an exception of him.

Too, it suddenly struck me that his beard itself was a suspicious point. As a rule, only missionary priests or Russian priests wear beards, and he had the appearance of being neither. And yet, if assumed for purposes of disguise, it would have entailed a long and patient process, for it was a real beard. Home-grown, so to speak. There was nothing artificial about it. But I wondered what the man's face would be like without that thin red mask.

He had not only taken pains to arrange a false alibi, but he had lied himself, and — which was still less what one might expect in a man of God — he had practically forced little Marcel to lie in order to support his story.

Pucci croaked, scratched, and fluttered clumsily down from the chair. The bird had been in the lounge with me just before Marcel had entered it the previous afternoon. After Marcel's first words I had seen nothing but Marcel. And then it had been all excitement and turmoil. I wondered where Pucci had gone. I wondered what he had seen. I wished there were some way to wrest from him the knowledge that might be back of those bright, shoe-button eyes — eyes that looked as knowing and secretive as his mistress's eyes.

He could not, however, talk, and naturally never did, then or thereafter. That is, he had never been taught to say words. It is a mistake to say he didn't talk, for he did, on occasion even quite volubly, and his expression and powers of conveying emotion were nothing short of marvelous.

This time Pucci croaked as disconsolately as he had scratched, sidled over to the priest and pulled himself up on his knee whence he scrutinized the beard closely, head tipped on one side in a way that was curiously disparaging and disillusioned, and which coincided with my own views in the most extraordinary fashion.

There was suddenly an impatient rustle of the newspaper, and behind it the priest's red beard and angry eyes appeared. I did not realize that I must have been looking, as I felt, faintly amused at the cockatoo's cynical expression until Father Robart snapped:

"Well, have you stared at me enough? And is it so amusing an occupation?"

It was true enough: I had been staring. But I could not resist the opening his words gave me.

"As a matter of fact, I was watching the cockatoo," I said, "and thinking of what Marcel told me."

I was looking directly into his eyes, and it was with interest that I noted the singular way they became fixed and rigid like a cat's. His face, too, looked suddenly rather yellow back of that flaming thin beard. Presently he said, his yellow-gray eyes never wavering in that rigid secret stare into mine:

"Marcel? And what was that, since you've introduced the subject?"

I hesitated, resolved in a fraction of a second that I was doing no harm, and replied:

"He told me the truth about the story you gave the police concerning your whereabouts the night the unknown man was murdered. He said you were not ill and that he was not in your room with you."

It occurred to me that he had braced himself for it; had perhaps known what was coming. He said coldly:

"Well?"

I shrugged, and promptly resolved not to indulge in that gesture again until my shoulder had healed.

"Well?" I said, with his own inflection. His eyes remained still, and yet it seemed to me there was an angry flash back of them. Clearly he resented the implication that it was not my place to speak.

He remained stubbornly silent for a moment, but he was not of the temperament to keep his feelings in leash for long. Fully conscious of the seething rage back of those still yellow eyes, I took out my cigarettes. In a leisurely fashion I leaned forward, extended the package toward him, and said pleasantly: "Do have a cigarette."

He made an angry motion with his hands and sprang to his feet.

"Oh, you are insulting!" Father Robart cried. "You are insulting!"

"Oh, come now," I said mildly. "It is scarcely an insult to offer a man a cigarette. *Hey — don't step on the bird!*"

He looked down and hastily swerved just in time to prevent Pucci's sudden translation to undoubtedly a warmer spot.

Pucci croaked again and fluttered strugglingly upward to a chair and looked at the priest with his suspicions confirmed. There was no doubt, indicated Pucci's cocked head, that this man's affairs needed looking into.

The priest in the meantime muttered something that sounded very much like "Damn the bird" and was most unsuitable to his cloth, and had regained his threatened balance.

"Why, Father Robart!" I murmured in a reproaching way.

He stood, a long black figure, with the wind sweeping the skirts of his robe outward and threatening his shallow shovel hat. In spite of his trappings he looked anything but pious. Still, priests are but mortal, and perhaps the mysterious illness that had brought him to A— had made him a little more peevish than ordinary. Peevish, however, was scarcely the word; the man was glowering down at me, he was fairly bubbling with wrath, but he was still silent.

"Father Robart!" I said again in gentle reproach. "Such words from a man of God. — May I trouble you for a match?"

His rage bubbled over at once. He took a menacing step or two toward me, his long black arms looking, I must say, anything but feeble.

"I suppose," he said, "that you've told the police."

"No. Not yet."

"Why?"

"Why what?"

He forced himself, I thought, to take a long breath and to become steady.

"Why have you not told the police what you've just told me?" he asked more coolly, but with the still look deepened in his light eyes.

"I haven't had time," I said with a degree of honesty. "I had more important matters to explain to them yesterday. But it's my duty, of course, to inform them of it."

"It doesn't matter," said Father Robart. "Having no alibi is nothing."

"Nothing at all," I agreed. "Still, I suppose the police will ask — why has this man been at some pains to prepare a false alibi?"

It was then that Father Robart, who'd been easy enough to bait so far, surprised me.

"A question that is easily answered," he said coldly. "In these unsettled times, when the Church itself is assailed, it is unwise for men of the Church to permit themselves to be entangled in any way with such things as —" He made a gesture toward the north wing of the hotel, with its shining glass wall looking down at us and the little iron stairway at its end. "As *that*," he said conclusively. "Keeping myself completely clear of the thing was merely another duty, Mr. Sundean, which you who talk so glibly and familiarly of duty will understand." With which he said good-morning in a way which hinted at triumph and turned sweepingly away.

The dignity of his departure was, however, somewhat marred by the cockatoo's making a sudden clutch at his soutane with a long gray claw, and hanging on for dear life, and squawking like a very devil, and having to be forcibly released. During the releasing I think he nipped the priest slightly, for the priest uttered suddenly an enraged ejaculation

and put his finger in his mouth in a most un-
dignified way, and altogether it was a confused
moment or two before Father Robart resumed
his exit, which was, then, a ruffled and hasty
affair and gave me some small pleasure.

Pucci, perching on the chair, gave me a diabolically knowing look, shook his feathers
gleefully, and all but chuckled. It was not out
of the question, it occurred to me, that he
had a natural antipathy for churchly vestment.

"And what," said Sue behind me, "did you
do to Father Robart?"

I sprang to my feet. She was standing there,
glowing in the fresh cold air of the morning.
A spark of laughter was dancing in her eyes,
and her cheeks were pink. She wore some kind
of tweedish-looking jacket and skirt of a soft,
warm gray, and a scarlet beret was perched
on one side of her bright hair, and there was
a touch of something scarlet at her throat, and
she looked altogether very nice.

"Nothing," I said slowly.

Her face sobered.

"Why — what is the matter? What have
I done?" she asked in a small voice.

"Nothing at all. Nothing. There's nothing
wrong." I realized that I was babbling and
drew myself up short. After all, I could
scarcely tell the girl that I wished she wouldn't
manage to look like that. She would say, and

rightly: Why on earth not? And I would say as rightly: No reason at all. It's nothing to me. Nothing to me. Nothing — I was babbling again; fortunately not aloud this time.

"We were only talking," I said more lucidly. "The priest and I. He explained the matter of his false alibi."

"Oh," she said, looking still faintly puzzled, and her eyes no longer laughing.

I told her of the result of the encounter, and she listened gravely.

"It sounds," she said when I'd finished, "rather reasonable. At least I think it will sound rather reasonable to the police."

"Perhaps," I agreed. "Nevertheless — I think the priest is not what he seems."

She looked suddenly white again, as if my words had brought her too suddenly back to the horror that had visited the old hotel; she glanced up at the north wing and then swiftly about the blankly shuttered windows and said in a kind of whisper:

"You don't think Father Robart — Oh, no, I can't consider it. We can't think that the murderer is here. Here among us. All the time. That would be too dreadful. Why — we would all be — gibbering idiots." She was shivering all at once; her small fingers were trembling.

"I don't know," I said honestly. "I don't like to frighten you, but you must remember that it is at least a possibility; you must re-member that and take no chances in these dark old corridors. — Good God, how I wish you could leave!"

"It isn't just flattering to think that you want me out of the way," she said lightly, although her eyes leaped to mine.

"There's nothing I should like better," I said brusquely. "I'm sorry, but I can't be light-hearted about it."

Her smile vanished. She said gravely:

"Let's not begin that again. I can't leave even if I would."

"Very well," I said briefly. "I'm sorry I seem to have thrust my opinion upon you."

It was, of course, petty. But she tried me very much.

She said at once: "On the contrary, I am the one who ought to apologize, since I actually did thrust myself and my affairs upon you."

She spoke very stiffly and coldly, and I for-got my own exasperation. I felt puzzled and dismayed; she had been so nice to look at, and it had been a pleasure — a strangely trou-bled sort of pleasure but still a pleasure — to see her and have her with me, and now we were all but quarreling. It was silly and stupid, and I did not understand it, for I had only wanted to be sure she was safe.

She leaned a little toward me and said suddenly:

"Don't look like that. You've been everything that's —" after a pause she said "kind,"
and I felt pleased and yet rather let down.
"I'll be very careful. I won't take any chances
at all. But I can't believe — it's mad even
to consider the murderer's being one of us
here in the hotel. Don't you see that it is?"

"I don't know," I said morosely. "I should
say this crazy, dark, silent, old place might
harbor — anything."

She shivered again and moved unconsciously nearer me and cried: "Don't!"

"I'm a fool," I said briskly. "I'm an idiot.
You're quite right. There's nothing for you
to fear in the hotel."

It was just here that Pucci uttered derisive
comment in the way of a wicked chuckle, and
I qualified my statement: "That is, nothing
definite. Don't look so — so little and white
and scared," I concluded insanely and wondered fleetingly if I had entirely taken leave
of my senses, and thus would continue to bab-
ble anything that entered my head, or whether
it was only a temporary affliction. I earnestly
hoped it was the latter, and Sue said:

"I'm not — that is, I won't be scared. More
than I can help at any rate," she added honestly. "Is your shoulder better?"

"Why, yes. I suppose so. It doesn't hurt."

"Of course it hurts. I loathe people who pretend nothing ever hurts them. It's nothing but wicked pride. Are you going to be like that, Mr. Sundean?"

"No," I said. "It really isn't bad. It's only stiff and sore."

"Has the doctor been here yet?"

"No. Now then —" I hated to drag her back to the problems before her, but still it had to be done, so that she might get her millions — her glittering, damnable millions — "have you asked Lovschiem for the envelope you had him put in the safe?"

"Yes." Her eyes had darkened again.

"He gave it to you?"

"No."

"No!" I had expected it. "What excuse did he give? Here, do sit down."

She took the chair absently, and I drew one near her and sat down also, and Pucci at once flapped and sidled and clung till he got onto my knee and then finally to my shoulder, with his head very near my mouth in a conspiratorial way. It was an attention I did not relish, and I took him firmly down again.

"He said," Sue told me gravely, "that — he'd lost the combination." She waited for my explosion; I could tell by her voice that she fully realized the weakness of the excuse.

"But, good Lord," I said, "can't the man open his own safe without directions? And even so, would he have only one copy of the combination? That's just silly. He surely didn't expect you to believe it!"

"Yes," she said reluctantly. "I think he did. You see, it really is a new safe. I know that, because I've been here, you see, and I remember when it came. And it actually is a little difficult to open, and I've seen him obliged to follow the directions and perhaps try two or three times before he could get it open."

It seemed, somehow, a maladroitness inconsistent with what I should have expected of Lovschiem.

"What's he going to do about it?"

"Well, he said that if I were very anxious for the papers he would send to the place where he bought the safe. But if I could wait he would perhaps find the paper on which he'd written the combination."

"And you," I said sternly, "said you were in no particular hurry and could wait."

"Yes. But I think that was better than to show my anxiety."

"Yes, I suppose so." Confound the man; suave and fat and slippery as a fish! "But if I were you I should lose no time in telling Lorn about it. After all, he's your brother's official representative. And it seems to me that in spite of the possible forgeries of which your brother speaks, still, the records you have might go a long way toward establishing your identity."

"Here's the doctor," she said abruptly. "You'd better let him look at your shoulder. *Bonjour, monsieur —*"

The wound was doing very well, the doctor indicated some twenty minutes later in my own room. He said a number of things I could not understand, I replied in English, thanking him, with a fullness and warmth which I judged he would consider suitable; I walked back through the corridors and to the door of the lobby with him, and we parted most amicably, having held an earnest conversation for half an hour, during which neither, I was convinced, understood one word that the other spoke.

Lovschiem was at the desk. He bowed greasily to the departing doctor and then to me, inquiring how my shoulder was doing. Through the window I could see Sue, the wind touching her cheeks to pink, and her crimson scarf flying, talking with the doctor and even walking slowly toward the entrance with him.

"Better," I said shortly to Lovschiem. "By the way, Lovschiem, where does this priest come from?"

"The priest?" repeated Lovschiem doubtfully. His little eyes were speculative. The dirty jewels on his fat dark hands winked maliciously at me.

A distinct change had come over Lovschiem during the last two days. Yet it was a change difficult to define: it lay just perceptibly in the uncertain, continual shifting of his eyes; in his unstill hands; in his bad color. He was frightened, glistened uncomfortably, and looked as if he had truly not slept; but there was something more than fright and weariness in his face and hurried, fumbling speech. Had I not felt as I did toward Lovschiem I should have called it a queer sort of perplexity. Now his fat paunch pressed against the edge of the tall desk as he made a pretense of looking through the register. I thought it a pretense because, with so few clients in his hotel, it was not likely that he would fail to know as many details about each as came his way.

"M'mm," he said slowly. "Paris, I believe. Yes, Paris. He's come here for his health, you know."

"How long has he been here?"

Lovschiem raised his glossy black eyebrows and shrugged.

"Three weeks, perhaps. I have it all here. Why do you ask?"

I did not reply. I was looking at the bright pamphlet which came into sight as he moved the register. He followed my gaze and with

235

a sudden movement pulled the register again toward him, so that it covered the printed booklet again completely.

"See here," he said with unctuous amiability. "I will show you the date he arrived. You do not doubt the good faith of a priest, Mr. Sundean! Look — see the date — almost three weeks to the day." I followed his fat forefinger, and looked at the date, and thanked him briefly, and walked out of the lobby.

I was conscious of his eyes following me and thought it likely that if I wheeled suddenly I would catch a look in them that was not so amiable. And I was wondering, not why a railroad time-table was there on the desk of a hotel lobby, that was common enough; I was wondering why he had covered it so quickly and tried to turn my attention from it. Trivial, of course — but his manner had been too hurried, too purposeful, far too amiable.

The matter had, however, no apparent significance, and there is something very insipid and bland and innocent about a railroad time-table.

"Ah, good-morning, Mr. Sundean," boomed a voice so startlingly near me that I all but leaped skyward. It was Mrs. Byng, of course; or rather a bundle of shawls and fringes from which Mrs. Byng's nose and voice, each equally belligerent, emerged.

"And how's the shoulder?" she shouted. "Come over here and sit down. There may be eventually a ray of sunshine in this corner. A nice fix we're in, I must say, two murders in the place and here we are caged up like rats in a trap. And we're like to stay in it, if those idiotic police have their way."

At a commanding gesture I sat down in the chair beside her.

"Nice girl," she went on without perceptible pause. "Pretty. Who's she talking to, the doctor? Yes, I see, it's him. Pretty girl — pretty girl." She paused, snorted rather after the manner of a war horse plunging into the fray, leaned nearer me and said in what passed with her for a whisper: "Pretty but queer."

"Queer?" I repeated, looking from the formidable nose to Sue, standing over near the gate, and back again. "Queer?"

"Queer." Her terrifying eyebrows, wide and black and active, hovered threateningly over the high bridge of her nose. "That's what I said. Queer. You know the night that poor man was murdered? Well, what was she doing turning out the lights?"

"What do you mean?"

"I mean why did that girl turn out all the lights in the hotel?"

237

"But she didn't," I said.

The woman snorted again.

"Didn't, h'mm?" she said scornfully. "I saw her do it with my own eyes."

CHAPTER XII

Of us all Mrs. Byng was the only one who was not, in a manner of speaking, partially protected by her own preoccupation from the full horror of the grisly situation into which we had been flung.

I don't mean by that that any of us felt at all normal or comfortable; the secretive old place surrounded us too closely for that. It had shocked us out of normality, and it hemmed us in with violence and murder, and we could not for a moment escape that fact.

At the same time, the thing that was most urgent with me was not that feeling of horror and uncertainty that we all partook of, but was, naturally, my own danger and Sue Tally's. I think that was true with Sue, too; at least to some extent her preoccupation with her own urgent affairs and problems protected her from the full shock that otherwise the really gruesome business would have induced.

Lorn, while not exactly callous, was more

accustomed to crime than the rest of us, and while I doubted if he had experienced anything so peculiarly ugly before, still he was able to approach the matter from a more intellectual viewpoint, and he too had his preoccupations; there was Sue's affair, and there was my own which it was to be hoped would entail the discovery of the murderer.

Lovschiem was frightened and nervous and had a bad colour; still, I felt somehow that he regarded the two murders as incidents. This notion may have been colored by my conviction that Lovschiem's fat jeweled hands were not completely clear of the crimes themselves; still, there it was.

The priest stalked about, a long black puzzle which I felt definitely now was more than a little suspicious itself; he might be honestly a priest and honestly preoccupied with keeping his own black skirts clear. On the other hand, he might be no priest at all.

Madame Grethe, too, kept her thoughts to herself; but one caught hints of them in her green eyes, where the cat-like look of secret reflection had deepened, and in her face which, when one came upon her unexpectedly, was set and rather haggard and had lost something of its smiling self-assurance.

Even the little maid Marianne was lost in grief and a kind of sullen, brooding resentment.

So it was only Mrs. Byng who was left a prey to horror and fear and morbid reflections. She showed the strain of it in her face, which was drawn and weary, and had great black circles under her hollowed eyes. She was, however, too gallant an old war horse to admit it openly. And she was not without her own unexpected role in that strange and tragic drama.

But I think she felt more poignantly, perhaps, than anyone else the dread of the mysterious unknown hand that reached so silently and powerfully and struck at its victims.

There was even, we knew later, a ghastly kind of order about the affair. One obstacle after another was, as it became necessary, removed. And when it became necessary to remove an obstacle, to sweep aside a life that threatened the safety or the success of that hidden force, it was done swiftly, mercilessly, without warning, and I am now convinced, without a shred of compunction.

It was all a part of a deep-lying program; an incredibly fixed and undeviating purpose. There was actually a horrid and ghastly kind of order about it. I think we felt that then, instinctively. We knew it later.

Mrs. Byng's words at that moment had given me a rather bad jolt, and I don't remember that I said anything for a moment or two. Then, conscious that her sharp eyes might be reading more than I chose they should read in my face, I said:

"Isn't there a possibility that you are mistaken?"

"Not in the least," she said promptly. "I'll tell you how it was. I didn't tell the police and shan't, for I rather like the girl. But this is what happened. Do you know where my room is?"

"It's on the second floor, isn't it?"

She nodded. "Number 11; it's just there at the turn of the corridor from the south wing, where the lounge is, you know, into the middle section of the hotel. You pass it every time you go toward the north-wing corridor. Well, anyway, there's a — what do you call it? — a switch box in the south-wing corridor just across at an angle from my door. You wouldn't see it unless you were looking for it, as it's in a sort of cupboard. The night that man was murdered up there on that landing I wasn't sleeping well. The wind was howling and shrieking and rattled my windows till peaceful rest was out of the question. I heard some noise, however, during a temporary lull of the wind —" (that was when, I thought to myself, the wind had lulled so suddenly and I'd heard the footsteps on the stair. It had been a lucky thing for me, that sudden lull. She was continuing:) — "a noise that sounded as if it came from the hall. Now, as you might surmise, we are very quiet here; a noise in the hall around midnight and past is unusual. So having nothing better to do I got up and went to the door and opened it a little. The light was burning dimly in the hall, and that girl was standing there at the switch box; the door of the little cupboard was open, and she had her hand on the big switch, the one that controls the whole hotel — I looked the next morning to make sure — and just as I looked she pulled it, and the light went out in the hall. I went back to bed and —" concluded Mrs. Byng with a fine feeling for climax — "thirty minutes or so later was hauled out by the police for murder."

"But — are you sure it was Miss Tally? Couldn't it have been Madame Lovschiem?"

"I've got good eyes, Mr. Sundean. It was Sue Tally."

"But the light was dim," I hinted.

"Look here," she said peevishly. "You don't have to believe me unless you want to. I know what I saw." She looked at the girl standing under the entrance arch and then back at me and said scornfully: "Do you think I'd ever take bobbed hair of that color to be that great red wad Madame has?"

I didn't think so. But I pressed the question,

though I spoke less bluntly.

"What was she wearing?"

"Some kind of black coat. Besides, she's much slimmer than Madame Lovschiem; has good bones. The secret," she added harshly, "of beauty is good bones. Shows breeding, too. Anybody can have pink cheeks and bright eyes; it takes race to make bones. It's going to be another bad day: wind all day and no sun." She had swerved suddenly and crossly, and Sue was walking toward us.

Just before lunch Sue and I went for a short walk. At Sue's suggestion we tried to leave the horrors that surrounded us with the hotel that held them, and she pretended most convincingly not to see the two blue-caped figures that followed us.

It was a rather strange, quiet little interlude, that walk out across the old cobblestones and onto the bridge where we looked down on gray water and up to gray cold skies and Sue sang *"Sur le pont d'Avignon"* and *"Le coeur de ma mie est petit, si petit, petit."* She had a funny, clear little soprano that hadn't an ounce of what you'd call voice about it and was gay and soft and pleasant to hear.

We talked too, a little; and Sue presently asked about what I'd been doing and where I'd been stationed, and we talked about Mexican laborers and their perpetual *mañana*, al-

ways *mañana,* and about chicken gumbo in
New Orleans, and about the remains of the
old Chisholm Trail stamped indelibly with the
beat of the hoofs of thousands of yellow-
backed Texas steers with shining long horns.
It all seemed far away and in another and
clearer world.

"You like our West, don't you?" she said.
And I said yes, but it was changing, as somehow one always says.

Then we veered to older places: Burmese
temples, squat and gold, and cold desert night
winds, and finally Moscow. She said:

"What a strange life an engineer leads. It
must be rather nice: that feeling of adventure
— always change, with adventure lurking
around every turn."

"That's what I thought, at first. Now I know
there's a lot of monotony and impatience about
it. Even change isn't always pleasant, you
know. And you think sometimes very long-
ingly of the pleasures of permanent things —
the same routine, the same home year after
year, the same people. An engineer misses all
that, you know, unless he remains in cities,
and somehow it is a little difficult to remain
in cities. I'm always finding myself on the very
fringes of civilization. But it's all right if you
just don't marry. An engineer should not
marry."

"Ah," said Sue. "And why?"

"Not unless he's prepared to give up wandering about and have a permanent home somewhere. Either that, or his wife has a bad time of it; it isn't easy for a woman, you know, for she's got nothing to do. No home, no children — or if she's got children they have to be sent off to school somewhere — no kind of society, living in all kinds of wild places — camps, tents, shacks, hideous little hotels — no family, no friends — no music, no theaters, no gayety. A woman of courage can make the best of primitive ways of living: it's the terrible blankness that breaks her spirit and saps her courage."

"She's got her husband," said Sue.

"No, she hasn't. He's gone all day and busy and happy and preoccupied with his work. A spirited woman can't live day after day and month after month and year after year in that appalling nothingness. It doesn't sound bad just to talk of it; the experience is rather tragic. I've seen things — no, an engineer has no business to think of marriage."

"Oh," said Sue in a rather chilly way, and we walked back across the bridge and toward the hotel without talking any more beyond a few rather strained and commonplace remarks.

Lorn did not turn up until after lunch, and

he came straight to me. We selected a spot in the court where we were not apt to be overheard, and he said he'd been busy all morning. He was, however, rather dejected-appearing, if a man of such immobility of expression can be said to be dejected. The police, he said, were very busy, and things didn't look any too bright for me.

"There's one thing that may help you, however," he said. "And that's the gun. They are tracing it, and while it's rather slow work, still it may prove to have had no connection with you."

"*May* prove!" I said hotly. "I never saw that gun before. Which reminds me, I haven't any gun with me, and I need one."

"*Need* one?" murmured Lorn, looking morosely at me.

"Of course I need one," I said impatiently. "But I don't plan to shoot anybody with it, so you needn't look like that. The fact is the only gun I possess is in my trunk, which is probably in Madrid by this time. And considering that I've been openly attacked twice since I arrived at this place, I think it's not out of the question that I should feel a little more comfortable if I were armed. Surely you've got more than one and can loan me one."

"I thought that's what you were going to

say," said Lorn gloomily. "And if you shot at somebody and didn't miss and my gun was found I'd be in a nice kind of pickle, now, wouldn't I?"

"I promise you I won't miss if I can help it — always providing I need to shoot," I said warmly. "However —" as he looked still more dubious — "you'd be in no worse fix than I'm in right now. I've got to be able to protect myself. And you know what would happen if I'd try to buy one."

"You'd be in jail in an hour," said Lorn with disheartening promptness.

He finally admitted, however, that he'd got two small automatics, and if I would do nothing rash with it, he might be persuaded to loan me one. I was grimly amused at his using the word rash, which seemed altogether too mild in connection with the violence which occasioned it.

"Have the police traced the poison yet?" I asked.

"Not that I know of," said Lorn. "They've sent to the Paris laboratories. It seems to have been something a little out of the common run of poisons. I don't imagine it's anything very strange and unusual — the kind of thing that you hear a lot about but seldom meet. I did discover, however, that no car had been found. I had Miss Tally show me as near as she could the spot where she left her abductor's car, and it's quite close to the hotel, and a strange car has not been found. There was only Lovschiem's own car, and Miss Tally doesn't know whether that was the car in which she was abducted or not. There's no way she can tell. It's possible, of course, that if her abductor was in conspiracy with Lovschiem he used that car. But there's no way we can make sure."

"Either that or the abductor went back to his car and drove away, and the murdered man was not her abductor — and thus, then, his death was not necessarily connected in any way with Miss Tally."

"Possibly," said Lorn.

"Or — that he had an accomplice who removed the car."

"Perhaps."

"Or the accomplice was Lovschiem, and it was his car, as you say."

"Perhaps," said Lorn again. "But don't forget the man in the courtyard."

I wished momentarily I could get out of my head Mrs. Byng's unexpected story of the lights going out and Sue, and said:

"The man in the courtyard may have been the priest?"

"Ah —" said Lorn. He was looking at the blank white paving at his feet, but his voice had a kind of "now-you're-getting-warm" feeling about it.

"What's your opinion of his taking the trouble to arrange a false alibi?" I asked.

"Well," said Lorn cautiously, "it's not an argument for his innocence."

"He says he wished to keep entirely clear of the whole affair; it seems he dreaded any connection with it on account of his position. A mere matter of discretion, according to him."

"Oh," said Lorn, giving me a quick look. "So you taxed him with it."

"It couldn't do any harm."

"Perhaps not," said Lorn slowly. "Still, if he should prove to be the murderer —"

"Do you think he is?"

"He might be, I suppose," said Lorn. "Although his story and papers must have been in order, or the police would have had something to say before now. They've looked us all up very busily, you know. A— hasn't had such a run of telegrams and cables in a long time. Still, things of that sort can be forged, and it takes time to verify such matters. Do you think it was wise to let him know your suspicions?"

"It could only place me in danger," I said. "And that, in the last three days, has been nothing unusual. Besides," I added maliciously, "I shall have your revolver."

"Not," said Lorn suddenly firm, "if you're going to use it. Besides, it's only two days and three nights. This is the third day."

"Have it your own way," I said fretfully. "But don't you think the police ought to investigate this priest a little more earnestly? I'm convinced that he's not what he appears to be."

"Yes, I suppose so," said Lorn. "Though I don't like bringing matters to a climax until we've something to go on. The murderer must be desperate; so desperate that he thinks nothing of killing. Is it wise to urge things on too rapidly without more definite evidence? Isn't it better to do things as quietly as we can?"

"Do you mean you're keeping your own counsel in matters you've discovered?" I asked at once.

"No," said Lorn. "I was referring to the danger to Miss Tally if we hurry things too much. We ought to be in a position to prove any accusations we bring — prove them, I mean, so completely that Miss Tally will be in no further danger."

"You mean if we push this matter about the priest too far before we can actually prove he is the murderer —"

"If he is the murderer —" interpolated Lorn gently.

"— he's apt to take the — er — swiftest way to — get what he wants."

"Yes," said Lorn quietly. "And having killed twice, the murderer isn't going to be too careful not to kill again. Of course, though, I'm not saying it was the priest — or rather, if you are right so far, the man who poses as a priest. I'm not even saying that the same person killed both men, although it is a probability. You can quite see — can't you, Mr. Sundean? — that while you and I have many surmises, we have very little definite proof. The police will have definite proof — I don't know in which direction their proof will tend, but it will be certain."

"But the *time* —" I said impatiently.

"Not so much time has elapsed, Sundean. It seems long, of course, but it's really been very short."

I thought over what he had said, and partially agreed, although I was impatient for something real and vital to be accomplished, and I felt strongly that positive steps ought to be taken to ward off the danger to Sue which little Marcel had died to warn us of.

"If Miss Tally were only out of it —" I said thoughtfully.

"Yes," said Lorn. "I agree with you there. I made a mistake in upholding her in her decision. I know her brother, and it will be a difficult thing to prove her to him if she deviates from his definite instructions — he's that kind of fellow. Curiously suspicious — something of a neurotic — certain that everyone he knows has his eyes only on his wealth. A strange sort of chap. But at the same time I've come to the conclusion that I was wrong; I was seeing only my side of it — you understand, Sundean, that in a sense I'm her brother's representative. I think it's only fair to her to urge her to go — tell the police the whole thing, if she will. There is very little chance that they will permit her to leave; none, in fact, that I can see. Still, we must leave no stone unturned." He paused, staring into space, and shook his head in a way that, in a man of his conservatism and phlegmatic temperament, confirmed my own fears for Sue. "I don't like the looks of things, Sundean. I'm doing what I can. But I don't like it. Not a bit. After all," he added in a morosely businesslike way — "after all, Mr. Tally wouldn't thank me for letting his sister be —"

"Stop that," I said sharply, and as he looked at me in a startled and uncomprehending way, I added: "It's your business to protect her. Are you actually sitting there saying in so many words that you doubt our ability to do so?"

"You needn't talk like that, Sundean.

There's no use in your getting so upset about it. You know I'll do my duty. And I know you'll do — well, far more than one could expect of a stranger," he concluded dryly.

"Then you are going to tell her she'd better ask the police to let her leave?"

"Yes."

"That's good," I said. "Now then, about the priest — and did you know that Lovschiem refused to give Miss Tally the envelope out of his safe?"

We talked for some time. I think I managed to convince him that the priest's good faith was at least questionable; and he agreed with me that Lovschiem's excuse about the combination of the safe was pure fiction and not too artistic fiction at that. He was still, however, much more interested in the doings of the police than in anything else and did not feel, as I did, that the center and explanation of the whole thing lay secret in the depths of the hotel.

He rose finally to leave; buttoning his brownish tweed coat and turning up the collar and pulling down his hat before facing the wind from which the court was a little protected, and thus only his nose and darkish deep-set eyes showed, and he looked suddenly much more aggressive and dependable. I might say now that I did not know and never did discover just how Lorn managed to get on such good terms with the police and to keep on such good terms with them; I suppose it was one of the secrets of his profession, and it was extremely convenient to him, certainly.

However, by that time our relationship had developed a kind of tacit agreement which divided our activities. Lorn, leaving the responsibility of Sue's immediate welfare largely to me, was thus left free to pursue his own way, while I passed on to him any bits of information I happened upon, as I judged them important. It was an arrangement which promised to work very well. It was only at the last that Lorn and I diverged sharply in our theories.

A gust of wind followed him out of sight. It was growing colder in the court. With the early approach of night, the wind had begun to grow stronger and more vicious in its sudden gusts. To this day a sudden cold whipping of the wind will snatch my memory back in an instant to those mad days at A— and I am once more walking cautiously along those cold dim corridors, ears alert to any sound behind me, eyes strained upon every shadow, or I am watching the flying shadows of the court from the eerie glass walled passage outside my door, wondering if that flying shrub conceals a figure, or if this angle of the walls

255

holds a too-substantial shadow — or peering across to the tiny lobby where I can see the cockatoo and a glint of Grethe's gold earring — or waiting over a fire in that massive shadowy bedroom for Lorn or Sue.

And listening — always listening through the sweep and rush of the wind and the rattle of windows and the creak of old floors for a step — a movement, a breath that would give warning of the thing that struck so swiftly and with so deadly an aim. Always listening for some physical manifestation of the power we all, God knows, had reason to fear.

The wind stopped only fitfully during the whole of the time, and somehow it seemed to be part and parcel of the insane affair. The continual blowing and creaking and murmuring; the dust in one's eyes and nose and gritting between one's teeth; the rattle of the old shutters, the bending and swaying of the vines and the shrubs, the whole witch-like, malicious confusion of it was so bound up with that ugly confusion and distortion of human law and human instinct that must take place where there is murder, that it all seemed one piece. I am not an imaginative man; engineers like exactness and are inclined to discredit impulses and feelings that cannot be definitely labeled. Still, there were times when I felt that the continual confusion and feeling of things surging and moving and threatening was making me, too, out of touch with normality and the beautiful logical base of reality. And that I might start shrieking and cursing the wind — and, since I am not readily affected by things I cannot reckon with definitely, I could only guess what a particularly sensitive person's reaction must have been.

A strong gust of wind blew dust in my face and whipped the cape of a policeman out beyond the wall as if to warn me of his watching presence, and I rose and entered the hotel.

Lovschiem was at the desk stroking the cockatoo with one hand and adding accounts with the other. The lounge was bare and empty and cold — somehow, we all managed to eschew the lounge that day, passing through it hurriedly because we must, and never lingering there.

The tiny lift stood dark and empty, with its doors open behind the little iron gate as if to show that now no one was hiding there.

There were voices in the parlor, however, and I swerved to glance through the door. Mrs. Byng, her eyebrows traveling agitatedly, was there, knitting furiously; Grethe's predatory red head was bent over some lace she was making, and she looked unwontedly quiet, though there was a kind of tenseness about her, like a cat waiting at a mouse hole, tensely biding her time until she could pounce. Sue was reading something aloud, in a clear and quite steady voice.

I could not fathom the look in Grethe's green eyes; I was not particularly taken with Mrs. Byng, although I felt a little sorry for her. But at that moment I heartily admired them all. It took courage to sit quietly there in the musty parlor so near the lounge where Marcel had died, with the gloom and silence and secrecy of the old hotel enclosing them.

Father Robart was sitting near the bar (in a room which always managed to look particularly bare and cold with its garish old calendars and desolate bar) reading his perpetual newspaper. And as I turned toward the stairway Marianne passed me with a whisk of her white apron, on her way kitchenward.

The coast then was clear.

Most of the afternoon I spent in the gloomy upper reaches of the old hotel. The portion of the hotel surrounding the well of the lounge, as well as the middle section, was to me full of unexplored possibilities. The north wing I did not immediately approach, for it had no third floor, as did the rest of the hotel; I knew the bedroom floor fairly well already, and on the ground floor there were merely storerooms which I knew had been examined. But, then, the whole place had been searched — how

thoroughly I did not know. Certainly searching the great dark rambling place for clues
was very like searching for a needle in a hay-
stack.

It was by no means a pleasant afternoon,
and I was very little wiser at its end, although
I was cold to my bones and more than once
wished Lorn had given me the promised revolver and I had it ready in my hand.

For I was gradually convinced that I was
surreptitiously accompanied in my search, although I do not know to this day who accompanied me except that it must have been
one of two people.

And I can't honestly say that I saw or heard
much to arouse my suspicions. There was only
an intangible feeling of someone patroling the
dark corridors near me, of someone whisking
around shadowy corners just ahead of me, of
rooms — dark and shuttered and cold — but
just quitted.

More than once I whirled, sure that there
was someone just behind me, and several times
hurried my steps to catch a clearer glimpse
of something like a shadow at a turn of an
angle ahead of me.

And another time, when I had paused at
the gallery of the cold, deserted top floor and
was looking down into the well of the lounge
with its foreshortened palms and the frivo-

lous-looking wicker chair on which little Marcel had died — was it only twenty-four hours ago? — as I say, I had paused there, and was thinking of Marcel and the shot from the lift and the musty shuttered rooms with their elaborate furnishings and their darkness — when I suddenly experienced that curious feeling that I was under close observation from somewhere.

I'd felt it, more or less, during my prowling through the dark upper stories, but not so strongly. It had been more as if some ghost had taken a fancy to haunt my footsteps — disturbed possibly by my intrusion into his rightful domain, for if ever a place looked haunted it was that rambling old hotel; yet, if ghostly, that conviction of unseen presence was still strong enough and menacing enough to give me an extremely chilly and uncomfortable feeling up the back of my neck.

But now I felt a presence more definitely. And I'd no sooner realized it than, out of the tail of my eyes, I caught a sort of movement on the lower gallery.

It was only a flicker, and it was gone, though I leaned far out to look.

Yet, Madame Grethe, Mrs. Byng, and Sue were still in the parlor, and I took the pains to walk to the lift shaft whence I had a view of a part of the lobby and could see Lovschiem still bending over his desk. I could not, however, see beyond the door to the bar, so the only alternative was the suspicion that Father Robart was my ghostly companion.

I had become, by that time, very circumspect in my actions, and I took greater caution about opening doors into supposedly empty rooms and was careful not to outline myself against any windows, thus providing a target. Had I needed warning, which I did not, the silent, dark little lift hanging there at the ground floor would have supplied it.

But, as I say, I was little wiser, and the one definite clue — which I was not, as a matter of fact, at all certain was actually a clue — was as impalpable and ghostly as was the feeling of a menacing presence stalking the dim-stretching corridors with me, just out of my sight and reach.

I found it when I visited the two rooms, thirty-four and thirty-five; from the window of one of the two I had caught that wild glimpse of a haggard and terrible face. The face which I refused to believe was Sue, which she herself unwittingly denied, and which still was so like — so terribly like her face, with the square-cut hair framing it, page-like.

Neither of the rooms appeared to have been occupied for some time. They were both cold and unaired and musty. It was only accident that I took my way across the heavy carpet of the latter, and going to the window, pulled back its curtain and squinted in an effort to see through the slits in the shutters in order to discover just how much of the second-floor corridor, directly opposite and across the court, the watcher's gaze could have encompassed. I realized at once that I couldn't see through the shutters satisfactorily and was reaching out my hand to pull back the doors of the window and properly unlatch the shutter when my hand arrested itself in the very act.

The shining glass was cold; the shutters behind it dark. My breath against the glass had misted a small patch, and in that little patch suddenly I saw very clearly the whorled imprint of fingertips. Four of them and a thumb. They were very clear, sharply definite. They were spread as if the hand had pressed heavily against the glass. And they were small and slender. No man's hand had made them.

Five small fingerprints. The question was, When had they been made? And, more urgently, Who had made them?

The possible significance of the little prints — prints that with a breath and a touch of my cuff I could everlastingly destroy — drew my attention from my surroundings.

Fortunately the door creaked. I've often

wondered what might have happened if it had not creaked. Things might have been very different. But it was old and hadn't been opened and closed much in its last years, and the hinge creaked.

I'm sure I saw the door move. I'm sure I caught the glint of a moving high-light in that darkish room. Then I flung toward it, pulled it open, and was in the corridor. There was, however, nothing but dimness and mustiness and increasingly shadowy walls and dark carpet winding past blank doors. Nothing.

And, as it proved, those ghostly little fingerprints had never a need to be photographed and ticketed and carefully documented. They served their purpose wholly in their own ghostly fashion and added their own small link to the gradually accumulating sequence of the chain that was so strangely woven and was in the end so dreadfully like a noose.

The incident of the door had finally convinced me of the folly of lingering unarmed about those dark stretches of halls and untenanted rooms, and I returned speedily to the second floor and to my own room. Once there, in the welcome light, with the shutters open to their fullest, I convinced myself once and for all that the clumsy, enormous wardrobe was merely an enormous, clumsy wardrobe and nothing else, and that there was no secret or hidden entrance to my room.

With an aching shoulder I emerged into the corridor. It was dusk by that time, and I had an impression of lights in the court below.

I knew, now, the general plan of the hotel; I knew the locations of the various tenanted rooms; all on the second floor. I had not, it is true, penetrated the storerooms in the wing below my own room; the time had been too short. I knew that the switch box was exactly where Mrs. Byng had told me it was, and that she could scarcely have failed to recognize Sue. I knew that the priest's room was off an intersecting corridor not far from the angle where I'd caught a disturbing glimpse of a moving shadow on the previous night. And I knew about the fingerprints which I had not destroyed.

Beside me was the door into the White Salon. I had opened the door, I remembered, in the darkness of the night when the odor of tobacco smoke had roused me. I opened it again and stepped inside.

The shutters were closed, and in the dusk I could see little. I found and pressed the switch, but there was no light in the high, ornate crystal chandelier. As my eyes adjusted themselves to the gray gloom, however, I could make out objects — carved armchairs and sofas, and a heavy gilt mirror above a large fireplace, and in one corner a great piano that loomed up darkly, so large that there was a sort of cavern of shadow under it. The Pope's piano, undoubtedly. Its dark unwieldiness and the look of waiting that an old piano always has — as if it were patiently waiting for the hands that had once touched it — gave the last touch of morose somberness to the room. I went out hurriedly, closing the door sharply behind me to shut in that waiting piano and those waiting chairs, and I wished the dimly cavernous White Salon with its musty air and its silence were at a happier distance from my own room.

Momentarily I paused in the long narrow corridor with its closed doors on one side and its glass wall on the other to look, as somehow I always did pause to look, down into the court and over the whole sweep of surrounding windows and encircling walls.

Lights were on in the lobby. The light was already swaying under the entrance arch, and thus above the gate that was not yet closed. Two policemen were in the court, huddled under their capes and leaning against the inner wall, which sheltered them to some degree from the wind. Lovschiem and Grethe were in the lobby. I could see into the parlor, since the light was shining there and the window facing the court yet unshuttered; Mrs. Byng and Sue were still there.

I turned and walked along the north corridor, turned into the main section of the hotel, and started again toward the corridor running to the lift.

The whole upstairs was silent and deserted and unbelievably empty. My footsteps made no sound on the carpeted corridor. Thus it was, I suppose, that as I passed the closed door to Sue's room I distinctly heard someone moving about beyond it.

And it could not be Sue, because I had just seen her sitting there in the parlor.

CHAPTER XIII

It was perhaps the maid, on a legitimate errand. It could only be Marianne or the priest or Lorn; all others were accounted for. But I must know who was moving about in that room.

A little back toward the north corridor again was the small niche where I'd seen Lorn and Sue talking that first day of his arrival. I quietly retraced my steps toward it.

It was a longish wait; so long that I was finally convinced that it was not Marianne in the room, for no business could keep her there for that amount of time, and all my suspicions of the afternoon and my ghostly company crystallized and became focused. Here was something definite. Something entirely physical.

The place was silent and deserted; the red carpet looked dim and faded in the half light; the heavy curtain near me smelled of dust.

I scarcely shifted my eyes from the spot

where, if the door opened, it must swing outward. And I was beginning to think it might be a ghost after all when the door finally moved. It opened only a little at first, as if to permit a reconnoitering glance along the corridor, then more fully. Something slid out and obscured my view of the closing door. I had no time to make sure I was concealed by the curtain, for the swift black shadow bore swiftly down upon me — and in another second it had glided silently past me.

It was Father Robart, of course. He did not see me, and I remembered what Lorn had said and did not intercept him as I longed to do.

He was walking swiftly, silently, his head bent and his red beard flaming. He was looking with narrowed eyes straight ahead. Afterwards I tried to think whether he'd carried anything in his hands, but I was only dimly conscious of his long black arms ending in white blurs that were hands, and I could not be sure.

Then he slipped around the corridor of the intersecting passage which led to his own room, and I emerged.

There had been something terribly furtive about him. I wished Lorn had been with me and realized suddenly that here was what amounted to convincing evidence against the priest.

Not, however, evidence that he had murdered.

I brought up sharply against that.

Slowly I took my way down to the lounge and from there — because I didn't like the air of the place and the memory of little Marcel's sprawled body which it induced, and still didn't wish to talk to Sue and Mrs. Byng just then — into the deserted bar. It was small, and there were tables and chairs and, when I'd discovered the switch, a light. The long bar itself looked as always very gloomy and unused, and the prints on the walls garish, and it wasn't too warm. But I had food for thought — such thought that I was oblivious of anything else, although I did keep a sharp lookout for Lorn.

He arrived perhaps two hours later, and I told him of the convincing evidence against the priest.

Lorn's dark eyes brightened a little, but otherwise he was not much affected. He looked at his watch.

"It's dinner time," he said. "And I'm deucedly hungry. Come on up to my room with me while I wash and tell me the whole thing again."

We went, and while I urged that something decisive be done immediately, he listened very gravely.

"It does look bad," he agreed finally. "But I don't like to hurry too much. There's no evidence against him regarding the murders, you know. Still — we can't leave Miss Tally in danger. Will you leave this to me, Mr. Sundean?"

"Not if you're going to do nothing."

He looked at me thoughtfully, finished drying his hands, dropped the towel, and said with an air of decision:

"You think I'm slow and too cautious. Well, that's true; but I'm inclined to think my mistakes would hurt you more than anyone else."

"I'm not worrying about myself, but I don't want that devil to get his hands on Miss Tally!"

Lorn's eyebrows went up a little.

"He won't," he said quietly. "Miss Tally will be under our eyes all during dinner. He'll scarcely attempt anything then. And immediately after dinner we'll have Miss Tally go to her room, lock the door, and one of us can guard her door while the other goes to the police. Does that suit you?"

"Yes," I said, not liking the impression he gave of indulging a childish notion of my own. "I'll watch her door," I added stubbornly.

"That's good," said Lorn dryly. "Then I'd better inform the police. Let me see — just what shall I tell them? That Father Robart arranged a false alibi; that you saw him leaving Miss Tally's room surreptitiously — and that you are convinced, in spite of his papers and claims being under investigation by the police, that he is not what he seems, being, in fact, no priest at all but —"

"But possibly a murderer!" I said. "And I'll thank you to remember that."

Lorn remained cool, and I felt instantly ashamed. After all, certain though my conviction was, I hadn't given him much to take to the police.

However, we went quite amicably down to dinner fully intending to carry out Lorn's plan.

Thus it was something of a shock when the priest did not appear at dinner.

When it became increasingly evident that he was not going to appear at all.

When we discovered that he was not in the lounge, not in his own room, not anywhere about the hotel.

With Sue safe in her room and promising to remain there we went together to the courtyard and told the police stationed there.

The priest's coat and hat were gone from his room, but nothing else. The obvious inference was that he had managed to escape — exactly how, no one knew, for the police said no one had passed that way, and Paul, in the kitchen, with another policeman, was equally sure he'd not gone that way. But he had disappeared completely, however and wherever he had gone. I'm sure it was not twenty minutes before the police were at the railroad stations and at every garage in the little place, combing them for news of the missing priest.

But there was no news. There was some excitement and a great deal of activity and inquiry and running about, but there was no news of the vanished man. It was exactly as if the earth had opened and swallowed him.

He had glided past me in the corridor and turned the corner and vanished from the haunts of men.

For I was the last one to have seen him — or at least the last who admitted seeing him — which fact did not improve my standing with the police. But with his escape, naturally, the tide of suspicion turned strongly his way, and it was not even necessary to tell the police of the reasons for my own suspicions regarding the man.

At the first word of trouble Mrs. Byng retired to her own room, barricaded the door but watched through her window the comings and goings in the courtyard. Sue, I think, hidden behind the window curtains, watched, too. The Lovschiems were noncommittal, so far as Lorn and I could tell, though Lorn's eyes were alert and not at all dull during what conversation they had with the police.

But Lovschiem was ingratiating and bland,

and Grethe cool and secretive, and if they had any guilty knowledge of the priest's escape they kept it very conclusively to themselves. I myself was inclined to think they had known nothing of it. For one reason, I had caught no hint of any collusion on their part with the priest. And for another reason, it seemed to me that there was still that look of strained and anxious perplexity back of Lovschiem's small dark eyes and fat glistening face. And if Madame Grethe's green eyes waited warily and bided their time, then there must be a reason for that feline patience.

Altogether it was near midnight before things settled down. Lorn and I finished talking — a talk that was eager enough but that went in circles of baffled surmise and could come to no out-and-out conclusions — and finally went upstairs again. We stopped at Sue's door and told her simply that the priest had escaped, and I thought from the look on her face that perhaps she had not believed in the man after all and was relieved to know he was gone.

It was my suggestion that Lorn and I take turns patrolling the corridor that night before her door but she wouldn't hear of it. And it did seem possible that with the priest — or, rather — the pseudo-priest, as I was convinced he would prove to be — with him gone our troubles might be at an end. That night, I thought to myself, I should rest better than I had since coming to the old hotel.

"I shall be perfectly safe," said Sue reassuringly. "Good-night."

With the feeling that there was still something I wanted to say, I lingered a moment. But Lorn lingered, too — and after all, whatever I had wanted to say didn't seem to get itself into words. So finally I said good-night, too, a bit brusquely, and waited to see her turn back into her room, with the light shining on her bright hair, and to hear the click of the key and the sliding of the bolt before I turned away.

"I'll take the revolver you promised to loan me now," I said to Lorn.

"Very well." He looked and I think was reluctant. "But don't do anything rash with it. I've got it here in my pocket."

But if with the revolver making a comfortable little sag in my pocket and the knowledge that the gliding black presence of the priest was no longer haunting the dim corridors of the place I had thought things would be better, I was never more mistaken in my life.

Through the middle corridor I walked boldly enough. It no longer seemed so important not to make a target of myself under or against any of the scattered lights. But when

I opened at last the door leading to the north-wing corridor and met the blast of icy air that always rushed to meet me — and heard the rattle of windows, and saw the glancing light in the court below and the flying black shadows, and then at my other side the diminishing vista of blank, dark wall and blank, closed doors — somehow things seemed no better for the priest's departure.

They seemed, if anything, worse.

But though my footfalls were audible there (that corridor floor being bare and cold), none of the black doors opened, and when I turned involuntarily as I reached my own door — turned with that twitching of neck muscles that is a remnant from primitive forbears who stalked and were stalked in jungles — the corridor was yet empty and cold and dark and bare.

Yet that was the first night, I'm sure, that I reached cautiously through my opened door into the blackness beyond, groped for the light switch, and turned it on before I would enter the room. And even when the light flooded the stuffy, elaborate room, I entered cautiously, my revolver in one hand. And I looked in the wardrobe and the bathroom and all about before I closed the door.

There was still no key; I may as well say now that though every night I promised myself to get the key, every day I failed to do so for one reason or another. However, by that night I had worked out a nice system of barricade by means of a small straight chair and the large carved table. The flat blotting pad with its advertisements of the Galeries Lafayette and the attractions of the Côte d'Azur, and its piece or two of hotel stationery, the red cloth, the inkwell with dried ink, and the broken pen point, all of which the table had held, I had swept into the drawer.

With the knowledge I now have I understand why that night was the worst night I spent in A—, bar none. Then I only knew that it was cold and uneasy and terribly long.

Sleeplessness was until that night almost unknown to me. That night sleep was out of the question.

I smoked, I read an old magazine that turned up in the table drawer, I paced the floor, I spent a long time making notes of the ugly business and trying to draw some conclusion from them — but rose finally, stiff and cold and cramped, and crumpled up the laborious notes and threw them into the ashes where they smoldered and smoldered, while I stood watching them, and at last fell into brown flakes without once bursting into honest flame.

The mattresses of the bed were stuffed with bricks; the great square pillows were adamant slabs of rock. All around me was that desolate, dark wing, far away from the rest of the hotel — and empty and cold.

Yet not silent, for there were mice in the walls, and the windows creaked — and not exactly empty, either, for I felt all along that there was someone or something in that wing with me. It was only a feeling; my reason was all against it. But there are times when reason has no place in the scheme of things.

However, there was no more tobacco smoke floating mysteriously from nowhere. And beyond the occasional skittering of a mouse between the old walls there was no sound of a living thing.

Yes, it was a long and cold and strangely horrible sort of night.

Morning, however, brought news. The priest had not been found, and the police had discovered no one who had seen him after his mysterious escape from the hotel. But they had discovered the owner of the gun. It was a man by the name of Michael Stravsky. And a photograph of the dead man had been mailed to the gunsmith, and he had said that without a doubt it was a picture of the man who bought the gun.

"That must be the murdered man, then," I said. "Michael Stravsky."

Lorn nodded. His face was impassive as

ever, but I think he was actually as excited over the development as I was.

"And it was a bullet from that gun that killed Marcel?"

"Yes. They extracted two bullets, and it was that gun."

"But the man was dead long before that gun was used to kill Marcel. If the murdered man was Stravsky that very fact links the murderer of Stravsky and the murderer of Marcel. Stravsky's murderer searched his pockets, took the dead man's gun, among other things, and later used the gun on little Marcel."

"Perhaps," said Lorn. "He would feel safe in getting rid of it as he did. Simply tossing it to the lounge floor, knowing that, even if it were traced, it could do him no damage. I tell you, Sundean, this is an exceptional criminal. It took nerve to do that."

"It took," I said hotly, thinking of Marcel, "a devil. I thought the gun would eventually prove to belong to the priest."

"I thought so myself," said Lorn. He pulled his coat tighter about him. We were talking in the courtyard. Inside in the little lobby were several policemen with Lovschiem, fat and protestant and frightened in the midst of them, and Madame Grethe listening coldly at one side.

"Michael Stravsky," I said again musingly.

"So that's the name of the murdered man. But who is Michael Stravsky?"

Lorn shrugged.

"That's what the police are asking."

"Why are they questioning Lovschiem now? Trying to discover if he knew the man?"

"I suppose so," said Lorn without much interest.

"Do you think he did?"

"I don't know. It's possible."

"Stravsky — he might have been in cahoots with the priest."

Lorn nodded impatiently, as if I were very slow at arriving at the conclusion.

"There's another thing," he said. "The poison was a compound of nicotine. No, no —" he forestalled my inquiries quickly — "that's all I know now. I'm off to the police station. Perhaps I'll know more when I get back. Ah-h —" He hesitated and looked a little embarrassed, as if he had just remembered his more pressing duty, and then said: "You don't mind just keeping an eye on Miss Tally, do you?"

I didn't mind. But I believe I managed to say so without undue warmth.

In the hall upstairs I met Sue. She looked tired and pale even in that dim light, and hadn't, she told me, slept well.

"I felt — haunted," she said and then

laughed a little tremulously.

Well, I had felt that way myself. I said:

"I'm delegated to 'keep an eye' on you this morning. Lorn wants to hobnob with the police."

"The police? Have they made any discoveries?"

Briefly I told her what they were, and she listened thoughtfully. After a moment she shrugged her shoulders.

"There's nothing we can do, I suppose, but wait," she said. "But the inactivity is rather bad. — Come," she said suddenly. "You must see the show piece. I'll show you the famous Pope's piano. Or the Pope's famous piano — whichever you please. It's probably pure humbug either way."

I followed her through the dim corridor, admiring as I went her graceful smooth carriage, the slope of her shoulders, the proud way her head bent on her slender neck. It was only later that I wondered what inexplicable whim had prompted her to offer, that morning of all mornings, to show me the Pope's piano.

It was just at the turn from the middle corridor into the north wing that an unexpected thing occurred.

She was wearing again the gray tweed suit and crimson scarf at her throat, and as she

entered the north-wing door the scarf floated
out, caught on a projecting latch — caught
and held and all in a second whirled her around
sharply against me and into my arms.

It was very sudden, and it caught me off
my guard, and there was no one near, and
the corridor was dark and empty and still, and
my arms were tight around her and holding
her close to me, and her hair brushed my face.
And immediately the empty corridors and the
hotel and the world ceased to exist, and there
was nothing but darkness and warmth and Sue
in my arms with my mouth against her mouth.

Then Sue was a small figure in the darkness
apart from me, her face a white blur. And
I was trying to steady my voice so I could
speak — say something, anything — and my
heart was pounding as if I'd been running a
race, and I wanted her in my arms again, and
I dreaded what she might say. It's true that
a kiss is only a kiss. But the girl was Sue.
It made such a difference.

"I'm sorry."

I waited. I thought of trying further apol-
ogy. I thought of saying I hadn't had time
to think — but that wouldn't sound very well.
I thought of trying to explain, but there didn't
seem to be any explanation.

Then all at once Sue spoke. She spoke in
a breathless little voice that I'd never heard

before, and I could not see her face clearly. But she said coolly enough:

"Weren't we going to look at the Pope's piano?"

I believe I said yes; we went through the door, and Sue's scarf didn't catch that time, and we marched along the corridor and reached the door of the White Salon.

I opened the door and then paused.

"It's dark in here," I said, with perhaps a note of warning in my voice.

"Well," said Sue, and there was just a spark of laughter in her eyes, though her mouth was still red from my kiss. "Well — open the shutters."

But as she followed me into the large, empty, funereal room the laughter fled.

"How cold it is!" she said with a shiver. "And how musty." She followed me to the window and held back the curtain while I flung back the window, which let in a breath of crisp fresh air, opened the shutters, and as the gray light crept in closed the window again.

The light did nothing to remove the gloom that hung over the old room. Even the flowered carpet and the gilt cupids on the mantel mirror looked garish and desolate and ugly.

The color had gone from Sue's face.

"It isn't exactly lively in here," I said, "in

spite of the frivolous furniture."

"The furniture makes it worse," said Sue with a shudder. "However, there's the piano."

It loomed up in the shadowy corner — enormous, dark, long, like a great black coffin on legs. Neither of us was in a hurry to approach it.

Sue looked about her, walked over to a long, white table with a faded pink velvet cover which stood under the dead chandelier, and paused there meditatively.

"Dust," she said, drawing a slim forefinger across it.

Then she turned, selected a carved fauteuil with gray satin upholstery that was faded and worn, and sat down. She looked small and oddly modern and trim in the old room with its elaborate and ornate elegance. But the silent gray shadows had laid a kind of pall over her; she was pale, and her eyes were very dark, and there were purple lines of sleeplessness faintly smudged under the white eyelids. Even her soft hair looked less bright. She had clasped her hands over her knees, and she was looking soberly at the worn carpet under our feet — a carpet whose garlands of roses were all dimmed and shabby and dusty-looking.

"I suppose you know," she said thoughtfully, "that Mr. Lorn has changed his mind; he wants me now to tell the police about the whole thing and try to get them to permit me to leave."

"Yes," I said.

My voice sounded loud and harsh in the strangely quiet room. There was an element in that silence which was making me uneasy. I wondered if I had done well to bring Sue to such a deserted and far-away part of the old hotel. I glanced about me again.

There was no place for anyone to be in hiding — unless it was behind the window curtains. And I'd already looked there. So there was no one but ourselves in the room. That was certain.

Therefore the eerie feeling of a presence somewhere near was only a feeling. I sat down near Sue, but in such a position that I faced the door into the corridor. The little bump made by the revolver in my pocket was a satisfaction: I remember slipping my hand into the pocket and how welcome was the touch of it to my fingers.

"You intend to do it, of course," I said firmly.

She looked at me then.

"You think it is best?"

"I've thought so all along." Why was I so strongly impelled to turn and look behind me?

"I suppose you and Mr. Lorn are right," said Sue wearily. Her voice broke off and changed, and her glance flickered rapidly over the room, and she said with sharp impatience: "What *is* the matter with this room!"

"It's been closed too long," I said prosaically, though I knew what she felt. "And it's cold."

"It feels," she said unexpectedly, "as if all its ghosts had come back to haunt it."

"Let's leave it to the ghosts, then."

The room had all at once become intolerable. Its silence brooded; the cold was musty; the shadows dim; there was an intangible feeling of — well, it was actually something like menace hanging over it and us. Instinct bade me get Sue out of the place.

But in that little moment of silence between us came a very strange and startling thing.

Someone — somewhere near us — sighed heavily.

It was a long sigh — long and struggling and inexpressibly weary. It was distinct and unmistakable and dreadful in that chill, breathless silence.

Our eyes leaped to meet. I was on my feet. So was Sue. Neither of us spoke.

Then I went to the piano. It was dark in that corner. I held the revolver in my hand.

There was no one there.

I lifted the lid of the huge shape.

After a moment my fingers dropped the revolver into my pocket again, and I used both hands to support the lid and then one to touch cautiously something inside.

"What — ?" whispered Sue.

I closed the lid. It was, then, in very truth a coffin.

"Please leave. Leave at once."

Sue did not move.

I was thinking that the crowded thing under that lid couldn't possibly have uttered that heavy, struggling sigh. It was too long dead.

CHAPTER XIV

It was quite naturally the priest's death that brought things to their climax, that was in itself the beginning of that preordained denouement. For it was, of course, the body of the erstwhile priest that we found that morning, huddled and crowded in its black robes in the depth of the coffin-like piano. It was the priest, and he had been poisoned, and the poison, said the commissaire, wiser now, was again nicotine. There was a small puncture in the skin of his right arm, and the poison, it appeared, and Lorn agreed with the police when he told me of it, had been administered quickly and deftly with a needle. It was, added Lorn more dryly than usual, a very quick-acting poison. The priest would have had practically no time to call for help.

It was to be expected, too, that the murder of the priest would sharply deny my previous calculations. Everything, to my mind, had pointed toward the priest's guilt. But now he himself was a victim to the insensate plan that reckoned murder, and murder by poison, only a counter.

The first murder had been that of an unknown and, till very lately, unidentifiable man. The second murder had been that of a waiter — shocking enough as a crime, it's true, but still Marcel had been in the eyes of the world a person of little importance. And his death had been considered, and rightly, I thought, to have been induced by, and a result of, the first murder.

But the murder of a priest — that was different — even though he might prove to be only a masqueraded priest. It was not only the fact of a third murder in a few days that roused the town and the police to a higher pitch of excitement and energy. There was also the fact that it proved that the murderer had escaped all efforts of the police to discover his identity, and that he felt so secure in his safety that he dared another brutal murder under their very noses.

Moreover — and what was more important from our point of view — it suggested forcibly that there was a dark and evil purpose alive in that old hotel which was not yet consummated.

If there had been few clues about the first murder and only my own evidence, which was little enough to go on in the case of Marcel's death, there were no clues at all for the third. The priest was dead by poison and had been dead for from seven to eighteen hours, and that was all they knew.

The police sent promptly to far-away Paris for assistance; from something Lorn said, I believe there had been in the town one of those subterranean political wars brewing which had previously intervened and determined the commissaire to settle the matter if it was possible without help. But the third murder proved too much for his faith in himself and his wish to inspire his political opponents with a sense of his own ability. Or perhaps it was the pressure of public opinion that grew too great for him.

He also temporarily increased his force, so that instead of our being simply clapped into jail we were, to all practical purposes, held prisoners by the numerous guard which surrounded the hotel and overflowed into the courtyard and rambled uneasily through the corridors and went to the kitchen, where Paul supplied them with such frequent drinks that there were several occasions, I'm sure, when, if the murderer had popped up under their noses like a rabbit and declared his identity, they might as readily have welcomed him as a comrade as have given chase. It is perhaps not strange, under the circumstances, that while this guard might have been supposed to act as protectors as well as jailers they were not wholly successful in either role, as you will see. And by the time the detectives from Paris arrived the thing had already marched to its swift and violent ending.

The intervening time seems long in retrospect but was very swift in experience, for we were so caught in the rapid, dangerous swirl of events that everything beyond our immediate peril was crowded out of our consciousness.

After the first dazed moment following my grisly discovery in the White Salon, I realized that if Sue had been in danger before, that danger must now be immeasurably greater.

So in the end Sue and I both went to call the police and tell them of what was there in the White Salon. We went together, for I could not bear to let her out of my sight in that menacing place.

I don't remember that I told her what lay in that black coffin, but somehow she knew. I do remember our calling from the very landing where I had stumbled upon the dead man whose murder had ushered in the dreadful business, to the policeman in the court below. And I remember how he sprang to his feet and stared up at us, and how his jaw dropped, and the blank astonishment in his face when he comprehended Sue's rapid French. And that he had visibly to try several times before he could pucker his open mouth sufficiently to give the shrill whistle that brought two other policemen tumbling into the court and eventually up the little winding stairway to bring in their wake turmoil and search and inquiry again. The whole thing couldn't have taken more than four minutes, but it seemed at least ten.

But the thing that stands out sharply in my memory is the thing that happened on the very second preceding their entrance into the White Salon.

I had left Sue under their eyes on the landing and had myself turned back into the corridor and then into the room. I suppose I had approached the great piano merely in order to show them where the body lay, for I could hear their hurried feet on the stairway. It was only chance that I stood in such a position near the piano that a wisp of white on the carpet caught my eyes. I bent involuntarily and took in my hand a small handkerchief. It had been concealed from my eyes until then by a massive carved leg of the piano. It was a woman's handkerchief, but it was the faint scent clinging to it that brought it upward nearer my face. It was a familiar scent; a faint delicate whiff of a fragrance that swiftly brought Sue to my mind. Then I recognized it: it was faintly like gardenias.

There was no time to think, for the steps were at the open door of the White Salon. But I knew that during our moment together in the ghostly room Sue had not been near that end of the piano. And I slipped the thing into my pocket as three blue-caped figures burst into the room, and the air began to crackle with excitement and furious questions and sputtering exclamations.

The whole thing was like a repeated nightmare with the results that I have mentioned. It was noon before I had a quiet word in the lounge with Lorn and Sue.

Lorn had, of course, turned up hot-foot at the first news of the new tragedy. And he felt, as did I, that the thing of supreme importance was to remove Sue at once from that death-ridden place. And Sue at last agreed.

"I can't stand it any longer," said Sue. She was white and frightened and taut-lipped. "If the murders are, as you believe, actually the result of a scheme to rob me of my inheritance, let's make an end to it. Heaven knows, I'd rather lose every cent of the money than be even remotely the cause of such — such —" She shuddered and said in a breathless way: "It's as if I caused it all."

"Nonsense," I said brusquely, not liking the look in her face or the way her little hands twisted themselves together. "You aren't the cause of this. The cause is the scoundrel who's back of it. Don't look like that."

"We can't even know with certainty," interposed Lorn dryly, "that this last murder has anything to do with your inheritance."

"Don't put me off like that," flashed Sue. "You know what you think, no matter what you can prove."

"Yes," agreed Lorn imperturbably. "I know what I think. There is a plot against you. The peculiarity of the terms of your identifying yourself and receiving your money practically invites such a thing. And I'm willing to admit that this — er — priest's — surreptitious visit to your room links him with you and your five millions. You see five million —" he shook his head gravely and said in a slow awed way — "five million dollars is an enormous sum of money."

"Why do you think the priest was killed?" asked Sue.

"Wel-l," said Lorn slowly, "there are two hypotheses. Either he was an honest priest who accidentally knew too much about one of the other murders and his knowledge was so dangerous and so incriminating that he had to be silenced at once; or he was, as Mr. Sundean thinks, no priest at all."

"If not a priest, then what?"

Lorn shrugged.

"If not a priest, then certainly a conspirator."

"Remember his searching Miss Tally's room."

Lorn looked at me soberly.

"You are sure that he carried nothing in his hands when you saw him come from her room?"

"I saw nothing."

Lorn turned to Sue.

"And you are sure nothing was gone?"

"Yes," said Sue at once. Her eyes met Lorn's steadily, and her expression did not change, although it seemed to me that Lorn's gaze became sharper.

"If he had come upon the object — token — whatever it is that is to prove your identity," ventured Lorn speculatively and rather guardedly, his eyes still searching Sue's face, "then that would provide a motive for his murder."

"Of course," said Sue briefly. "Although that would presuppose several different people trying to obtain the — token."

"Two, at least," said Lorn. "Not counting your eventual substitute."

Sue shivered.

"I think now you are both right," she said. "I will go to the police this afternoon."

There was a short silence.

The lounge was empty except for us and bare and chilly. Above us were those blank gallery railings, and all around us the secretive dark old hotel.

The Lovschiems were in the lobby. I had watched them carefully during the morning's inquiry and excitement, but they were guarded, both of them — guarded and wary and inscrutable, although Marcus looked frightened under his mask and glistened more than usual. But Grethe was cool and calm, her face set in properly and innocently shocked lines, and her green eyes shining and cool and unfathomable.

Mrs. Byng had promptly — or as promptly as the police would permit — retired with her shawls and her temperament to her own room, where she was, I had no doubt, well barricaded. Marianne, no longer hysterical but dark and sullen and remote, was in some nether region with, I supposed, the chattering cook.

Only the cockatoo remained diabolically unperturbed. As I watched he flopped awkwardly to the floor from Grethe's graceful shoulder, waddled along it to the door to the courtyard, and paused to examine with handsomely flared crest and a knowing and speculative eye the boot heel of a policeman who stood there. He opened his curved beak dubiously, paused to scratch with vigor under one wing, and I said thoughtfully:

"If we only knew exactly where the danger lies."

"When we discover that, we will have the murderer," said Lorn. "It may not be as complete a mystery as you seem to think. Things have a way of breaking suddenly."

"Perhaps. But yesterday, I felt sure the man pretending to be a priest —"

"You don't know yet that he wasn't," said Lorn softly.

"Do you want to bet that the police won't discover his papers to be forged?"

"Oh — no," said Lorn temperately. "He probably was no priest. But it's better to be quite sure of these things before resting a case on them."

"Well, in any case, I felt he was the murderer. Now — I don't know — someone certainly killed him. And there's the nicotine again, to link it with the murder of the man called Stravsky."

"Yes," said Lorn slowly. "If the priest had taken anything yesterday from Miss Tally's room we might come nearer to understanding the affair."

Sue said nothing. Presently he continued:

"But since Miss Tally assures us that he found nothing —" He shrugged again and left the obvious conclusion unspoken.

"In the meantime," I reiterated, "the thing to do is to go to the police and tell them all that we know and beg them to permit Miss Tally to leave."

"Unless," said Sue rather tremulously, "it would only be to take myself also away from protection."

"I'll go with you," said Lorn.

"Oh, I'm not changing my mind again," said Sue at once. "Surely you can intervene for me, Mr. Lorn, with Francis, if he disapproves."

"I can try," said Lorn rather dubiously. "But it's the only thing for you to do, Miss Tally. You are in a position of great danger. I'm afraid I made a grave mistake in backing you up in the first place. It hasn't been fair to the police, and your safety lies in their discovering the criminal. And they should have every facility to do so. That is," he corrected himself somewhat hastily, as the meaning of the expression in Sue's little white face reached him, "at least to some extent your safety lies in their discovering the criminal. Our only hope is to try it, though I fear the police will make you stay, even after they know the story."

There were voices in the lobby: someone had just entered from the outside. We could hear Grethe's fluent French, then some scattered English phrases in a strange voice. It was a man's voice.

I followed Lorn's blank gaze into the lobby: a man stood there. A stranger; the light from the window was full on his face. He seemed to be explaining something in English to Grethe and Marcus, for we caught a brief English word or two.

Then, with all the effect of a curtain in a theater, Grethe appeared suddenly in the door of the lounge. She stood there a moment, her sleek body framed against the light. Then she crossed swiftly to Sue. She was smiling, but her eyes were calculative, guarded. She said:

"Your brother has come. He —" she turned toward the man who somewhat hesitatingly had followed her — "this is Miss Tally, monsieur."

I was on my feet. I was barely conscious of Lorn standing just behind me. Sue was standing too, looking white and incredulous, and even her lips looked pale and stiff. Her eyes were wide and fastened on the newcomer's face as if in frantic effort to recall it. And her little hands had clutched themselves pitifully together.

"Francis," she said in a whisper.

He was fairly tall, moderately slender, and blond with grayish eyes. He wasn't altogether handsome, for his features were a little too fine for a man, and his mouth was not firm. He wore gold-rimmed spectacles, which gave him a pedantic look, and he was muffled up in coats and gloves and a woolen scarf. His eyes back of the spectacles were very sharp — as sharp as Grethe's, who was watching him with an expression that indicated strongly that here was at last the mouse she'd been waiting for. He smiled a little uneasily and cleared his throat and fumbled with his gloves and said, in a rather uncertain voice:

"Sue, I suppose."

She said nothing, just looked at him, and as no one else spoke he seemed to feel that his greeting was a bit lacking in something, for he put out his hand and smiled more blandly and said:

"It's difficult to know just how to greet you, Sister. We are almost strangers."

"Quite," said Sue in a frozen small voice, and laid her hand momentarily in his.

Francis Tally was growing more at ease. He looked at me and then discovered Lorn.

"Ah," he said at once. "How do you do, Lorn?"

Lorn stepped forward. He was quiet, unobtrusive.

"How do you do," he said in an unexcited way, quite as if he'd known all along that brother Francis was about to turn up.

"Everything going well?" asked Francis Tally easily.

Lorn's eyebrows lifted a fraction of an inch.

"Not exactly well," he said. "Still, Miss Tally is quite safe."

"This," said Sue, "is Mr. Sundean."

Francis Tally looked sharply at me. So did Grethe, but in a more knowing manner.

"Sundean?" said he.

"He has been very kind," said Sue stiffly, as if words were extremely difficult. A curious look crept into the man's face, but he extended his hand cordially enough. And exactly then Marianne, in the dining room, sounded the clattering bell which announced lunch.

"It's — lunch," said Sue in a relieved way, as if she snatched at the interval. She added: "You'll share my table — Francis?"

"Good," said Francis, also looking relieved. "I had a very early breakfast. What's the trouble here, though — why all the police about the place? I had a very devil of a time getting them to let me in."

For a full moment no one spoke.

Then Sue said in a voice that did not belong to her:

"I'll tell you after lunch."

He looked puzzled and I think would have questioned further, but Grethe silkily intervened.

"You'll want to wash before lunch," she said, smiling pleasantly into his eyes. "I'll show you to a room. We are — er — temporarily without a porter."

Lorn coughed. I realized that for the first time in my knowledge he seemed to be what in another man I should have called thoroughly disconcerted. He said:

"Er — Mr. Tally — you'd better — er — see the police first."

"See the police?" Tally paused in the act of turning to follow Madame Grethe.

"Yes," said Lorn. "You see — well, the police are here because — there've been three murders here in the last few days."

"*Three murders?*" said Francis Tally. "*You don't mean here?* Right *here* in the hotel?"

"Yes. We are all practically jailed here for the time being."

It struck me that Francis Tally was either an extraordinarily brave man or he was extraordinarily callous. But then, of course, he hadn't lived through the horror of it. He said:

"H'mm. Well. What's the reason for it all?"

Lorn's hidden dark eyes went to Madame Grethe. He said cautiously:

301

"I don't know. But I doubt if they'll let you stay here."

Luckily for you, I wanted to add. Madame Grethe forestalled me. She said graciously:

"Oh, nonsense, Monsieur Lorn. Things are bad enough in the hotel as it is. Surely the police won't drive patrons from our door. If Monsieur Tally wishes to stay here with his sister, as, of course, he does wish —" her brilliant green eyes were smiling into the young man's — "leave it to me. I will see that it is all settled with the police. Your room, monsieur?"

She turned away with a gesture that brought Francis Tally after her. I suppose we all moved to watch them cross the lounge. Grethe led the way up the stairway, her body undulating gracefully under the green silk, and her red hair gleaming. But even cool Madame Grethe had not wished to use the tiny lift that hung there.

Then I turned to Lorn. But he was suddenly withdrawn, his eyes veiled, his expression exactly as animated as that of a chair.

"Did you know he was coming?" I asked quickly.

He did not look offended at my implication that he was concealing that important bit of knowledge from Sue and from me — a knowledge that, if he had had, in fairness he ought to have shared.

"No," he said quietly. "I didn't know."

"This puts a different complexion on the affair."

"Yes," agreed Lorn remotely. I wondered what he was thinking, but the unwontedly disconcerted look had entirely left him — had left, in fact, so completely that I doubted whether it had ever been there. He added:

"In the meantime we may as well go to lunch. After all, one must eat."

I hadn't looked at Sue, and she'd had time to pull herself together. I could have wrung her precious brother's neck when I saw the still look in her eyes as I finally turned to her. There was, of course, nothing I could say. She walked beside me into the dining room.

It was a strained and dreadful meal. Not even the food was good, for Paul's hysterical nerves had apparently had their outlet in burning what was burnable and seasoning too wildly or not at all. The hors d'oeuvres were flat and tasteless, the fish crisp, and the only thing entirely edible was the cheese.

Marianne came and went, still sullen and dark and wary.

And the four of us in that still cold dining room tried to eat and drink like civilized people when I've no doubt our combined desire was to flee from the place. Mrs. Byng did not arrive at all. The priest's table was still by some oversight set with the silver and glasses of the previous night, and it was rather dreadful to see it there, facing me, and remember how I'd last seen that flaming red beard. That thought spoiled even the cheese, and I sat there crumbling bread and not wishing, somehow, to leave the room until Sue left.

It was true that she ought to be safe now, if she was ever safe, with her brother and his detective; at the same time I was perfectly aware that Francis Tally's unexpected arrival might well give a last horrible impetus to the dreadful wheel that was revolving so ruthlessly, guided by unseen hands, there in the black depths of the old hotel.

Francis Tally himself was admirably cool. He was also stoic, for he ate his lunch, crisp fish and all, with gusto. The two, Sue and the newcomer, talked very little, and their every word was plainly audible in the silent white room and consisted of commonplaces. He told her what boat he'd sailed on; and when he'd landed — three days previously, it appeared. She assured him in that stiff voice that did not belong to her that, yes, it was cold. And, yes, the wind was apt to blow like this for a week at a time.

It was directly after lunch that Sue and her brother retired to the parlor. Lorn, always a bit mysterious, became suddenly more mysterious and, it seemed to me, more active and even a little agitated under that mysteriousness. He disappeared before I could get a word with him. Not that I really wanted, just then, to hear his customarily unperturbed half-statements.

For I had even then that feeling of approaching climax; of haste; of urgency. There were things that must be done. If the views that I was beginning vaguely to entertain proved to be faulty and clumsy and entirely incorrect, why, then, no one but myself should ever know it.

It was Marianne, dark and sullen and brooding, who came upon me in the dark corridor near the dead priest's room, where I'd been watching my chance to dodge a promenading policeman (who kept his hand on his revolver, and his back to the wall at the end of the corridor, in a nervous but at the same time rather disconcertingly ready manner), and to get into the room. I knew, of course, that the police, and in all probability Lorn himself, had searched the room, and doubted if my own search would be in any way illuminating; still, I was in a frame of mind to snatch at straws. Marianne, giving me and the policeman dark looks of equal doubt, indicated by gestures and a shower of French that I was to follow her. I did so; I wished I could talk to Marianne

— there was something rather guarded about her morose surliness. I wanted to know what, if anything, she was guarding back of her lowering black eyelashes and sullen red mouth. Sue and Lorn, mysteriously returned, and Francis Tally were waiting for me in the lounge with Grethe, eager-eyed and, I had no doubt, as eager-eared, hovering near, and Marcus Lovschiem's glistening face watching from the lobby.

They were going, it seemed, to the police. And Sue wanted me to go with them. Francis, puzzled, I imagined, had acquiesced; I suspected his consent had been a bit reluctant. Lorn's face told nothing, but Sue's eyes pleaded, and I accompanied them.

A number of policemen accompanied us, and our passage through the streets caused quite a stir in the town, though I noted it only absent-mindedly and that because so many children and so many dogs seemed to spring up beside us.

I did not, of course, understand much of the interview with the commissaire and the *juge d'instruction;* that is, I did not understand French, and neither, it developed, did Francis Tally; Lorn and Sue translated swiftly for us, but sometimes forgot momentarily to translate, which was maddening. They told the whole story of the inheritance, of the abduction, of the token, of the reasons we had for believing the murder centered about it. They were constantly interrupted and questioned. It was a difficult hour, and the conclusion was what I should have expected but somehow had not.

The police did not believe their story. They listened, they questioned, they even grew excited and, I thought, sent a telegram or two; but they did not wholly credit it.

Well, of course, it was extraordinary. Still, it had happened.

At any rate, they politely forbade the plan Francis Tally advanced to leave with his sister the coming morning. Even when his fine-featured face flushed and became angry and he shouted a bit, they still refused. They were polite; they were regretful; but Monsieur must see that it could not be. They could only assure us that the detectives from Paris would arrive tomorrow and then, we gathered, it would immediately be over, the murderer in jail, and everything settled. And as far as that goes they may have been speaking the truth; we were never to know as to that.

In the end our progress back to the hotel was in the nature of a retreat.

It happened that Sue walked beside me. She had pulled on a heavy coat of some rough woolen stuff that was fur-lined, and the dark fur collar came up over her chin, and I could see only the straight line of her nose and the dark sweep of eyelashes against her cheek and a blowing wisp of bright hair beneath her crimson béret. She said nothing on the way back through white, wind-swept, cobble-stoned streets winding narrowly between shuttered stone houses with tall, peaked roofs. In the courtyard once more, a chance movement brought her momentarily very near me with the others — Francis and Lorn, that is — ahead; a policeman was at her other elbow, but she took the chance of the man's not being able to understand English.

She whispered, her eyes on Francis Tally's sloping shoulders:

"I've lost the token. I can't show it to Francis. It's gone."

"Have you told him?"

"No. No — he must not know. What shall I do?"

Lorn turned to hold open the door to the lobby, and Sue was obliged to pass ahead of me and ahead of Francis into the lobby. Lovschiem was waiting, rubbing his hands on which the jewels sparkled. The cockatoo chuckled.

CHAPTER XV

It was in all likelihood that curious and dis-
tasteful gesture of Lovschiem's that suddenly
convinced me that he was again in the saddle,
so to speak.

He'd been ever since Stravsky's unsolved
murder vaguely uncertain, definitely perplexed. He'd had, like Grethe, an air of waiting, but in his case it had been anxious waiting.
Uncertain waiting. Where she had been poised
and alert in her secretive patience, he had
been, somehow, worried, inept, hesitant. It
was as if his course of action were not definitely mapped; or as if he thought more of
its possible failure than of its possible success.
His eyes had been veiled, darting, nervous. His
face had glistened and had had a bad color.
His flabby hands had hovered irresolutely, as
if they could not decide upon any certain action but must hesitate over the ledger and over
the inkwell. His continual smile had been no
longer bland.

But now all at once there was about him a perceptible air of decision. It was as if he knew now exactly what he was going to do. There was briskness in his bulky shoulders; briskness in his fat rubbing hands; confidence in his bland smile, and decision in his darting eyes. Even the dirty jewels seemed to wink and glimmer with a sudden access of evil and knowing energy.

"So," he said in a congratulatory way. "So you have gone to the police. You have arranged things. You may now leave my poor hotel. That is good. That is good. Not that I want my guests to leave me, but it has been a bad time here."

He advanced in an ingratiating way toward Sue.

"I am so glad, Miss Tally, that your brother has finally arrived. Sorry you are to leave us. But glad he has arrived. We have tried to make you happy here in our poor way. But it has been a sad time for this young miss," he added, turning sympathetically to Francis Tally, though, oddly, he avoided meeting his eyes.

"But it appears that we are not leaving," said Francis Tally.

Lovschiem's gesticulating hands arrested themselves in the air. He looked so suddenly and completely at a loss that it was almost ludicrous. In an instant the new decision was wiped out of his glistening fat face.

"But — but why?"

At once I knew that whatever this new course of Lovschiem's had been it must have included Sue's immediate departure in the company of her brother. Why?

I listened to Francis Tally's reply. He had seemed ill at ease and not too likable at first; he was more at ease now but no more likable.

"Some absurdity about waiting for the detectives from Paris. I don't know what they expect to discover. But the police won't let us leave. They'd rather subject us all to the danger of staying here in your murderous hotel —"

"Monsieur," gasped Lovschiem parenthetically. "An unlucky accident. Only an accident."

"— than let us go to a safer place. It's outrageous. What can we do about it, Lorn?"

There was a moment before Lorn replied. He seemed to be seeking some way out of it, judging from the thoughtful, remote look in his dark eyes.

I was thinking of Lovschiem's curious use of the word accident. It was a flagrant understatement. All that horror summed up in the one word accident!

Then it occurred to me that perhaps he used

311

the word for the simple reason that that was exactly what he meant. Perhaps it had been largely accident from his point of view. An accident which had set awry his carefully laid plans that had only righted themselves to be — or I was no judge of looks — set at odds again by this unlooked-for tenaciousness on the part of the police.

But again I asked myself why he had wanted Sue to leave at once with her brother. Was it possible that I was all wrong in my judgment of Lovschiem? Had been wrong from the beginning? Was it possible that he was merely an uninterested but sincere friend to the girl — had known nothing of her inheritance, nothing of the things that threatened her, nothing of the whole ugly affair?

"There is nothing we can do just now but wait," said Lorn finally. He spoke quietly but with a slight air of reservation.

"Wait!" exclaimed Francis Tally impatiently. "Waiting seems to be all that any of you have been doing. Wait! What for? More murders?"

"I assure you it has been enforced waiting," I said. "And no pleasanter for us than it will be for you."

He turned slowly toward me. His spectacles winked in the light, and there were hard lines suddenly about his eyes and thin mouth.

"Well," he said, "it's a little different with you. I understand you are actually under suspicion."

"Not at all." Sue's words came crisp and clear. "Not at all, Francis. Mr. Sundean was a victim of a mistake on the part of the police. He is entirely cleared."

That was not quite true, of course; I could only wish I were entirely cleared. I hadn't liked the way the police looked at me that very afternoon.

"Really," said Francis, with only faint skepticism.

Sue's cheeks went pink, and I said quickly: "Your Mr. Lorn helped me out of it."

"H'mm," observed Francis, looking at Lorn, and Lorn immediately said:

"I did so at Miss Tally's request. It did not — interfere with my — er — other duties."

If I had ever been in doubt as to whether Lovschiem knew what Lorn's purpose there was, the doubt was dispelled then. Not only did Francis Tally's and Lorn's words make clear the tie between them; Lovschiem's fat face was already knowing and unpuzzled. Probably little Marcel had not been the only one in the hotel who listened at doors.

"Really," said Francis Tally again.

"Well —" It was Madame Grethe entering from the lounge. Her green gown caught highlights in its curves, and the white cockatoo clung to her shoulder, looking inquisitively from one to the other of us. "Well," she said again. "Will the police now permit you to leave?"

She heard of their refusal with a face that did not alter a shade in its suavely amiable lines. Watching her, it was difficult to believe — as I certainly had believed, watching her husband's reception of the news — that that refusal affected any plan they might have made. Either it had not, or she was a better actor than her husband. Perhaps the look of secret reflection in her catlike eyes deepened, but her face remained smooth and friendly, with only dark lines under her eyes and a certain pinched look about her nostrils showing the strain of the last few days. Grethe was always friendly; usually amiable.

When Lorn, who had explained dryly and briefly, finished, her soft shoulders rippled slightly under the silk, she lifted one squarish but very white hand to caress the cockatoo's neck and said:

"Ah — well — the detectives from Paris will do something. The police here —" She left her sentence unfinished meaningly. "We may have you here for several days more, then. Heaven send they be better days."

She said it quite honestly — at least, that

314

was the effect. I heartily agreed with her.

At the same time I'd have thought more of it as a wish if I had been entirely sure it was Heaven and not Madame Grethe herself with whom the responsibility lay. I reminded myself that I hadn't, actually, a shadow of a clue against her, and moved nearer the register which lay open on the tall desk at my side.

Grethe had turned to Sue and was talking of her leaving them in a very frank and pleasant manner — a manner which nevertheless contrived to emphasize Sue's long year with them and, somehow, the friendliness of the Lovschiems toward Sue and her mother — while Francis and Lorn, equally noncommittal in expression, waited and perforce listened.

As she talked I was looking with interest at Francis Tally's name scrawled across the open page, and trying to recall the interwoven initials below his typed signature in the letter Lorn had brought. It was true that he had recognized Lorn; true, which was more important, that Lorn had recognized him. Still, as Lorn himself had said, it is well to prove things before resting a case on them. I could not recall the exact characteristics of those intricate initials with enough accuracy to compare them with the signature. I must ask Sue to permit me to look at the letter again.

But there was something about that page

that was wrong. Something that had nothing to do with Francis Tally's signature.

There were three names on it: my own, David Lorn's, and Francis Tally's. It was exactly the same as it had been when I looked at it last, which was on the occasion of David Lorn's arrival — exactly the same except, of course, for the addition of Francis Tally's name.

Yet it was not as it had been when I signed it at the top of the page.

Something tugged and pulled at my memory a second and then made itself definite, so definite that I wondered that I had not seen the discrepancy immediately upon my looking at the page at the time of Lorn's arrival.

It was simple, trivial. And yet by reason of its very triviality must be somehow important.

There wasn't an ink blot.

And there had been an ink blot on that page when I signed my own name, under the cockatoo's suspicious eye, the very evening of my arrival in that ill-omened hotel.

Now there was no ink blot. Yet there were no signs whatever of erasure; the page was smooth and glazed. And there was my own name in my own writing.

They were talking behind me, but I did not hear what they were saying. Under cover of the conversation I leaned nearer the book and, luckily, caught a highlight from the window near by on the glimmering surface of the paper.

Then I was sure. My signature was still in my own handwriting; that was true. But it had been traced on that page with a sharp instrument and then followed with pen and ink. And it was not too well done; with police it wouldn't have stood a test one moment. Even I, no policeman and, God knows, no amateur detective, could readily discern the forgery.

But the forgery began and ended with my own name. Lorn's and Tally's signatures were clearly not traced.

Why, then?

The explanation was simple and swift. Something had made the removal of that page imperative. It had become imperative after my arrival and before Lorn's. And it was nothing of an innocent nature, such as a bad tear or more spilled ink, for Lovschiem, in such a case, would have merely asked me to register again and explained the need for it. No, the very fact of careful and painstaking forgery of my name proved that there was a hidden and probably incriminating reason for it — incriminating to whom, I could not know, although it pointed strongly to Lovschiem, and was thus practically the only material clue I had so far discovered which led to him.

The removal of the page had been defter than the forgery, for there were no signs of it at all, and since the page had been in the first quarter of the book there was no chance of discovering the loss of the other half of the sewed-in sheet, owing to a gap in dates of registry, for that other half would have been, of course, in the latter part of the book and among still blank and unused sheets.

Suddenly I realized that I was looking too long and too closely at the page. There were still voices behind me, but I looked up quickly and met Lovschiem's eyes. I endeavored to look blank and unconcerned. I even said in a casual way to Tally, "Your home's in the South, then," as if I'd been only guilty of idle curiosity.

There was no way to know, however, whether my small ruse succeeded with Lovschiem or not. His eyes still followed me when I left the lobby, and as I started upstairs I glanced back from the landing and saw him bending over the register.

Lorn and Tally had drifted into the chilly parlor again, and Sue had made some excuse about taking off her coat and was also coming upstairs. I did not wait for her until I had passed beyond the gallery and into the corridor and thus was beyond the range of vision of anyone on the first floor.

When we reached the little niche in the corridor I stopped. There was no one in sight; we were visible from only one or two doors, and they were closed; not even a policeman was to be seen up and down the length of shadowy deserted corridor.

"Now then," I said, "tell me all about the token."

"But I don't know," said Sue in what was almost a wail. "It is just gone. And I thought it was so safe."

"When did you lose it?"

"Sometime last night."

"You don't mean anyone got into your room during the night?" I was frightened. I had her by the arm, gripping it so hard that she winced.

"Oh, no, no! The door was locked and bolted all night."

"When, then?" I asked, only a little relieved.

"I don't know. I looked at it — the token, you know — yesterday about noon. Last evening after dinner you told me the priest had been in my room, but the place where I — where I had hidden the token —"

"Your slipper," I said grimly.

"*What!*"

"Of course. One of your scarlet slippers with the silver heels. It was probably in a hollow in the heel."

"But you — how could you know that?"

I hated taking time, especially when it was so simple.

"Oh, you wore them so much — wore them that first night when you had been out to walk on the bridge — would you wear scarlet evening slippers with narrow high heels for a walk along cobblestones unless there was a reason?" I was impatient.

"But I didn't wear them in the daytime," she protested.

"Naturally not," I said. "But there wasn't so much danger then — or you probably thought there was not. Or perhaps you removed it during the daytime. Or perhaps it was very well hidden. Go on — when did you discover it had been stolen?"

She looked at me a moment before she said: "It *was* well hidden. I felt safe about it — when I glanced at it (it was in the heel of the right slipper) — it showed no signs of being tampered with. I thought I could have told at once if it had been removed. So I said the priest had taken nothing from my room. I only discovered it late last night. I felt I must be sure, of course — and I — opened the heel and the token was gone."

"What did you do?"

"Nothing. There was nothing I could do then. Everyone had gone to bed; I — I was afraid to venture out into the black corridors." She shivered, and I said quickly, taking a long breath at the thought of what might have happened had she done so:

"That was right."

I felt rather as if I had walked without knowing it to the very edge of a precipice and only looked down at the last step. Suppose she'd gone out into the corridors — murder-haunted — black —

"That was right!" I repeated inadequately. Then that feeling of urgency, that there was not much time, nudged me, and I went on: "But you should have told us at once this morning."

She hesitated, looking at me with steady but troubled eyes.

"But I couldn't tell Lorn."

"Couldn't — oh — oh, I see. After all, he's in the employ of your brother. And your brother's interests would come first with him."

"Exactly," said Sue. "And I couldn't search the priest's room this morning myself. I was still, somehow —" she paused, and her breath caught a little as she admitted — "afraid — afraid — you had warned me too well. But

I was just going to tell you, in the White Salon, you know when —" She stopped completely there.

So that was why the priest was murdered. He had had the token, and someone knew he had it and murdered him. A small incident in the lust for that waiting gold.

This left three possibilities — that is, if we granted that the priest had stolen the token, and I thought I was safe in doing that — first, the murderer had taken it from the priest, and it was in his possession. Second, it had been on the body of the priest, and the police now had it: this I thought was highly improbable, as the murderer had had hours after the priest's death to search the body unobserved. Parenthetically I thought of the hideously uneasy night I had passed trying to sleep in that death-haunted wing. The third possibility was that the priest had hidden the token successfully or had passed it immediately to a possible accomplice; this last was also unlikely.

"Do you want to tell me what it is?" I asked rather diffidently.

"You mean you want to try to find it again for me?"

"If I can," I said briefly.

She considered this gravely.

"It's rather dangerous knowledge," she said at last. "And I must be able to tell Francis

322

that I have kept it a complete secret. That, of course, is the pressing thing. I didn't intend to ask you to find it for me. I think that's rather a hopeless task now. And besides, I — I have already placed you in too much danger. The thing I wanted to talk to you about is what to do now. What to tell Francis. Oh, it's — it's so dreadfully ironical. If he'd only got here one day sooner. He's waiting now, I suppose. He hinted that when we returned from interviewing the police we would go into what he called the — 'formalities.' He means, of course, the token."

It was true that that was the urgent and immediate thing. How to meet Francis's inquiries at that moment. To tell him lamely that the thing had been stolen but that we were searching for it would be to convince Francis once and for all that Sue was only another impostor.

"You'll have to bluff your brother. Get the papers from Lovschiem; make him hand them over; give those to your brother to digest. Then refuse to show your own token until he shows you his — I gather they are identical? The chances are he will be reluctant to show his. He'll be afraid it is a trap. He will tell you it is you who are the defendant, so to speak. That it is up to you to prove yourself to him. Not his place to prove himself to you.

323

Which is, of course, true. However, you'll hold out; you'll say you also are afraid of a trap — or rather you'll indicate it tactfully. Don't hesitate for an instant. Be firm and cool and sure of yourself."

"Yes, I can do that," said Sue.

And it was true; she could — no one better.

"But suppose — suppose he believes me — suppose he is ready to match his token with mine. Suppose," she said with a ghost of a smile which did not lighten the tense look in her eyes and the taut line around her mouth, "suppose he calls my bluff."

"He won't," I said with more confidence than I felt. "He'll want to think about it awhile — talk it over with Lorn. And in the meantime perhaps —"

Her eyes quickened, and she grasped at the hint that I had not intended to convey.

"Do you mean —" she whispered — "that you — that perhaps — that you know something — are on the trail of —"

"No, no," I said at once. "I've only a faint notion. Don't bank on it. Don't hope for anything. I mean it. I'm counting on Lorn and Lorn only. Unless the Paris detectives get here first."

It had not convinced her. I could see by the eager questioning look in her eyes that it had not. I felt vaguely embarrassed. I had no pretensions to the rôle of detective. I was clumsy and inexperienced and had no notions of the logical, conventional method of approach. I even preferred the adventurous, active type of fiction, with more emphasis, I fear, on muscles than on brains, to a tale of the keenest and most miraculous of fictional detectives. I suppose the lure in such tastes is one of contrasts; an engineer gets enough and too much pure reason, the immediate and material relation of cause and effect reduced incontrovertibly to figures, in his own profession; he's apt to thrill a little more authentically over a splendid sea battle or a vigorous man-to-man fight, even in the newspaper, than over a case of deductive reasoning.

Still, I would be the last to deny that two and two must make four — it's never very difficult to add; the difficulty lies in being sure of the digits in which you are adding.

It was the uncertainty of the digits that troubled me now. I said:

"This is your handkerchief, isn't it?"

She looked at the delicate wisp of white that I drew from my pocket. She had been, I think, about to question me further, for she looked faintly impatient at the interruption. The impatient look, however, was succeeded by a puzzled little frown.

"Why, yes," she said. "I believe it is. At

least, it looks like some I have, and it has a scent that I use. I couldn't be sure, though. It's a quite ordinary handkerchief — linen, hand-made — rolled hem and drawn threads — you can get dozens of them in any store in France. Why?"

I did not explain. I said: "I found it on the floor. Will you come with me a moment? I know your brother's waiting and you mustn't be long, but it will only take a moment."

She looked further puzzled but went with me toward the north corridor. As we passed through the door I think she recalled the thing that had happened there only that morning — though it seemed long, long ago — for the small lobes of her ears were suddenly pink. Her scarf, however, did not catch.

At the end of the corridor I asked her to stand for a moment before my door. I marked her height against the window. I did not need even to go to the lobby whence I had seen that flying silhouette. Even allowing largely for the angle of my perspective from the lobby, Sue was at least a foot shorter than that brief silhouette had been. I ought to have known it at once; still, Sue had been so prominently in my mind — I had left her in that room, and there was a flying silhouette in black before the opened door — so brief a silhouette that, strive though I might, I could remember only a black figure with flying black skirts.

There was still neither time nor need to explain then to Sue. I said:

"Do you see that room up there on the third story — the fifth shutter from the corner of the middle section? About number thirty-four or thirty-five: were you up there at all the night of the first murder?

I don't know what she was thinking of me just then. She looked perplexed, but Sue was never dull.

"No," she said directly.

"Another thing," I said. "And forgive me for all this pointlessness." I hesitated here; the thing I was about to ask was not entirely pointless. I plunged on, however:

"Mrs. Byng says she saw you turning out the hotel lights the night of the first murder. She says —" Sue's eyes were widening. Her face was white and suddenly set. "She says," I went on miserably as I saw that my very inquiry must suggest to her that I'd believed Mrs. Byng, "that she saw you at the switch box, there in the corridor near her door. That she saw you pull the main switch, and that the lights went out at once."

"And you believed her?" said Sue rather sadly.

"No." I had her hands and almost had her, suddenly, in my arms. "No! I didn't believe her. Not when you told me where you'd been at that time."

She pulled back away from me.

"I don't know what Mrs. Byng saw or thought she saw," said Sue. "But I told you the exact truth. About everything."

"I know. I know. Tell me, is Mrs. Byng friendly with you?"

"Why — no," said Sue. "But not unfriendly, either. We've had very little to do with one another. Scarcely talked at all."

"You wouldn't say, then, that she'd ever been particularly interested in you?"

"Heavens, no," said Sue, seeing what I meant and forgiving me simultaneously. "If you mean Mrs. Byng may be — suspect — that's absurd. She's exactly what she seems."

"I'm beginning to think I don't mean anything. You'd best go along to your brother. He'll grow suspicious. I'll go with you to the lounge."

"It's not going to be easy," said Sue. "Facing him, knowing all along that if he suddenly produces his own token I cannot produce mine to match it. I was almost ready this morning to give up the whole thing — when you and Mr. Lorn advised my going if the police would permit, and I knew besides that I had no longer the means to identify myself. I was ready to go. After all — why do I want five million dollars?" She said it thoughtfully, as if she really did wonder why.

"Five millions," I said rather bitterly, "is not to be regarded with disrespect. And in this case, if you are in for a penny you're in for a pound."

We were walking back along the north corridor. In two or three days at the most she would go completely out of my life; she would remember me, I thought, because she could scarcely forget A—. But it would become gradually an indistinct and blurred memory; it would grow inactive and unalive, blurred and erased by the full and varied days she would live.

One crowded year is longer than ten leisurely years. In one year at the most I should be crowded completely out of her thoughts and be merely a figure, dim and not poignant in any way in her memory. I wondered fleetingly where I should be myself in a year; probably in some far-flung outpost of civilization — lonely and very near the earth and stars — and I would look at those stars and see Sue against a desert night — Sue with her soft bright hair and her crimson lips that I'd kissed and her eyes holding mine and shining mysteriously.

It was then that I knew what a devastating thing it would be never again to see her advancing toward me. Never again to catch the gay little challenge of her mouth that was a smile. Never again to watch the gallant lift of her chin, the light in gold gleams on her hair, the delicacy of her hands and her beautiful body.

Yes, it was devastating. It was like being caught in the vortex of a cyclone that you hadn't seen coming.

But even in that destructive moment — and it isn't easy to know suddenly that your only moments of high and magic living are counted and are few in count, and that they'll go swiftly and irretrievably and finally, and you'll be left to flat and sober marking time, doing this, doing that, with only a dimming memory of the full tide of life — even in that moment I knew I could not tell her. I could not tell this girl with the golden millions.

I wished she'd gone that morning before her brother came; I wished she'd given up her claim as she said she was about to do — I wished all manner of insane things.

And something said: You won't feel this tearing at you for long; it would be unendurable if you did but you won't, for even the memory of your love will grow dim and faint.

And that, of course, was worse, and if Sue had turned just then, if she'd faltered or hesitated or looked to me for help, the whole thing would have come out. Like most engineers, I am by nature inarticulate; it isn't so difficult to get a bare record on paper — that's habit; but it's only once in a while, under great pressure, that I find the key that turns feelings into speech, and then there's no damming up the flood until it is spent.

But she didn't turn. And by the time we reached the stairway I had walked through heaven and hell and emerged. I loved her, and I was going to give her up. I was even with my own hands helping erect that hateful, glittering path along which her little feet would walk away from me.

Well — I emerged. It is by no means a unique experience. And after all, I'd rather have had it than not. So there was no good making a fuss about it.

It was almost a relief to wrench myself back to the business at hand. The business of helping Sue acquire those damnable millions which not only severed her from me but which threatened her — threatened her — threatened her.

And time was pressing.

Francis was still in the parlor. As we walked down the last steps into the lounge, Lorn came suddenly from the parlor.

"Your brother is waiting for you," he said, and paused, his clouded dark eyes meeting Sue's gaze. He looked peculiarly uncertain and

331

ill at ease. The effect he gave of not having concluded his sentence, and thus of having still something he must say to her, was so strong that both Sue and I paused too, motionless, waiting for what was to come. But if he'd intended to say something further he thought better of it; he made a rather strange little gesture with his hands, shrugged and walked away, vanishing through the lobby into the court beyond. She looked after him perplexedly, then turned toward me with a question in her face. But I, of course, could tell her nothing; I only felt that the detective's look savored, somehow, of warning.

Sue took a long breath, gave me a quick little nod, and walked swiftly toward the stuffy old parlor and the waiting man. There was a fine tempering of steel in Sue; she never lacked courage in a crisis.

I sat in the lounge in full view of the door and waited. After a few seconds I found it impossible to sit, and rose, walking back and forth, watching the parlor door, the lift, the galleries. After all, I'd seen little Marcel shot before my very eyes, and I had been powerless to prevent it.

And there was no denying the fact that with Francis's arrival Sue's danger was great. His arrival had forced the climax; now, if ever, the plot would need be carried to its swift conclusion, for once he was convinced of Sue's identity that plot must automatically collapse. And blind and groping about in the dark as we were — not knowing from what quarter trouble might come — there was every reason to fear that that conclusion might have an unthinkable, ghastly outcome.

With the token stolen, even the small measure of protection its possession had given Sue was gone; with that in the possession of the murderer the next step was inevitably to produce the substitute for Sue — and to silence Sue. And it must be done at once, if ever.

There was one faint hope. That was that whoever it was who had killed so swiftly, so mysteriously, with such ghastly silence and stealth, striking without warning there in the blackness of the old hotel and vanishing as mysteriously as he had come — whoever he was might possibly believe that, without that token, Sue would not be able to convince her brother. Her brother who, as a matter of fact, might be only too glad of a chance on which to base a refusal. After all, even to a brother ten millions might be better than five. It was strange and yet to be expected that from the beginning Francis Tally had been so important a figure in the tangle that I felt I had known him all along. That he was no stranger just arrived, but an active and integral part of the mystery.

But the faint hope was so very faint that it was almost untenable.

Sue's only assurance of safety lay in convincing Francis of her identity. And she was going to him empty-handed, without that token on which had been placed such ill-proportioned significance.

At any rate, she had the birth and marriage records; if Francis were only inclined to be fair and reasonable, those written records would go a long way toward establishing her identity.

It was with taut nerves that I saw Francis appear in the doorway, and heard him call to Lovschiem, and saw Lovschiem, after a moment or two, emerge from the parlor and waddle fatly toward his own rooms. He's going to his safe, I thought, and I lit a cigarette and forced myself to wait quietly. If Francis would only credit the evidence of that long-ago marriage certificate and Sue's own birth record, things might yet go well with Sue. Given time and luck, we might recover the token.

But I was not exactly easy. It was somehow not really a shock to witness Lovschiem's hasty return, his fat flurried hands, his agitation and his cries that he'd been robbed.

The safe had been opened, he cried, gasping and wheezing for breath. Miss Tally's envelope was gone. Nothing else. Only the envelope.

The strange thing about it was that his agitation was not affected. It looked to me to be real.

CHAPTER XVI

My opinion of the Lovschiems was going up and up.

It's true that Marcus was exactly as fat and greasy and sly-looking as he'd ever been, and Grethe as lithe and seductive and secretive with her waiting green eyes. But I felt sure, while I watched the resultant commotion that brought them all — Francis and Sue and Lorn and Grethe — into the lounge, I felt sure that neither Grethe nor Marcus had known of the theft of the envelope Sue had entrusted to them. I felt equally sure that they were honestly surprised, discomposed, and regretful. I was at last convinced that they had actually wanted Sue to have that envelope and to go away with her brother. Which conviction completely reversed my whole train of speculation regarding the Lovschiems.

At the same time, I was interested in discovering from the resultant conversation with its implications that they undoubtedly had known more than Sue believed they had known about her inheritance and the conditions of it. For Francis was not guarded in his remarks even before my ears, and the Lovschiems were obviously not puzzled by his allusions.

"However," said Francis crisply at last, interrupting Lovschiem's perspiring expostulations, "the papers in the envelope were not of first importance. It's true that my sister —" He checked himself, glanced at me, and made his first allusion to the secrecy of the affair. "I conclude that you've taken your — er — friends —" he gestured toward me and the Lovschiems, an inclusion which, despite my rising regard for the Lovschiems, I did not relish — "into your confidence regarding this affair."

"Only Mr. Sundean," said Sue. "Who has —"

"Well, well," Francis interrupted. "It's quite all right. The important thing —"

"But I did not tell anyone else," went on Sue firmly, refusing to be interrupted.

Francis glanced fleetingly at the Lovschiems. I followed his glance and was caught by a curiously still expression on Grethe's face. She met Francis's eyes directly, but there was a look in hers I could not fathom as she said very deliberately and distinctly:

"Miss Tally's mother told us something of the strange conditions under which Miss Tally would inherit money from her father. She told us in confidence, hoping that we would give what assistance we might to Miss Tally. She had no other friends." There was a nice lack of emphasis on the words "other friends," but they stood out definitely in their implication. "I hope I do not need to assure you that we have told no one. If there is, as we have feared, a scheme to rob Miss Tally of her inheritance, it is not one we have brought about by a careless revealing of her mother's dying confidence. We have even kept the fact of our knowledge from Miss Tally. We understood, of course, that it was a delicate matter and one that invited danger." She hesitated and then added only a little uncertainly: "We did not dream it would be such danger. But our hands were tied."

Fine and fair and careful.

At once my growing opinion of the precious two gave one feeble flicker and collapsed. It was far too fine and fair and careful. Grethe's eyes were too cautious, and they held too brooding a flame as they met Francis Tally's. I felt that her claws were unsheathing themselves, her white muscles gathering tensely. And a look at Marcus's face confirmed my feeling, for it bore a silly look of combined dismay, fright, and ludicrous relief as his quicker-witted mate spoke. It was, perhaps, like that of a canoeist who sees too late that he's rushing upon a rock and is only averted at the last fraction of an instant by a strong paddle in someone else's hand.

"Oh, of course. Of course," said Francis Tally carelessly, as if it didn't in the least matter. I wondered if he would be so careless if he himself had lived through those days with us. I thought not. And I also thought that had the Lovschiems been so honest and so fastidious they would have charted their course in quite a different direction.

"The point is," went on Francis easily, "we don't need the papers that were in the envelope. There is a perfectly simple way for my sister to prove her identity. And I suppose she is willing to do so at once and end this uncertainty."

"I'll match your own token, Francis," said Sue pleasantly.

Francis whirled sharply to look at her. Even Lorn, who had, as usual, mysteriously turned up at a crisis, seemed to sense something under her voice, and I caught his speculative, thoughtful look and wondered about it. There had been something queer about Lorn — some impalpable difference. It had come with Francis Tally's unheralded arrival, but it was nothing to which I had a clue. Nothing even that I could definitely interpret. It was only there: a greater watchfulness perhaps; a silent wariness. I wondered what it meant. What had he been doing — what, perhaps, had he discovered? There was certainly something very strange back of his guarded dark eyes as he watched Francis Tally.

"What do you mean?" Francis's voice went upward a note or two.

"Only that," said Sue still pleasantly.

Francis's face slowly darkened.

"But, my dear girl," he said, "it is you who must prove your identity to me. Don't you think you are reversing matters a little?"

"No," said Sue quietly. There was firmness under her voice, but it was still quiet and, curiously, there was a spark of gayety in the glance she flung toward me. I was interested to note that Francis's face was less bland. What would he say? What would he do? He shot a glance at Madame Grethe, who watched with her feline look of secret, guarded waiting. He said:

"You forget that I am sole arbiter of the matter. And in any case, Sister, I think it might be better to continue our conversation in a less public place. Shall we —" He motioned toward the parlor, and Sue preceded him, meekly enough, but with another glance at

340

me, into the room, while I conquered my inclination to tell him that he himself had hurled his private affairs at our ears, whether they were unwilling ears or not.

Grethe, with a sharp word to Lovschiem, vanished, Lovschiem followed her, and Lorn, looking undecidedly after Francis, as if waiting for some indication of Francis's wishes, sat down beside me. Neither of us spoke for a time: I was lost in my thoughts, and Lorn was equally engrossed in some mysterious speculations of his own.

"Well," I remarked at last, having reached a cul-de-sac in my reasoning from which there was only one exit, and that too incredible to take.

"Well enough, I suppose," he replied a bit grudgingly. He was watching the door to the parlor carefully. "Well enough."

I said bluntly:

"See here, Lorn, I've got a feeling that you know more about this affair than you are willing to admit. Is that true?"

His chin sank a little into the collar of the dark topcoat he still wore owing to the barnlike chill of the hotel. He had slouched down in his chair, and looked flabby and baggy-trousered and altogether ineffective.

"Yes and no," he said. "If I do know something, the time isn't ripe for it yet."

He flicked a look at me. I could read nothing at all in his clouded dark eyes.

"You're not telling me to mind my own business, are you?"

"Not precisely," said Lorn with rather startling candor, "but it might be better for you if you did."

He did not even look at me to see what I thought of his warning — if warning it was. He continued at once:

"Mr. Tally doesn't seem to want me. I'll just go along and take a look at this very opportunely robbed safe."

"Wait," I said quickly. "I've got the link between Stravsky and Lovschiem."

"What!" That time I did succeed in getting his full attention. I often felt with Lorn that he was enduring me, even quieting me; never that he was doing me the honor to give my efforts much regard or, even, attention. This time, however, he was interested.

"One that will hold water with the police?" he asked at once.

"Well — perhaps not," I said, thereby losing at least three fourths of his interest.

"What then?" he inquired with an effect of languor.

"The night of my arrival someone came to this hotel, registered below my name, and was shown to a room. Then he vanished. Even his name was removed from the register. Who was that man if it wasn't Stravsky?"

"How do you know that?"

For once his frank skepticism did not shake my conviction.

"I don't know it," I said, "if you mean by that can I prove it on the strength of the evidence we now have. But it's the logical conclusion."

"Indeed," he said dryly. "And from what do you draw your logical conclusion?"

I told him briefly, watching the parlor door and keeping half an ear for any untoward sound. He did look faintly more impressed when I'd finished, although he pointed out at once that I was building up supposition on the strength merely of a missing ink blot and Marcel's few scattered words anent the soiled towels in a supposedly vacant room.

"It fits," I said stubbornly.

"No," he denied me rather sadly. "It doesn't fit. It isn't in the least conclusive. It does, however, provide a line of investigation."

"Well, it ought to be of some value to you, then," I said. "I hope you don't mind my saying that it seems to me you need a few more lines of investigation."

He was not angry. And he heaped coals of fire immediately, which is unforgivable. He said:

"You think I'm making a complete failure of this, Mr. Sundean. I suppose it seems so to you. Well, I don't blame you. I'm sure I must seem incompetent and fumbling. But I'm really working hard. Harder than you think. And the result may surprise you."

"I hope so, I'm sure," I said, still disgruntled. "And there's one thing I'm going to say which I hope you'll credit more than my other occasional gems of wisdom and discernment. And that is —" I ground out my cigarette with a quick motion and got to my feet, where I stood looking down at him — "that is that Miss Tally is not out of danger. We both know that she's — willful; she may refuse to show her brother her token until he shows his own. They may both be afraid of traps, and the thing may be deadlocked for a little time. And Miss Tally, until she is accepted completely by her brother, is in greater danger than she ever was. The arrival of her brother has forced the climax. I hope you'll remember that."

Lorn rose too. He gave me a singularly long and strange look.

"Don't worry, Sundean," he said. "I'll remember that."

And that was all the satisfaction I had.

It was just then, however, that he heaped further coals on my head. He said slowly:

"I'm afraid I must warn you, Sundean, to

be — most circumspect in your behavior."

I was struck by the undercurrent of meaning in his voice. I had the feeling you have when, walking in deep woods, you see the brush near you waver silently with the passage of a stealthy and unseen body. It is a strangely sinister and primitive kind of chill that it gives you, and I felt it then, looking at Lorn and hearing his slow words.

"Why," I said, "what do you mean?"

"I hadn't intended to tell you. I explained to them that it was probably done this morning when you entered the White Salon and before you opened the shutters. But they are not convinced. Don't try to leave the hotel tonight, Sundean, and above all things, make no suspicious movement, for it will be as much as your life is worth."

"What on earth are you driving at?"

"The police found your fingerprints on the electric switch in the White Salon. They argue that because you tried to turn on the light it must have been night when you touched it. Ergo —" One of his slight baffling shrugs finished it.

Things about me were suddenly rather dim. It was true: I had touched it and tried to turn on the light late the previous afternoon. Just before my last glimpse of the priest. I remembered it all too perfectly. Lorn was watching me, noting, I felt, every shade that flickered over my face. I said as nonchalantly as I could contrive:

"I suppose they are preserving the clue for the Paris detectives?"

"Why, yes — naturally. I don't wish to alarm you, Sundean, but it is nothing to regard lightly."

I was so far from regarding it lightly that it gave me a small measure of satisfaction to discover from his words that my face hadn't given me away. Sue's danger and the press of events had dulled to a degree my sense of my own danger.

"I'm not regarding it lightly," I said. "I'm looking to you to get me out of it."

"Well — I'll do my best, of course," he replied a bit gloomily. "But I do wish you wouldn't go out of your way to leave clues."

"Look here, Lorn — who's the murderer? You must know by this time. Or you must have some notion. You've had days to do it. And it's a shocking situation."

"One can't hurry about such things," warned Lorn pessimistically. "One must be very sure of every fact. Must prove as one goes. One can't safely leap to conclusions in your own startling fashion. But there's one thing I must tell you, Sundean. I'd prefer telling Miss Tally directly. But I can't quite do that

346

under the circumstances. So — I'll tell you."

"Well?"

He paused, arranging his words; there was no shadow of feeling or expression in those cloudy dark eyes. He said finally:

"I think it might be as well for Miss Tally to delay concluding the negotiations for perhaps a day or two."

"What do you mean?"

"What I say. No more, no less."

I stared at him, trying to find explanation in his shadowed eyes, his quiet face — rather dark, with its promise of aggression belied by that womanish chin.

I did not say that at the moment Sue had no intention of concluding negotiations, no matter how much she longed to do so.

"He's your employer," I said musingly. "You don't quite trust him. Your reason for distrust isn't strong enough to permit your going openly against your employer and warning Miss Tally not to trust him. Yet you warn me, knowing I shall tell her." His eyes hadn't blinked, although I felt strongly that he didn't like my bald way of putting something that I daresay he imagined he had conveyed quite diplomatically; he was always a little fond of stiff and pompous language. "Come, Lorn — you've said too much not to say more."

"I can't tell you more now," he said in what

was almost an oblique kind of promise.

"You must. Time is too short."

"Very well, then, I refuse to say more," he replied obstinately.

I had a savage impulse to grasp him by the shoulders and shake his information or suspicions out of him then and there; and I might add that I've always regretted not doing it. At the time I had hopes that he had a plan up his thin brown sleeve; I was still, though less firmly, under the conviction that after all Lorn was at the helm and, despite our differences of opinion, might be able to carry through successfully. Might be able to guide our small ship safely around the rocks and whirlpools encompassing us.

If his method of work, his mysterious silences, his extreme conservatism baffled and annoyed me, I always remembered that in a crisis he was not inefficient and conservative and slow at all. Twice he had got me out of a very bad entanglement. It was actually owing to Lorn that we had made what small progress we had made. But I wished I had some way of rousing him to the swiftness of action to which only a crisis seemed to provoke him. He was from the beginning an incalculable person.

From the first we had not seen eye to eye in every matter, but it was after his half-hints and mulish obstinacy regarding Francis Tally that we diverged sharply in our different paths. And it was in only a few moments that, despite Lorn's warning, which could only be construed as applying to Francis Tally, we found ourselves ranged in two different camps, with Francis Tally and his employee on one side and Sue and me on the other. Yet in the end it was Lorn's effort more than mine that brought it about.

I say we were to become immediately ranged in two different camps. And it happened just then, when the muffled sound of voices in the parlor became more definite and clear and all at once Sue swept into the lounge.

Her cheeks were pink, her lips red, her eyes sparkling with anger; she looked spirited, poised, quivering — like a slender sailboat which has swept up from the trough of one wave to its crest and is poised to meet the next as gallantly.

Francis, angry too and showing it less pleasantly, followed her. His face also was flushed, his eyes were narrow back of those studious spectacles, his hands were working nervously.

Sue said, every word falling like a brittle little icicle and yet marvelously polite at the same time:

"I hope you don't mind my telling Mr. Lorn and Mr. Sundean of our talk, Francis. You

349

see," she turned to me, "I have asked Francis if he will permit me to have a lawyer represent me. I feel that it would be more fitting, considering the nature of the affair. But my brother thinks it is unnecessary —"

"No reason for it at all," burst in Francis. "I came here from America to settle things with this girl. To give her a chance at five million dollars — *five million dollars,* and she holds back and prattles about a —"

"I beg you not to interrupt me, Francis." I was faintly amused to note that as Francis grew angrier Sue grew sweeter and cooler, but it was a most infuriating sweetness and coolness.

"I'm most grateful to my brother to make such an effort," she went on. "Though perhaps it might have been made sooner — before I had been subjected to —" Her sweetness faltered a little there, and she swept on quickly, preferring not to talk of the horror that had dogged her days. "At the same time, I can't help feeling that just because it means — as you have reminded me so thoughtfully — five million dollars — because of the amount of the money involved, it is only fitting and suitable to ask a lawyer to conduct negotiations for me."

Francis's eyes were very narrow; I heard a slight rustle behind me, and I saw him dart a quick glance in that direction, and I had no doubt Madame Grethe had made her appearance.

"Come now, Sue," said Francis rather pleadingly. "Why make such a commotion about something that should be kept — er — in the family? All you need do is let me look at the token you have. If it is what it is supposed to be, the thing is done. I'll take you back to America with me, you'll have all the money you want. You'll forget this whole thing — do be sensible."

"But, Francis," said Sue so very sweetly that for a second or two I think Francis did not fully comprehend the enormity of her suggestion, "is there any particular reason why you refuse me a lawyer?"

There was an instant or two of silence before Francis's gathering rage rose to his lips. Knowing what I knew, I was rather proud of Sue, standing there facing him, using all her feminine equipment most deftly, carrying war gayly into his own territory when she hadn't actually one vestige of heavy artillery of her own. Attack, I thought, is the feminine weapon; defense would never carry weight. And Sue attacked so sweetly, so coolly — so gallantly from my own viewpoint, because I knew of her empty hands. I knew of the infirmity of her ground.

"Do you mean," demanded Francis, "that you don't trust me?"

"What a thing to say! *What* a thing to say!" cried Sue, giving a soft little ripple of laughter that stung Francis and that actually shocked me in its deceiving sweetness. All women can shock you that way.

She continued: "But why do you say it? Not trust a brother who's come from home to settle millions upon me!"

"Then," said Francis, again glancing past me to where, with a quick following look, I saw Madame Grethe standing, motionless, her green eyes shining — "then," he said heavily, "you do trust me?"

"Why not?" said Sue, her beautiful shoulders sliding gently upward in a ghost of that exasperating French gesture to which I have never seen nor heard a really clinching and suitable reply.

Then Sue, very suddenly, and in a totally easy and meaningless voice, said an extremely odd thing. She touched me with her eyes just before she said it, as if to be sure I was listening, but neither her words nor her look was illuminating. She said, her eyes then on Francis, and her voice quite flat and even a bit bored:

"Why should I not trust you? For now we see through a glass darkly, but then —" And there she stopped and carefully arranged her crimson scarf at her throat as if it had her entire interest. But her eyes through their dark eyelashes watched Francis.

Francis did not speak. He only looked angry and baffled, and his eyes sought Madame Grethe again.

There was a swift little swish of silk that broke the singularly tense moment. Grethe stepped forward and passed her round silken arm through Sue's. I did not like their propinquity. I did not like the smooth white cheek so near Sue's, the burnished red hair, the way those knowing green eyes slid suavely from one to the other of us.

But what Grethe said was entirely unexpected.

"Don't you think you are a little overcautious, my dear?" she said smoothly to Sue. "Forgive me for speaking, but I could scarcely help hearing you, you know. For your own good I must say this. It is better for you to do as your brother wishes. Follow the terms of your father's will and prove your identity to your brother and let him take you away. It is only a matter of form. And while I have hesitated to speak before, lest I make you feel unwelcome in this, your only home — still — still you must see what — what a thing you have brought upon us all."

She paused. Sue, standing there firmly and lightly poised, was somehow no less dignified for Grethe's pressing arm and gently admonitory air, which carried with it a kind of caressing, self-sacrificial tone — a tone that reminded Sue of any friendliness Grethe had ever offered her. I was glad to see that Sue was sternly unmoved. But I think she was still doubtful; still loath to discredit Grethe's motives in her own mind. And Grethe said suavely:

"Think what's waiting for you, dear. Five million dollars — five millions. The things you can buy. The things you can do."

It was just then that Sue's long, purposefully blind loyalty collapsed. She removed her arm quietly from Madame Grethe's clasp. She was too fine and proud to permit us to see the wound of mistaken loyalty. And with superb and sudden maturity she met the older woman on her own ground.

"Don't think for a moment, Madame Lovschiem," she said sweetly, "that I shall forget what you've done. And I'm sure my — brother — will feel most grateful to you in your attempt to smooth the way before us."

Grethe looked placid, then faintly puzzled, then suddenly comprehending. Her white lids dropped over her secretive eyes, and she said gravely, as if taking Sue's words at their face value:

"Don't thank me, my dear. I've only done what I could do."

"I'm afraid I'm not thanking you," said Sue quite frankly. "You see, it wasn't altogether kind of you, to keep what my — my mother — told you a secret from me. It was a reticence which is not of a nature to maintain my confidence in your friendship. You and your husband are the only people in A— besides myself who knew of the circumstances of my inheritance."

I think Sue had not actually intended to say so much. I think she was wounded, she was conscious that Grethe was suddenly on Francis's side and that she must fight them both, and that she was new to that dreadful niggling warfare which can exist so hideously between two women. But knowing she must fight whether she liked or not, she struck a little too blindly, choosing in her haste a weapon whose sharpness she did not quite comprehend. But its very unexpectedness frightened Madame Grethe. A common woman, inherently vulgar, in spite of her quick wits, she had probably many times taken Sue's reticence for timidity; her restraint, her quiet dignity — all those marks of breeding — for stupidity. Where Sue would regard friendship highly, taking it for granted that a friend would offer the loyalty and truth and lack of ulterior motives that Sue herself, with her finer instincts, would offer, Grethe would only feel that Sue was stupidly young, stupidly credulous. And now that Sue struck boldly with a weapon Grethe herself would have used, Grethe understood and was frightened. Though, to be sure, only a close observer might have caught her fright in the sudden leaping of her eyes, in the way her sharp white teeth closed suddenly over her red lower lip, in the placative manner in which she addressed Sue and put an end to the situation with less adroitness than one might have expected of her.

"You are tired and unstrung," she said. "Otherwise you would not speak in such a way to me. To your only friend. To —"

"I have other friends," said Sue, cutting into Grethe's soft speech without visible compunction. Her eyes went to me, and Grethe went on suavely, pretending rather unconvincingly not to have heard.

"The trouble is we are all tired and nervous and upset, and no wonder. I'll order tea, and we'll all feel better." She walked with a swish of green silk to the bell and pushed it with her square, vigorous white thumb. "Then we'll talk the matter over more amicably. Do sit down, Mr. Tally. Come now, my dear — let's not quarrel."

Blissfully Sue's little smile flashed. I liked

her being able to achieve it. She said with a quiver of mirth in her voice: "I'm not quarreling. I'm only telling you what I think. I'll go and call Mrs. Byng if we're going to have tea. She won't want to miss it."

She turned quickly toward the stairway, and Lorn started to follow her, but I sprang ahead of him.

"I'll go along," I said, and we were on the stairs before anyone could stop us. I caught a green flicker from Grethe's eyes and heard her saying sharply something about Miss Tally's new acquaintance, and then we passed around the landing.

Sue was flushed, panting a little. But as we emerged onto the gallery and the somber gray light from the skylight fell upon her, I caught again that blessed little flicker of laughter in her eyes and in the corners of her mouth. She'd seen the collapse of a friendship, and she'd fought a vulgar and unscrupulous woman, and she'd faced her brother gallantly and victoriously on sheer nerve and courage, and she'd escaped the whole thing unscathed and able to smile.

We turned from the lounge well with its blank galleries and tiny group waiting down below — Marianne had answered the bell, and we could hear Grethe's crisp syllables directing her — and went along to Mrs. Byng's door.

Sue knocked. Mrs. Byng did not reply immediately, and I said in a low voice: "Don't knock again for a moment. I want to talk to you."

She glanced up and down the corridor. Away at the end a policeman's blue coat and tight trousers came into view. She said:

"Here. In my room."

She opened the door. I've never known why I remembered in that hurried moment to enter it first in order to look about — habit, I suppose — that hasty habit that arose suddenly and forcedly out of grim necessity. At any rate, that's what I did while she stood there in the corridor.

The room was empty. No one was about. It was only the quivering of the door to the massive wardrobe that caught my eye.

CHAPTER XVII

My first thought was: Sue is safe in the corridor, out of range of any revolver shots. From the second of Marcel's death on, I had ever that fear for Sue in my mind. I could guard her from many things, but not from a sudden spitting revolver.

Then I had flung across the room, my own revolver in one hand, and had my other hand on the latch of the wardrobe door. In that second the door had stopped its brief motion and was firm, though I'd heard no noise.

"Come out!" I said.

There was not a sound inside the wardrobe. I started to fling open the door, and the door resisted. I pulled and exerted all my force, and it still resisted. It was during that moment that I was conscious of hearing a voice in the hall, but only faintly.

The key was not in the lock. Was it possible that the thing was locked from the inside? I'd never known a wardrobe door to have an in-

side lock; it seemed an extraordinarily pur-
poseless thing; still, my acquaintance with
massive carved wardrobes had been slight, and
in any case, the important thing was that in
this case evidently the keyhole extended
through the door. At least, I could not get
it open, and there was someone inside the
wardrobe.

I glanced about for a chair or table I could
swing at the door. It was not a courageous
thing to do — unless, of course, whoever was
inside started shooting at me — for the first
sound of either a shot or a blow on the door
ought to bring help. And in that glance I saw
that Sue was gone. I dropped the chair and
was at the door. I was in the corridor. Sue
was not there.

The corridor stretched dim and empty and
mysterious. Even the prowling policeman was
gone. The thing in the wardrobe must wait.
Where was Sue?

I tried to call to her: Sue — Sue. I believe
I did call out, but my voice must have been
husky and strained, for although she was very
near — she said afterward that she did not
hear me, did not even know that there was
someone in the wardrobe.

I ran down the hall, past Mrs. Byng's door,
and into the intersecting corridor. A policeman was coming lazily from the back of the

main wing, and I tried to tell him what was wrong, but he could not understand me and neither would he follow me, and altogether I wasted a moment or two. And then, with him trying to detain me — and I daresay I looked rather mad — I ran back to the corridor that passed Sue's room.

And there was Sue in the very act of opening the door of Mrs. Byng's room and coming from it into the hall, talking contentedly with Mrs. Byng in the room beyond as she did so.

I stopped abruptly. I got my breath, and when I saw the policeman's puzzled eyes on my shaking hand that still clutched the revolver, I stuck it and the hand into my pocket. The relief was so great to see her there, not a hair on her head touched, that I felt actually a little dizzy and queer.

"There you are," I said breathlessly.

She looked at me unconcernedly then as I came nearer with more attention.

"Mrs. Byng opened her door and spoke to me — asked me to step in her room a moment." She saw, I suppose, something of my feeling in my face, for she added quickly and anxiously: "I thought you heard her speak. — What is it?"

"There's someone in the wardrobe in your room," I said rapidly, recovering myself. "Tell this policeman, will you?"

Her eyes darkened with fright as she spoke quickly to the man. His own face took on suddenly an acutely uneasy look, but he had the grace to turn rapidly toward her room, and we both pressed through the door. He glanced at the wardrobe and said something to me with a questioning gesture. Sue and Mrs. Byng were back of us, and I called over my shoulder for Sue not to come into the room. Then I crossed to the wardrobe and pulled at the door.

And it swung readily open.

There was no shot. There was no motion. There was no sound. There was only a sort of vacant space where Sue's gowns had been pushed back on their hangers.

Well, I knew what I'd seen. I knew the wardrobe door had not budged under my hand, though I'd pulled hard and it could not have been stuck. But the policeman either didn't believe me or didn't want to believe me, and in either case the effect would have been the same. He questioned me, through Sue, shook his head doubtfully at my replies, and still more doubtfully when Sue admitted that she hadn't seen the wardrobe door moving and he did not even seem to think it advisable to search for a possible intruder. He said, Sue told me, that it was no great wonder that we in the hotel saw things which were not. Which infuriated Sue and gave me a kind of grim amusement, for by that time I didn't see myself that there was much use starting a search for the person who had beat such a hasty and skilled retreat during those few moments when I'd been in the main corridor.

But I was interested to note that the wardrobe lock actually did go clear through into the inside, and *the key was on the inside.* Certainly no place for a key in a wardrobe. The policeman looked only a little puzzled when I pointed this out, and said, through Sue, that it made nothing. I said finally to Sue:

"You and Mrs. Byng go on down to the lounge to tea. I'll go with you to the stairway and watch until you are safe in the lounge. Promise me to stay near the others." It ran through my mind that it was in the very lounge, with all its commanding galleries and doors and the lift itself, that little Marcel had been killed. But I had been the only other in the room, then — I and the cockatoo. It would be safe for Sue with Lorn there, and her brother and Mrs. Byng and even Madame Grethe. Safer, perhaps, with Madame Grethe than without.

The policeman, relieved, vanished. Mrs. Byng, having apparently added several further layers under her outside clothing, stalked beside us, looking for all the world like a tall and very untidy bolster. As we emerged into the galleried space I glanced over it down into the lounge. Grethe and Francis and Lorn were still there, with Marianne's black hair shining near the tea table. Sue followed my glance and lifted her eyebrows inquiringly, and I shook my head. Yet it didn't seem possible that it had been Lovschiem in that wardrobe.

"Later," I said rapidly to Sue, referring to my wish to learn just what Francis had said and how we should go about it to recover — or seek to recover — the token, which was of course the pressing thing. We must recover it and have it ready for Francis's possible capitulation. She understood me, but she looked troubled. Mrs. Byng passed a little ahead of her at the top of the stairs, and in the rustle of that lady's numerous garments Sue leaned toward me and said quickly:

"Soon. It's important." She started to follow Mrs. Byng, looked back at me, hesitated, and then added with a kind of catch in her breath: "Be very careful."

Then she ran lightly down the stairs, and I watched her shining bright hair.

In another moment she was with the others in the lounge.

I went down the service stairs which led from beyond Marianne's room.

Paul, his egg-shaped bald head shining

without his tall white cap, and his little black shoebrush mustache looking very electric and alive, was peeling potatoes in the kitchen and talking vivaciously to a listening policeman. He did not see me; neither did the policeman, and I went past them into the narrow passage that led through the unused middle wing, mostly composed of a great banqueting hall with a waxed floor, but which looked as though it had not seen a dance or a banquet in at least a hundred years, and straight through it to the ground-floor storerooms of the north wing.

I knew that these storerooms had been searched, not once, but several times, by the police. I knew that their only connection with the floor above them was by way of that narrow passage and up the service stairway. I knew that they were practically unused and that neither the police nor Lorn had connected them in any way with the strange affairs that had taken place in and near my own room.

It was, I must admit, with some trepidation that I approached those empty, dark rooms. I walked lightly and cautiously, with my revolver openly in my hand. Fortunately, the shuttered windows gave some light, for I had no flashlight, and if there were electric lights I did not find any.

The rooms were large, dark, and silent. I

gave the first few rooms, which were bare and empty, only a glance and went farther along to the room which lay directly under the White Salon and under my own room. One large room stretched shadowily along what I judged was the full length of both the upper rooms, and here I managed to open a shutter.

The dim light permitted me to see more clearly the dusty cobwebby conglomeration of old furniture, barrels, boxes, a few old lamps, some outdated small tin bathtubs, and a great supply of wooden trestles and planks which I suppose made the banquet tables on the rare occasions when there was need for them. It was this room that I examined thoroughly, even though, as I say, I knew that both the police and Lorn had been over every square foot of the old hotel.

The ceilings, unfinished and with rough beams, were very low — a matter which not only accounted for the annoying little flight of steps in the corridor of the middle section, just before you turned into the north wing, but also, probably, for the fact that the rooms there were used only as storerooms. The pipes for the central heating which presumably supplied the upper floor of the north wing ran openly through these rooms, and I looked with some interest at the spot where they passed into the radiators of my own room and to the White Salon.

But it was among a group of barrels in a corner of the room that I found what I found; something that the police could easily have found had they known what I knew, and something Lorn would have immediately discovered had he given my statements any weight in his own mind. From the first Lorn's efforts and mine seemed a curious sort of example of too many cooks spoiling the broth. I was for a time held back from pursuing my own notions of inquiry by the feeling that I would do better to guard Sue as well as I might and leave the inquiry to Lorn — the detective, the professional, the man who knew what to do. And Lorn also from the first never felt, I am sure, that my own suspicions and contributions were of any particular value. In Lorn's mind I played an entirely different rôle than that of investigator.

Not that the thing I found was incriminating to anyone. But it did go far to prove a possibility that was in my mind. For it was an eiderdown, a new, little-used eiderdown covered with red silk, and it was wadded up and thrust into the bottom of one of the barrels which was then turned upside down.

For some time I stood there holding the thing in my hands, following a terse train of thoughts. Sue's abductor had been, she thought, slender — lean. Someone had used an eiderdown in that room very recently; I could tell it was recent from the way the wrinkles fell out of the thing, and the fact that it was still dry and fresh-smelling and not musty and dank. The odor of tobacco smoke very late one night had floated up through the hole in the ceiling where the heating pipes went through and which was so loosely and clumsily constructed that it was no great wonder my room above was always cold and draft-swept.

But could that strange sigh we had heard so clearly that very morning in the White Salon just above have come from such a distance? It had been a perfectly human sigh, and it had been the final impetus for my present search. The tobacco smoke had been not quite tangible; it might have been explained by only a strangely shifting current of air. But that sigh had been wholly tangible. Someone near us had sighed, and there was no one near.

I considered it thoughtfully, testing it in my mind against Lorn's scorn.

But I dared not linger too long in that empty, rapidly darkening storeroom. I had seen, I thought, what was to be seen. I didn't like the feeling of the place, with the dusk increasing in its corners and crawling steadily nearer me; and with the approach of night

the wind was beginning to whisper and murmur and wail around the old dark building.
And there was the urgent matter of Sue's
token.

I made my way (not without qualms, for
during my short stay in the cavernous storerooms twilight had fallen with the complete
suddenness of winter, and the whole place was
a hollow, black stillness with shadows that
seemed to move, but still couldn't have, and
my footsteps echoed against the old walls) —
back through the dreary banquet hall — less
dreary now that shadows clothed it, but also
less positively empty, and reached the lighted
kitchen door.

Paul's white cap was bending over a steaming kettle, and I stayed there for a moment,
actually relishing the light and the smell of
things cooking and the warmth.

For a moment the chef didn't see me, as
I was still in the little passage outside the
kitchen and outside the area of light. I think,
however, as I turned away he caught just a
glimpse of the motion, for I heard behind me
a kind of howl, something dropped and clat-
tered, and there was a sound of hissing steam.

The upper reaches of the place were again
deserted. Not a gendarme was to be seen in
the long, half-lit corridors. It was true, however, that the presence of the police there was

a rather silly and hysterical gesture. There were too few of them actually to police the rambling, wide-flung hotel, and, anyway, a dozen murders could have been committed under our and their noses without anyone being the wiser until it was too late. But then I have never understood French psychology. I have heard, of course, that they have the best police in the world, and it may be true. It *is* true that, owing to the peculiar conditions of the thing, none of us, not even Lorn, had full knowledge of their procedure, although Lorn learned a great deal of it.

It was not at all difficult to get into the priest's room. I would have liked learning more about the missing token from Sue before I searched that room, but as it developed it was not necessary, and I wanted, of course, to take advantage of the opportunity at once. I knew that the place had been searched by the police and by Lorn, in all likelihood, but it must have been a cursory search, for, as far as I could see, every effort was being made to maintain the *status quo,* so to speak, for the arrival of the detectives from Paris.

And anyway, while I had no doubt the coming detectives would have found and rooted out the secret of the thing, ordinarily it would have attracted little if any observation.

For I found the token.

Although it was in a large degree accident that I found it. I had approached the heavy window curtains and was drawing them back to get more light in the room when one of my fingers slid somehow through the thick chenille cords of the enormous tassel hanging from the red rope that controlled the curtains. And in slipping ran upon something that was not soft chenille and was not tassel.

I worked very cautiously, there in the gathering darkness, pulling at the thing carefully to extract it from the large bell-shaped tassel; and when I finally had the bit of folded paper in my hands I was obliged to turn on the light, which I'd avoided as long as possible in order to myself escape attention, so as to examine it.

It was a jaggedly triangular piece of paper — a thin piece with small print. And the instant my eyes fell on the print I knew I had found Sue's token. It was a torn half of the chapter about love in first Corinthians. As I glanced at the page I saw a word here, a word there, that made suddenly bits of old and familiar phrases and automatically finished themselves in my mind — "with the tongues of men and" — "tinkling cymbal" — "understand all mysteries," and toward the bottom, "face to face; now I know in part" — "and the greatest of these . . ."

That was why Sue had said what she'd said. Had said it so flatly, with such an effect of casualness, while she'd watched Francis so carefully.

And — it recurred to me with significant force — Francis had not finished her quotation. Had looked faintly puzzled and baffled. Had, so far as I could see, failed entirely to catch its meaning.

The token itself surprised me, for somehow I had expected it to be some kind of jewelry — I don't know why. It was, however, remarkably efficacious — simple, easily hidden and preserved, and practically impossible for anyone who discovered its secret to duplicate owing to the necessity for duplicating not only the edition of the Bible from which the leaf had been torn, but the jagged edge where it was torn and with whose words the matching half in Francis's possession must exactly coincide.

There was something pathetic about the little scrap of paper — something that drew me to Sue's father; I could see, somehow, a silent man, silent and wounded and bewildered, choosing, perhaps unconsciously, the chapter about love for its symbolism — hoping his two children would eventually be brought together by it.

But I had no time, then, to speculate on

the tragedy of the lives from which had grown with such grim logic this other tragedy of a different nature. For the implications of Francis's refusal to recognize Sue's one offer at compromise were important. He had either failed to recognize it purposely, not desiring to do so, thus tacitly conceding Sue's claim in the presence of witnesses. Or — he had not known it for what it was.

Either alternative was significant. That, then, had been what Sue wanted to tell me — wanted to tell me soon. She had trapped Francis, and doubtless she had drawn the same conclusions from it that I had.

And there was Lorn's curious warning about his employer — inexplicable until now. I must see Lorn at once; I must force him to tell me what he had meant. And I must tell Sue that her token was safe.

My back had been, foolishly, turned to the door. I don't know whether it was some sound or rustle that touched a little tocsin of warning in my subconsciousness, or whether it was only that strange age-old instinct that tells us when eyes are watching us. At any rate, I was suddenly aware of it, and I whirled and clutched for Lorn's revolver. The door which I had closed was open.

It was open and gently moving and revealing about six decreasing inches of blackness.

I heard nothing. I saw nothing except that decreasing area of blank dim corridor. I flung toward it and was in the corridor, but there was nothing but dim walls and blank doors to be seen. I had not the faintest notion where to start looking for that ghostly observer, and I was suddenly acutely aware that I was outlined quite sharply against the light streaming from the priest's room back of me.

I went back into the room, closing the door firmly. I returned to the position where I'd examined the scrap of paper and saw with some dismay that the door itself was completely visible to me from a mirror opposite. I, then, and the thing I'd held in my hands had been clearly visible from the door.

After a moment I folded away the token — it rolled up and slid into the hollow of my pencil (the little cylindrical chamber where lead is stored) very easily — turned out the light, and let myself cautiously into the corridor. It was not an altogether comfortable situation. Clearly it behooved me to walk with care.

All this had taken time — more time than I realized until I reached unmolested (although something kept me glancing back over my shoulder) the gallery looking down into the lounge. Sue, to my great relief, was still there, and Mrs. Byng and Lovschiem and the cockatoo. Mrs. Byng was knitting furiously, her eyebrows going up and down at a terrifying rate, Sue was looking rather tired and pale, and her eyes kept going toward the stairway, and Lovschiem was smoking, his cigarette was in a long amber holder that looked strange and slender in his fat hands, his jewels glittered and winked in the light, and his face glistened, and he stared at the floor as if there were a picture on those blank tiles that frightened him.

Only the cockatoo was devilishly unperturbed; he was perched coolly among the débris on the tea table, dropping his head to drink the residue of tea from the various cups, and cocking his head on one side and smacking loudly and with the air of a connoisseur following each taste. As I looked, his shoe-button eyes discovered a cake left on somebody's plate. He slid toward it, gathered it greedily into one scraggly gray claw, and lifted it to his beak for a highly approving bite and cluck. Mrs. Byng said, "Drat the bird," in a voice that was tinged with a kind of belligerent pride, and Pucci clucked again, looked up and saw me, and began to flap his wings fiercely and chatter and behave altogether as if he were convinced that I was about to take his cake away from him. Mrs. Byng, and of course Sue and Lovschiem, looked up at once. But I only saw Sue and the glad look that leaped to her eyes as she saw me, and I thought she'd been anxious about me.

I nodded and then turned away from the railing as I heard someone walking along the corridor behind me.

Lorn's brown figure loomed out of the dimness.

"Well," he said. "Where have you been? You weren't in your room."

"You are the very man I want to see," I said. Mutually conscious that those in the lounge below could, in all probability, hear every word, we walked farther back along the corridor. I said in a low voice:

"Why did you warn me about Tally?"

He hesitated, and looked uneasily up and down the dim length of corridors with their occasional faint glints and intersecting lanes.

"I told you I could not yet explain."

"You mean it's something you aren't sure about? That you want to prove first?"

"Perhaps."

"And you still refuse to tell?"

"I still refuse." He spoke smoothly enough, still looking uneasily over my shoulder as if afraid we might be overheard. Then his glance shifted to meet mine and suddenly he stepped backward. "Why — what's wrong?" he said.

"You are going too far," I said. "But —

it doesn't matter. I'll tell you. You aren't sure of Francis Tally."

That time the faint scorn he always felt for me showed rather clearly in his face, even in the dim light.

"I should think that would be obvious," he said coldly.

"It is. Perfectly. But it isn't only that you think Francis Tally may not be square. It is that you aren't sure the man is Francis Tally."

He said nothing. He'd moved his head, and his face was now in the shadow.

"Hurry up. Answer yes or no. Is that man Francis Tally?"

There was another pause. All around us loomed the menacing, secretive, dark rooms. There was not a sound, not a breath of life from any of those black caverns surrounding us. Presently Lorn said quietly:

"I don't know."

Of all the things I had expected, that reply was the last one. It took me completely by surprise, and, as always, Lorn's quietness, his refusal to be stirred by my anger and impatience, his forgiving way of meeting my outbursts, made me feel vaguely ashamed, as if I were ungrateful to the man who, after all, had rescued me when I needed rescuing pretty badly.

I said rather feebly: "What do you mean

by that? He's your employer."

"I know," said Lorn. "And I don't mind telling you that his coming has worried me considerably. You see —" his voice sank; it was not too clear and audible to me, and I'm sure no one could have overheard him — "you see — it isn't a matter of a resemblance — a double. That kind of thing simply doesn't occur. But the fact is that, though I've seen Francis Tally, I've — well, I've not seen him, so to speak."

"What do you — Go on."

"Don't interrupt me, please," said Lorn crankily. "It's very simple. You see, when he came to consult me he'd just had a slight accident — had slipped on a wet street in traffic and got involved somehow with a taxicab and flying glass. It wasn't serious, he told me, but his face was heavily bandaged. At the time I thought nothing of it — and even if I had suspected it was only a dodge to keep me from seeing his face, I'd have thought little of it. People often are notional that way — I see it in my profession. That was, of course, fully six months ago. And I've not seen him since."

"Where was that meeting?"

"In New York."

"Was he the same general build as this man?"

"Of course," said Lorn impatiently. "Do

you think I haven't tried every test? Francis Tally is mediumly tall and slender — nondescript brownish hair, no spectacles, but he couldn't wear spectacles over his bandages. I couldn't see his mouth clearly, and the bandages muffled his speech a little. He even wore gloves — oh, yes, I'm willing to admit that he may have deliberately got himself up to give me no definite way of identifying him again. But whatever was the purpose, the fact remains that I can't tell whether this man is Francis Tally or not."

"There was a purpose back of it."

"Perhaps. He is naturally suspicious. Crafty. His letter would have told you that."

"But this man recognized you. Spoke first. Called you by name."

The scorn in Lorn's gaze made itself felt though he was still in the shadow.

"Have you failed to consider a possible connection between the Lovschiems and this man? Of their informing him carefully of everything they have managed to discover? In case — of course — he is actually not Francis Tally?"

"No —" I said slowly. "No — I've not failed to do that." Several things returned to me. Grethe's sudden activity after that period of curiously patient, catlike waiting; the way she'd looked at the newcomer when he floundered into the question of whether or not the Lovschiems had known of the token and the peculiar conditions of Sue's inheritance; the way his eyes had sought hers there in the lounge — had it been for guidance? Then I remembered the railway time-table and Lovschiem's covering it so guiltily from my gaze — guiltily when there was, so far as I would otherwise have known, no need for guilt.

Briefly I told Lorn of the time-table; he nodded thoughtfully over it, and he too, he agreed, had noted the curious effect the man called Francis Tally gave of looking to Grethe for help.

"The thing to do," said Lorn, "as I see it, is simply to sit tight until the Paris detectives come. They'll make an end to things in a hurry. I've done what I could," he said, as probably I looked, as I certainly felt, impatient with his failure thus far, "and perhaps I will still be able to accomplish something. I've not, I might say, given up hope."

"But, Miss Tally —" I said.

"We'll advise her to hang on to her token, take no chances, and wait for the detectives. In the meantime —" He paused, and then continued: "I may as well tell you, Sundean, that I've hit on a rather well-marked trail — not perhaps too well marked. Still, I think —" He paused again and finally said in a quiet way that, coming from the conservative, slow-acting Lorn, had quite the effect of a bomb — "I think I know what the motive power is."

"You mean," I cried excitedly, forcing him for once to a definite statement, "the murderer?"

He had turned his face again, and I could see his half-pained, half-reluctant expression. But he said quietly, "Yes.

"Don't ask me any more now, Sundean. And I must go. Tell Miss Tally what I've told you, will you?"

We walked together to the stairway. He went down, met Mrs. Byng and Sue on the landing, and as he stepped aside to let them pass gave me a meaning look. I watched, over the gallery railing, curious to see where he was going. He crossed the lounge and entered the lobby. At the desk I saw Lovschiem's heavy black bulk. Lorn paused and spoke to Lovschiem. Yet — of course, that did not mean that Lovschiem was, after all, the murderer.

There wasn't a scrap of evidence against him.

I turned to meet Sue and Mrs. Byng.

"I suppose," Mrs. Byng was shouting, "that we must eat dinner in this den of perdition. But don't worry, darling." She meant, of course, Sue, though at the moment she happened to be fixing me with a very penetrative look, and the endearing term gave me a swift impulse to retire with expedition. "Don't worry. I've a nephew in the War Department, and I shall cable at once. I should have cabled earlier had I not been suffering from a crisis of nerves. Such useful phrases the French have; crisis of nerves. That's exactly what it is, you know." She moved ahead of us in the narrow corridor, walking with a strange stiffness and lack of freedom brought on probably by her entangling garments.

Sue dropped back a little with me, and under the continued boom of Mrs. Byng's voice as she obliged with some of the more intimate details of her recent attack, I asked to see Francis's letter again. "Envelope and all," I said. "As soon as possible."

She nodded. "I'll get it."

Mrs. Byng, still talking, stopped in her own room, closed the door, and I heard her lock it. I went into Sue's room with her, which was this time empty, and watched while she rummaged in a drawer and brought out the letter. With Francis's arrival I suppose she no longer thought it necessary to carry it herself. She handed me the square white envelope. I took it and moved under the light to look at the address more closely.

"That light is very dim," said Sue. "I'll turn on this one over the table. Not that it's much better. They hate to waste voltage here."

She moved to the door; I heard it close and waited, staring at the envelope in my hand and noting the writing and seal and wrinkled appearance of it, for the little click of the light switch.

It did not come.

I heard her light footsteps behind me, and the bottom dropped out of the world.

"Put up your hands," she said coldly and crisply.

I felt the cold pressure of a revolver against my neck.

"I mean it," she repeated in a hard voice I'd never heard before. "Put up your hands."

CHAPTER XVIII

It was impossible to obey. In fact, and in spite of that ominous cold touch on my neck, I believe I was too numb with shock to lift my hands.

And my momentary inability to do so, as well as my shocked tardiness in grasping the situation, was very nearly fatal. I am convinced that I was never nearer death in my life than during that queer cold moment of utter paralysis of thought and motion.

Then slowly I turned. The girl backed away so that she still held me in range of that small revolver. And my heart began to function again. The girl was not Sue Tally — or rather she was not the girl I knew as Sue Tally.

For when I said slowly: "Who are you?" she replied:

"I am Sue Tally. I've told you twice to put up your hands. This gun is loaded, and I'm a good shot."

I don't remember actually thinking that if

she had been intending to pull that small trigger she would have done so when I turned toward her, but I suppose some such thought flashed through my head. I stood there looking at her. She was of the same general height and build as Sue but lacked Sue's fineness of wrist and ankle and delicacy of proportion. She was fair, too, and wore her hair like Sue's, only it was coarser and did not have the shining vitality that Sue's hair had. She was even dressed in a black velvet coat, long and tight-fitting to the waist, with a full skirt flaring below her hips. But she did not resemble Sue in the least. A general written description of height, weight, and coloring might have applied to them both, but they were not at all alike.

Then a horrified question crashed upon me. Where was Sue? What had happened? Where had she gone?

I must get rid of this girl: I must get that gun away from her: I must find Sue. There was no time to be lost, but I must proceed carefully.

"You don't want to shoot me," I said. "It won't do you any good. There are too many gendarmes in the place for you to escape."

"They are drinking in the kitchen. Paul likes having them there." She spoke a little contemptuously, but her eyes did not waver from mine. They were rather hard, knowing eyes, and her young face showed curiously sharp lines across the forehead and around the full mouth.

"I am Sue Tally," she reiterated, "and I want the paper you took from the priest's room a short time ago. Don't deny it, for I saw you. That paper belongs to me."

"So you are Sue Tally," I said thoughtfully. "I had suspected your presence for some time. Can't we sit down and talk this over more amicably? I'm only an innocent bystander, you know, caught in the hotel at the beginning of the affair and not permitted to go away."

She did not relax her hold on the revolver and eyed me suspiciously. I went on:

"Where have they been keeping you all this time? Hasn't it grown a little tiresome, dodging the police, hiding here and there?"

She bit her lip. I thought suddenly that there was something at the same time shrewd and stupid about her face.

She said: "It was easy enough. All but those nights in the storeroom. Come, give me the paper."

So it was she in the storeroom; I had not expected that, even though I had guessed that she was about somewhere, waiting to carry out her rôle in the conspiracy. But did her sudden appearance and announcement that she was Sue Tally mean that, after all, Francis Tally *was* Francis Tally and a meeting of the two was to be arranged? Or was it merely an expediency to get the token from me? And in the meantime — where was Sue?

"In the storeroom," I repeated sympathetically. "You poor girl. It must have been most uncomfortable. The smoke from your cigarettes drifted up to me one night. And I heard you a time or two — thought you were a ghost. Or mice. But where have you been otherwise? Surely not wandering about this hotel — someone would have seen you."

"Oh, it wasn't difficult to stay out of people's way. Anyway, at a distance I look rather like — this other girl. I had this coat made like hers on purpose. Of course, I've not been in the hotel all the time. I've been staying at Paul's — the cook's house. Very dull there — but I had no trouble getting into the hotel when I wished. Paul saw to that."

"Oh, so you've been staying at Paul's." I thought the girl had been bored and dull; she was probably not averse to talking to someone. Her hand did not waver with the revolver, but she was looking rather approvingly at me. "The Lovschiems haven't been treating you very well, have they?"

It was a lucky thing to say.

"No," she flashed. "They forget how important I am to them —" She checked herself quickly, but it was too late. I pretended to take no notice of the tacit admission. So I had been right about the Lovschiems from the beginning. And this was their substitute. I said:

"I've seen you before, you know."

"When?" she said incredulously.

"Looking from the third-story window — I suppose you were lodged there then — the night of the first murder."

She bit her lip again, and to my astonishment and intense discomfort tears came welling up into her too-large eyes. I should have preferred her to remain hard and shrewd.

"And Mrs. Byng saw you too — when you turned out the hotel lights. I suppose that was after Madame Lovschiem had said you must hide from the police who were coming."

She nodded without, I think, realizing what she was doing.

"They didn't tell me it would be like this," she said sullenly, the tears still hanging there in her eyes. "They ought to have told me."

Possibly I ought to feel a decent compunction for my not too diplomatic behavior. But I didn't — either then or thereafter. I was, even, too hurried for finesse. I said with sympathy: "You poor girl. They've treated you very badly, haven't they?" And I looked at her with crass admiration and murmured:

"So beautiful —"

As I said, she was fundamentally stupid.

Her eyes stopped looking faintly like oysters and strayed to the mirror. The second's wavering gave me the chance, and I sprang toward her and seized her arm, and then, with more difficulty, for she was strong, wrenched the revolver out of her hand. The danger had been that she would press the trigger and bring the Lovschiems to the spot. But in a second or two that danger was past, and I had the revolver, and she was standing there staring at me resentfully.

"You are ill-fitted for this," I said. "I know who you are — or rather what your purpose is here, of course. I suppose they promised you a lot of money to impersonate Miss Tally later on."

She looked at me sullenly. She said with a touch of defiant triumph:

"I've seen you, too, when you didn't know it. I followed you all over the hotel yesterday afternoon, and you didn't know it. But you nearly caught me there at the door of 34."

It was this girl, then, not the priest.

There were a hundred things I wanted to ask her then and there. But I dared not take the time. I must secure the girl some place — and find Sue. Find Sue. I shoved the letter I still held crumpled in one hand into my pocket and said:

"What have they done with Miss Tally?"

"Don't you wish you knew?" she said with more spirit than she'd yet displayed.

"I suppose you know that you are apt to be arraigned as an accessory before the fact in the coming murder trial — which is almost as serious as murder?"

"Arraigned?" she said. "Oh, they said they'd get me off."

"Who? The Lovschiems?"

She nodded.

"Well, they can't do it. Tell me, was it Lovschiem who killed Stravsky and Marcel and the priest?"

A startling change came over her face; she was no longer vacantly pretty, stupid, with a few bits of shrewdness pounded into her by the life she'd led. Her forehead and hideously thin eyebrows came down over eyes that shone with hate, and she was all at once powerful and vital. She said: "If it was Lovschiem, I'll kill him, and he knows it."

I said slowly: "So it was Stravsky. He was your connection —"

"Don't speak of him," she cried. "He was a man. Lovschiem's a jellyfish." She brooded a moment. "Prove to me it was Lovschiem, and I'll kill him. I'll kill him."

"Look here," I said, feeling rather as if I

had unleashed a revengeful panther. "Tell me where they've got Miss Tally, and I'll — if I can — I'll help you out of this. There's no use your staying on the Lovschiems' side of the fence. They'll only use you to pluck their chestnuts out of the fire."

She considered this, and I think I held my breath.

"You may be right," she said finally, giving me a black look. "But I don't know. They promised me a lot of money."

"What good will money do you? — Stravsky — can't be brought back."

It was not as brutal as I thought it might be. Clearly here was no gorgeous, indefeatable *"Mon Homme"* affair. She had been Stravsky's, and she'd grieved for him, and she wanted revenge. But still, she was fully aware that life was still to be lived, and that money was not a bad thing. She said again:

"They promised me a lot of money."

I dared not wait. I dared not tempt her with the necessary care.

"What's your name?"

She looked at me suspiciously and said stubbornly: "Sue Tally."

"Oh, nonsense. I know all about you. Come, what's your name?"

"Elise." I think she was rather accustomed to being beaten in life's struggles, for she said it dully. I felt, though I shouldn't have done, a gleam of pity for her.

"Tell me at once where they've got Miss Tally. Hurry up."

Probably I had strengthened what must have been a growing distrust of the Lovschiems; she had a primitive sort of mind, and my failure to press the matter went far toward convincing her that I was speaking the truth. Which fact gave a curious sidelight on her life. She said, watching me:

"She's in the White Salon, I suppose. It's the only hiding place. I was there. Grethe and Lovschiem pushed me, made me hide — *that* night."

Marcel's words flashed over me; while it was dark there in the corridor, he'd heard someone moving near him. And Elise said, "Lovschiem"; Lovschiem, then, was not the man in the courtyard. I said:

"What do you mean? Quick."

She hesitated. "In the fireplace. You won't see it unless you look for it. It's just an old cupboard up above the ledge. I was there this morning when you found the priest."

"What! Did you know the body was there?"

Fear leaped into her eyes again.

"No! No! I swear it!" Her words burst out in a rapid flood. "I was in the north wing, and I heard you and Sue Tally coming, and

I hid in the White Salon. First I was going to get behind a curtain — that's when I dropped my handkerchief — but to be safer I hid in the fireplace. Just got under the screen and pulled it down and waited. You'll see the place. But you and that girl talked and talked, and I was tired, and you heard me take a long breath and —"

"How did you — It doesn't matter." I checked my inquiry. No time. No time. But she caught it.

"How did I get away? While you and that girl were calling the police. I was scared. I didn't know what had happened, but it was simple to run along the north corridor and get away. You were on the stairway, and you had eyes for nothing but —"

I cut into her swift, confused explanations.

"Come with me."

She shrank back.

"Oh, no — not to the White Salon. They'll kill me, too."

I dared not wait. I dared not let her go, for there were too many things she could tell me. And I dared not take time to convince her.

"No, I'm not taking you there. Just to a room down the hall. Come. You'll be safe. Open the door cautiously and glance out into the corridor. Hurry up. Do as I say. Is there anyone about?"

She looked and shook her head.

"Come, then."

I took her to Mrs. Byng's room. She did not attempt either to cry out or to escape.

When Mrs. Byng opened the door, I simply thrust the girl inside. I said:

"I can't explain. Keep this girl here. Don't let her call anyone. Do you know how to shoot?"

Mrs. Byng was superb. She lifted her nose, gave a delighted sniff, and said:

"Give me the gun."

I wanted help, but dared take no longer. It had been a tedious business getting the information I'd had to have out of Elise. I ran through the corridors, hoping at every turn for the sight of a gendarme. There was none.

The north-wing corridor was as ever cold and wind-swept and dark, and the lights across the hurrying shadows in the court glittered only faintly, and I saw no one in the lobby.

Then I was at the door of the White Salon. There was no faint penciling of light below the door. Perhaps Elise had lied to me. I laid a cautious hand on the door knob, and holding my revolver before me tried to peer into the darkness of the room.

There was no sound, and it was entirely black.

I slipped quickly through the door, more

than expecting flashes of spitting fire to greet my momentary silhouette against the wavering light from the court. But there was none. Gradually I became convinced that the room was empty. She had lied, then; the story about the fireplace was not true. But somehow it had sounded true.

I went to it. My eyes were becoming accustomed to the dark, but I longed for some kind of light. Still, perhaps it would be better to work in the dark, if Sue were actually in some forgotten closet there near the fireplace.

But I could see no closet. And Elise had said in the fireplace. It sounded impossible now, facing that dim expanse that showed me faintly only a glittering mirror hanging above — a mirror which in the twilight looked like a black sea on a cloudy night — and below it the dim outline of hearth and mantel and rolling metal fire screen.

"Sue," I whispered in the silence. "Sue."

There was a little rustle.

It was a rustle that came from inside the wall somewhere, and it was about the height of my head. It was repeated; a kind of tap.

"How can I get to you?" I spoke in as low a voice as I thought would be clear.

There was no answer except that repeated rustle.

I bent over and rolled up the fire screen.

It rolled quite silently. I groped about with my hands into the space. There was nothing but tiles and concrete and cold iron fire dogs. The space, however, seemed very large. I ducked under the mantel breast.

A man could stand there easily, for I lifted my head with much caution, and it encountered nothing. There was that rustle again; closer now and clearer. The girl had said above the ledge. I groped into the darkness, met cold wall — and a ledge. It was quite high and was set in the wall that slanted inward on the right side of the old fireplace. And my groping hand suddenly encountered a little foot — two feet bound together at the ankles — and then two hands, bound also, trying to find me.

It was Sue.

I don't remember much of my whispered directions, and her slipping and sliding down until I had her in my arms and outside the cramped well in which I had stood and into the room, and the way I worked to get first the towel from her face and then the knots that held her little hands and her feet bound. But I got them off, and she stayed there in my arms.

She said, gasping, that she wasn't hurt, but she clung to me, and I could feel her heart beating, and her breath, and the warmth of her hair against my mouth.

I don't even remember what I said except that I kept fearing she was hurt, and she said again and again that she wasn't. Then all at once I realized that we must get out of the ill-omened room. I took her cautiously out of the White Salon and through the intervening corridor — no one saw us — into my room next door. They wouldn't think of looking for her so near the place where they'd left her. I put her in a chair — she was trembling with cold and with the reaction of released terror.

She was in the chair beside me, and I knelt and lit a fire, and the flames presently lit the room with dancing, flickering lights which touched her dear gold head and reflected themselves mysteriously in her eyes.

It was too dangerous to turn on the light just then, for I didn't want to call the Lovschiems' attention to that wing. So I made a quick circuit of the room and convinced myself that it was empty, and I propped a chair against the door to guard it against entry, and I took my heavy flannel dressing gown and put it around Sue, and, because I couldn't help it, there with my arms so close around her, I took her wholly into them and held her, and I kissed her and kissed her and was never so happy in my life.

And I had to stop and look at her wrists with red marks against the white and assure myself that she actually hadn't been hurt, and then kiss her wrists and her warm palms, and then hold her to me again tight in my arms with her dear little head in the curve of my shoulder and my cheek against hers.

The fire threw glancing lights and shadows. It was the sharp crackle of one of the heating logs that, crazily, reminded me of the small sharp spitting of a revolver and recalled me sternly to the business at hand.

Another picture that I remember very vividly out of that mêlée of pictures I took away with me was one of Sue sitting, wrapped in the dark red dressing gown, her bright hair tousled, and the flickering light throwing one side of her face in light and one in shadow, so that I saw the glow of her eyes and the way one cheek was touched with soft gold light.

She told me briefly how the Lovschiems had been there in the corridor beside her room. It had been so simple that I felt a kind of cold horror hearing it. She'd gone to turn on the light, and I'd thought she was safe — there — only ten feet or so from me. But as she was standing there in the door he — Lovschiem — had simply clapped his fat hand over her mouth and lifted her into the corridor and some woman flashed inside the room very swiftly and silently, and then the door closed, and Grethe whispered sharply that if Sue screamed they'd kill Sundean. The woman who'd gone into Sue's room had a revolver and would kill him.

So, said Sue, looking away from me, she hadn't screamed.

She let them take her to the White Salon and bind her hands and feet and put the towel around her mouth, and then Lovschiem had lifted her up on the ledge where there was a sort of space — like an old cupboard set there in the wall — and had told her they wouldn't hurt her if she made no sound.

Grethe had said, added Sue, that she was quite safe there, for no one would dream of the hiding place; even when you pulled up the fire screen and looked, there was only blank wall on both sides leading directly back to the fireplace proper and the chimney. The most you would think would be that the chimney was very far back from the hearth and that it was a very deep and wide wall.

I wondered what the Lovschiems, coming boldly out in the open as they were, had planned to do with Sue once they had accomplished their purpose.

"I have the token," I said rapidly. "It was hidden in the priest's room. It was accident that I found it. But I have it."

"You have —" She paused. "But how did

you know what it was? It can't be — you don't know."

"It was easy enough to guess, once I came upon it." She watched me draw out the pencil and unroll the small thin paper. I held it toward her, and she gave a little gasp and then bent nearer the fire so she could see the printed words more clearly.

"Why — you —" It was a sort of gasp. She was looking incredulously at the broken words.

"What is it?"

"This — this is the token — but it is not my half. It is my brother's half."

"Then your brother —"

She leaped where I was trying to reason.

"The priest — was my brother. The priest was Francis!" A look of horror and a kind of wondering blankness came into her face. "He was Francis. I'm sure of it. He came to see for himself. Without letting anyone know of it. He came secretly. Even Lorn did not know."

"How can you be sure?"

There was a queer kind of impatience in the look she sent me. "Oh, I know!" she said briefly. "It would be so like him. I had thought perhaps he would do some such thing; I even feared when I saw the dead man — the one on the landing, Stravsky — I even feared he might be Francis. But I could discover no resemblance at all to my mother or what I remembered of my father. But somehow — the priest seemed — Oh, I didn't dream *he* was Francis. The beard and all would have changed him. He had been educated in a church school — and well educated. He knew how to manage the — disguise. How and what to do." Her voice dropped into brooding, and presently she said, staring somberly into the flames: "He must have been like my mother." She drew a long shuddering breath.

"Don't," I said, wishing I had the gift of words. "Don't. You couldn't have helped it. Don't grieve. He — it's harsh but it's true — he was the cause of it all."

"I can't grieve for him," she said soberly. "I will later, I suppose — later, when I think how happy it might have been. Not now."

After a helpless moment I said: "But what of your own half? You'll be obliged to prove yourself to his lawyer — there'll be arrangements. I think I'd better cable the lawyer immediately."

She nodded.

"If," I added, "you are quite sure. You've only this to go on, you know." I motioned toward the small triangle of paper.

"Oh, I knew the man calling himself Francis Tally was not my brother. I knew that when he failed to catch the line I gave him. That was what I wanted to tell you. But, of course, you are right — we must prove Francis — that the priest was Francis — somehow. Yes, we'll cable at once."

"Then this man calling himself Francis Tally must be actually in conspiracy with the Lovschiems. Also this charming substitute they've kept in waiting."

"Substitute?" said Sue, roused. "They have the substitute already?"

I explained.

"And the point is," I finished, "we've got to hurry." They'd killed her brother — when they discovered their present plan had failed they would have some new plan for presenting Elise as Sue — with the brother gone it only doubled their gain from success. And any plan now was dangerous for Sue. Ten millions instead of five. I said:

"I see — Elise was sent to get the token I'd found; they must have your piece of the page; therefore, when she saw me with the priest's — Francis's — the other half in my hands, they jumped at the chance to give it to the man called Francis Tally so that he, in turn, might use it to convince you. — No, that's wrong. If they've got your token, they don't need Francis's —"

She nodded again, watching me, her eyes

bright in the flaring light of the fire.

"It doesn't click." I rose. "If they hadn't your own piece, it would. But since they've already got your half of the page, why should they trouble to convince you that this man is your brother? I'm going to call one of the policemen to stay here with you. Then I'm going to find Lorn —"

"Lorn should have known the priest was Francis!" she cried.

"He didn't. He wasn't sure about this new-comer for the same reason." I explained that to her, too, very briefly. "And then, if you can get hold of Marianne, I want you to question her. Ring for her and question her. I'm convinced she knows something; I have a faint hope that Marcel told her what he had seen. At any rate, question her, will you? Get everything you can out of her. But don't leave the policeman or let him leave you. I hate letting you out of my sight, but I've got to find Lorn."

I went to the door which led to the winding stairway and thus to the courtyard. Under the swaying light of the arch stood one of our guard, and, after making sure I was unobserved, I called and beckoned to him, and once in my room he seemed to understand very sensibly what was wanted.

I left Sue talking rather cautiously with him.

I did not like leaving her, even under that sensible and stalwart guard, but I thought that so long as the Lovschiems remained ignorant of her escape, things might be safe.

The corridors were as usual deserted. It was at the very door of Lorn's room that I met Grethe. She slid rather than walked out of it, closed it silently, and saw me.

CHAPTER XIX

It was the only time I ever saw fear in the woman's eyes, and that was for only an instant. Then one white hand went upward in a gracefully slow motion to her head; she tucked in a straying red wisp of hair and patted it nonchalantly, and she recovered her composure and said:

"Well?" and as I did not reply, for I was thinking of what they'd done to Sue and, which was worse, what they might have done but for Elise's stupidity — as I did not reply she leaned nearer me and slid one smooth soft arm through mine and said: "Are you looking for me?"

I said grimly: "I'm looking for Lorn! What were you doing in his room?"

It had flashed across me that perhaps they had decided to dispose of Lorn; perhaps they had discovered that he was, or thought he was, on the verge of discovering the murderer. And with this knowledge threatening them so desperately — Without waiting for her reply I thrust her aside and flung open the door and looked about. The room was empty, although it looked singularly untidy. Madame Grethe was smiling a little; her green eyes were narrow and were shining knowingly.

"Well?" she said again, her voice trailing upward.

"Where's Lorn?"

"Downstairs, I believe," she said coolly enough. "He was in the lobby with Lovschiem a few moments ago."

In the lobby.

I left her there — she watched me go with a curious look in her shining eyes, but said nothing.

My footsteps thudded on the stairs and echoed on the bare cold tiles of the lobby. It was thus, I suppose, that Lorn heard my approach. I was nearing the door to the lobby when I heard his voice, taut and sharp and strange:

"Sundean! Sundean! Hurry!"

I ran the last few steps.

They were both in the lobby — Lovschiem and Lorn. And Lorn had a gun in his hand, and it was trained straight at Lovschiem's fat paunch, and Lovschiem was standing there just beside the desk with his jeweled hands lifted high in the air and an expression of acute anxiety and fear and astonishment mingled in the strangest way in his glistening dark face.

"You've got the revolver?"

I had it in my hand.

"Yes."

"Keep this man here while I get the police. Don't hesitate to shoot. He's the murderer."

"*Lovschiem?*"

"Yes. I've known it for some time, but I've got the proof now. From Marianne."

Lovschiem's slack mouth moved and mumbled something and then was quickly silent again as Lorn's revolver quivered.

I said: "What is it?"

"His connection with Stravsky. She, the maid, heard them talking the night Stravsky was killed. They were in the court. She heard — steady, there, Lovschiem! — she heard Stravsky promise to get something for Lovschiem. Lovschiem warned Stravsky to make no mistake this time. The thing was, of course, Miss Tally's token."

Again a kind of mumble arose back of Lovschiem's loose mouth, and again Lorn's revolver quivered and the mumble ceased.

"Stravsky said he'd give it to Lovschiem *mañana*. Tomorrow. You know you are guilty, Lovschiem. Guilty, and you'll die for it. I'll call the police. Don't let him go, Sundean. Shoot to kill."

The door to the court whipped open, and cold air swept the lobby, and the door closed itself, and Lovschiem's terrified eyes shifted to me. This time the mumble was half coherent.

"I didn't — I'm not — I didn't —"

"What's all this?" It was Grethe from the lounge. Fortunately I had moved away from the door, so she did not approach from behind me.

"They say I murdered them. They say I killed —" Lovschiem's fat, beringed hands were shaking and trembling there in the air.

"Stop that," I said sharply to Grethe, and she stopped her stealthy retreat. "Come back here. Stand over there."

She gave me a still look but obeyed. Her eyes were no longer secretly aware, and her broad hands gripped the edge of the desk. But she said calmly:

"You'd as well not make a move, Lovschiem. I think our friend is rather likely to shoot us."

It was very still in the small lobby while our eyes met and locked. Very still except for the small rustle of the cockatoo scrambling from his perch to the desk. From the corner of my eyes I could see him sidle toward his mistress.

She did not move or shift her eyes from

mine as the bird caught her green sleeve and pulled himself clumsily in a curious kind of hand-over-hand movement to her shoulder. She was, probably, scarcely conscious of the bird clinging there, although his claws must have penetrated the silk and scratched the white shoulder beneath.

Pucci chuckled hoarsely and laid his wide bill alongside his mistress's warm red hair, and the wind howled outside, and the glycines danced, and blue shadows fled across the court.

But there was something wrong — something that didn't add — some quantity that was not right.

Pucci was pushing his bill into the red hair. He was pushing and pushing — no! He was pulling. He was pulling at something that was thin and white and folded and that finally came entirely from the mass of red hair. It was a thin folded paper. A paper of unmistakable thinness.

Madame Grethe heard suddenly some small rustle, and she moved her head and cried, "Pucci!" in a strangled voice.

I dropped my hand with the gun.

"Put down your hands, Lovschiem. Give me that paper, madame."

She did so. She did not hesitate, as I had known she would not. She took it gently and carefully from Pucci and put it in my hand.

The paper was what I thought it was. Lovschiem had still not moved, and I repeated:

"Put down your hands, Lovschiem. You didn't kill them. I know now."

"What — what —"

Grethe was leaning against the desk in her only display of weakness. She said: "Be still. There's no use talking. He knows."

A commotion of footsteps and voices arose outside, and the door was flung open and Lorn was there. Even in that hurried instant I was conscious of the singular look he gave us: it held surprise and a kind of disappointment and at the same time decision. Then he called something over his shoulder in sharp French, and the following policemen were in the lobby, too. Lorn pointed at me and said something very sharp, and Grethe said, "Ooh —" — like a scream, and the police fell upon me, and as I did not move they gripped my arms.

"So," I said above things to Lorn. "So that is the reason. You need a victim. You must supply them with a murderer."

"There's no use talking like that, Sundean," said Lorn. "You can't defend yourself. You know you're guilty. You'd better save what wits you have till the trial. You're guilty. They will find the poison in your room, where you

410

hid it. Where I —" his eyes touched Lovschiem — "where I found it and thus was convinced of your guilt."

A long shuddering sigh came from Grethe. Lovschiem was leaning with his fat hands spread out on the desk and his jaw dropped, staring at me. I was dimly conscious that the man who had called himself Francis Tally had appeared in the doorway of the lounge and was staring, too, as if struck dumb.

"Madame," I said to Grethe, "will you do me a kindness? Ask these policemen to free my arms for a moment. I won't try to escape — I couldn't."

It was perhaps the certainty in my voice that secured my momentary freedom.

I reached into my pocket, praying that I still had the two things I wanted, and I did. It went fleetingly across my mind that if Elise had not come exactly when she did I would have been sure then. But she came, and other things were urgent. Then, before their eyes I brought out the envelope in which Francis Tally's last letter to his sister had been sent. And I had also a small irregular piece of wax which I had found on the landing where the body of Michael Stravsky had lain.

There was not a sound while I fitted the broken wax to the half of the seal which still remained on the envelope. The two pieces fitted exactly and made one.

I said to Lorn:

"You have killed and killed for the Tally millions."

"Take him away! Arrest him! *Messieurs, faîtes vos met* —"

"You killed Stravsky and you killed Marcel and you killed the priest. You were here the night Stravsky was killed. You were here in the courtyard, hiding and waiting and biding your time. And when you killed Stravsky because you had witnessed the abduction and Sue's return and you thought Stravsky had got her token — when you killed Stravsky and searched him and took his gun and everything he had for fear of missing the token, you broke this wax from the seal of the letter you were bringing Sue from her brother. It fell there. It's going to convict you. But Stravsky didn't have the token. And you killed Marcel so he couldn't tell what he knew of you. And you killed the priest because you discovered he was the real Francis Tally and that he'd seen the real Sue and that spoiled your plan. You killed him, and that's where you got Sue's token, at last. Her brother had found it and taken it — perhaps to see if it matched his own. But you took it from his dead body. And you trapped yourself when you did that."

"Trapped —" whispered Greth.

"That proved that there was someone else after the token. Someone besides the Lovschiems. For it was gone. Yet the Lovschiems did not have it. And it was not on the priest's body."

Grethe said in a still way: "It's true. It was in his room. I found it."

Lorn had shrunk into his brown coat; he was only shadowed eyes and chalk-yellow face, and he no longer screamed at the policemen.

"You see," I went on, "you went too far to make me think Lovschiem was the murderer. You hoped he would try to escape rather than face the police, and that I would do as you told me, shoot to kill. You probably told the police I was threatening him with your gun. Your plan was to arrive with the police and catch me red-handed, for if Lovschiem was ever to escape he must do so then, and you thought you'd thoroughly frightened him. But it didn't work. You see, *you* heard the conversation in the courtyard between Stravsky and Lovschiem. You heard it yourself; no one told you of it. You had to be there at the time."

"Marianne —" The word came rather shrilly from the coat collar.

"Marianne couldn't have told you. The conversation was in English. Marianne cannot understand English."

"*Jim* —"

Sue was thrusting aside the man who posed as Francis Tally, and she was pulling Marianne into the lobby with her, and the gendarme I had set to guard her was there, too.

"Jim," cried Sue wildly. "It's true. Marianne has told what Marcel saw. He saw Lorn — *Lorn* — in the courtyard the night Stravsky was murdered. And then Lorn came back the next day, and Marcel recognized him. He told Marianne, but he was afraid to tell anyone. But he watched and listened and knew I was in danger. So he tried to tell you. And he was — killed."

It was then that Lorn lost his head.

It wouldn't have mattered whether he denied the thing or not, for they found the poison and the papers he had stolen from Lovschiem's safe hidden in his room. He had intended to plant the poison in my room after he'd turned me over to the police and it was safe to do so, but he hadn't had time.

As I say, the man lost his head.

For he wheeled suddenly and began to run.

He was out the door and was running blindly through the court with his head down. He was running wildly and dazedly and frantically, as a rabbit runs along the road ahead of an automobile.

Well — they caught him, of course.

When the detectives arrived from Paris the next morning they made short work of the whole tissue of horribly interwoven threads. One of the first things was the poison. (It was, by the way, hidden so simply that it was no great wonder it had not been found. The poison and the needle he had twice used and was saving for Sue when he should get her away from the hotel were in a small wooden pepper box; that curious, old-fashioned kind that grinds pepper as you turn the top and is in use in so many small Continental hotels. The only fact that would have drawn anyone's attention to it was that it remained in his room on a tray, and then you'd only have thought it was forgotten by some careless servant. Marcel might have noticed it, but Marcel was gone. And the papers were under the carpet.)

Lorn was the last man I should have expected to confess, but confess he did. After all, I suppose it was in his nature; inherent in that weak chin and of a piece with that blind funk that had sent him stumbling across the court in such futile and betraying flight.

It was late the next day before we had the whole story. The wind was still blowing, and the lounge where Sue and Mrs. Byng and I sat was cold. Mrs. Byng was knitting furiously, and Pucci perched on the table beside us and took the liveliest interest in the conversation.

"So," said Mrs. Byng, "the Lovschiems were actually in the business after all. The Lovschiems and the dead Stravsky and this young fellow who pretended to be your brother, my dear, and this Elise person who's been wandering about like a lost soul all day. Quite a conspiracy!"

"It arose very simply," I said. "Lovschiem has confessed to conspiracy. I gather that when your mother, Sue, told them of the money waiting for you it was irresistible. Like an apple ready to drop into their laps. All they needed was a little organization, and they had affiliations which provided the organization at once. The rest was simple."

"But how in the world," said Sue worriedly, "could they hope to convince a lawyer that Elise was — Sue Tally? The lawyer would be particularly suspicious, owing to Francis's murder."

"Why not? She would have the token. However, the Lovschiems did not know that the priest was Francis. They suspected me of being your brother at first; that is why Madame tried to keep me out of jail. She wanted me where she could watch me and discover my identity. But they thought the priest was

416

actually a priest. In spite of his disposition for snooping about — I beg your pardon, Sue."

"I've got to know," boomed Mrs. Byng, "how Lorn escaped from the lift after he had killed Marcel."

"He says he simply walked through the corridor while I was struggling with the police, dodged into a vacant room to avoid your coming and the others'; while you were all attracted to the lounge, he ran through the main section of the hotel and the north-wing corridor (which was the same route by which he had re-entered the hotel after passing me in the lounge a short time before and apparently leaving. He chanced returning that way, for he feared I would succeed in getting Marcel to tell me what he knew, although he himself was not sure of what knowledge Marcel had. He only feared it and listened from the gallery above and knew he must kill Marcel. He took a chance with the lift, but he had to. And chance favored him that time). There was less chance in walking down the winding stairway, sheltered by vines as it is, and crossing the court to the lobby door *after* Marcel was killed, for everyone was in the lounge. There was no one to see. Yes, chance favored him that time. But he preferred killing stealthily. By poison."

"And when he killed the priest — Francis Tally?"

"He returned again unobserved by way of the winding stairway, and later, when it was over, left the same way. The first time he had succeeded by lucky chance. The second time he watched and planned and dodged the police. It was dusk then, and the shadows made it easier. Then, too, the police did not watch him as carefully as the rest of us. The police, by the way, while they did not suspect him of being the murderer, still were not as confidential with him as he led us to believe. They had accomplished an enormous amount of routine work of which we were told nothing. Such as proving that the priest's — Tally's — papers were forged. But that came just too late. And finding the marks of bullets in the courtyard and a flattened pellet that they think came from Stravsky's gun. Stravsky's gun in Lorn's hands."

"But why did Lorn rescue you twice if his aim was eventually to make you the victim?"

"He wasn't ready for a victim yet. And he wanted Sue's confidence. And he knew that the police still would suspect me. I was in danger from him from the moment he knew that I knew of the broken seal. He dared not say or do anything that would emphasize its importance in my eyes. But I was his victim from then on. And he had a pretty plan to catch me red-handed. But Lovschiem didn't try to escape. And I didn't shoot. And Pucci found Sue's token —"

"In that hussy's hair!" Mrs. Byng was knitting with dangerous abandon. "And you knew —"

"I knew Madame Grethe had put something in her hair when she came from Lorn's room. Pucci pulled it out, and it was Sue's half of the token. I knew it must be Sue's half, for she herself had her brother's half. And it had come from Lorn's room."

"Then Lorn was acting entirely alone?"

"Entirely. It was a simple matter of greed. There was that extraordinary story. There were the millions. Why shouldn't he have them? Do you remember, Sue, how remarkably definite he was at the very first about the lines that a conspiracy against you must take? He'd thought it all out. He hadn't his substitute yet, as the Lovschiems had, but he thought that part would be simple."

Mrs. Byng snatched at the knitting which had dropped out of her hands and slid toward her knees. She picked it up, looked at it crossly, said parenthetically: "I've purled clear across this dratted thing," and asked:

"Did the priest — your brother, I mean, my dear — did he suspect Lorn?"

"Lorn says not. He's been — boasting a bit. He says he guessed the priest was Tally, taxed him with it, and they arranged a meeting in the deserted White Salon. Lorn, as I said, pretended to leave and sneaked back again without being seen. He realized that since Tally had seen the real Sue his plot was automatically ended. But Tally unwisely told him two things: told him he'd left the affair in the hands of his lawyer so, if anything happened to him, Sue could still prove herself and inherit the money. And he also told him that he had found Sue's token, had it with him, in fact, and that he was going to acknowledge her as his sister at once. That was only a few moments after he had found her token. I suppose Francis was doing a little boasting himself — had outsmarted the professional detectives, you know. But that settled Francis's fate then and there. Lorn was deft and quiet with his needle. Francis was of a strange nature — too cunning and too sure of himself."

"Elise says she was not near the north wing the night Stravsky was murdered until after his death, when Lovschiem hid her in the fireplace cupboard." (Parenthetically, I thought: With what military precision Mrs. Byng has rooted out and mastered every detail of the affair.) "So the black figure you saw must have been the priest. What was he doing there?"

I started to say prowling, but with a glance at Sue I said instead:

"He seems to have tried to keep a close watch on Sue. I imagine he simply saw the light and came down the north corridor to investigate. We can't know, however. He must have barely missed Lorn's own visit to my room."

Sue shivered and spoke.

"Did Lorn confess about the sword?"

"Yes. He used it for the very reason he told us a criminal who was clever might have used it. He saw you leave my room and had seen me leave. He slipped into the north wing merely to reconnoiter; he wasn't so hurried then, for he thought there was no possible chance of the body being discovered before morning. And the first thing he saw was the sword clock. An excellent manner in which to clog the issue and throw suspicions within the hotel, while he escaped and returned openly the next day. He took the sword and left the corridor just in time, I suppose, to escape Francis."

There was a short silence. I looked at Sue — Sue with her millions — Sue looked at Pucci, Mrs. Byng stared into space and her lips moved absently, and Pucci scratched. Mrs. Byng's cogitations became audible: ". . . and Stravsky arrived after Jim and, naturally, registered, since he was to be about the place for a while, and used momentarily the room

Marcel thought was unused. Marcel did not see him — that was luck for Lovschiem. Then, after Stravsky's murder, they had to change the register hoping to keep Stravsky's identity and thus any connection with them a secret. But why did Lorn shoot at you, Jim? Oh, how stupid of me! He thought you were pursuing him, and a man who's just killed and knows his kill has been discovered will shoot if someone pursues him. He shot at you and then escaped through the latched door of the gate."

"Yes. He knew it was there, for he'd seen Sue and Stravsky enter by that little inner door, but it took him a few moments to find the latch. Then he walked to a town near here and returned openly the next day to install himself as the protector of the girl he —" I stopped. The thing was over. But there were still parts of it that didn't bear thinking of.

"Then," pursued Mrs. Byng earnestly, "what happened to the car Stravsky had used when abducting Sue?"

"It was Lovschiem's car," I replied wearily. "All Lovschiem had to do was put it back in the garage."

Mrs. Byng gave me a sharp look, gathered up her knitting and Pucci, and vanished. Vanished is a singular word to use in connection with one of Mrs. Byng's substantiality, but that is what she did.

She left complete silence. There was nothing that might be said, and I could not sit there.

It had been bad enough while Mrs. Byng was talking to sit there so near Sue — Sue with her millions hovering about like florid yellow ghosts. With Mrs. Byng's restraining presence removed it was impossible.

Sue was near enough for me to touch. Just by putting out my hand I could have touched her.

I shoved back my chair and rose. Sue looked up, startled.

"I've got to pack," I said, my voice harsh against the silence. "I've got to pack. I'm leaving."

One slim hand went upward to her throat. I could not look at her, so I started toward the stairs and then came back and said briefly:

"I'm glad things have worked out for you. I hope you enjoy your — ten millions."

I had my foot on the first step of the stairs when Sue's quiet observation reached me.

"I haven't ten millions," she said.

"What did you say?"

"I haven't ten millions. A cable from the lawyer this morning said so. Something happened; I don't know what exactly yet. Anyway, it's gone. The ten millions."

I walked to her. I said:

"See here. Why did you take the dagger

from Stravsky's chest and replace it on the clock?"

"To protect you," she said steadily, and then looked up.

It is a mistake to say that the happiest moment in your life does not repeat itself, for it does, and even prolongs itself. Sue came up into my arms, and I loved her so much that there was nothing in all the world but my Sue.

She said she'd marry me and go any place with me.

Then she became silent and very thoughtful in my arms. She was so thoughtful that I lifted her face and looked and asked what was wrong.

"I was only thinking," she said, "that there's a million or so left. But it's too late for you to do anything about it now," she added hurriedly.